# LOST LOVER

### Crime and Passion, Book 4

## Mary Lancaster

## ARE YOU SIGNED UP FOR DRAGONBLADE'S BLOG?

You'll get the latest news and information on exclusive giveaways, exclusive excerpts, coming releases, sales, free books, cover reveals and more.

Check out our complete list of authors, too!

No spam, no junk. That's a promise!

### Sign Up Here

www.dragonbladepublishing.com

*Dearest Reader;*

*Thank you for your support of a small press. At Dragonblade Publishing, we strive to bring you the highest quality Historical Romance from some of the best authors in the business. Without your support, there is no 'us', so we sincerely hope you adore these stories and find some new favorite authors along the way.*

*Happy Reading!*

*CEO, Dragonblade Publishing*

Ghostly Lover (Novella)

**The Husband Dilemma Series**
How to Fool a Duke

**Season of Scandal Series**
Pursued by the Rake
Abandoned to the Prodigal
Married to the Rogue
Unmasked by her Lover
Her Star from the East (Novella)

**Imperial Season Series**
Vienna Waltz
Vienna Woods
Vienna Dawn

**Blackhaven Brides Series**
The Wicked Baron
The Wicked Lady
The Wicked Rebel
The Wicked Husband
The Wicked Marquis
The Wicked Governess
The Wicked Spy
The Wicked Gypsy
The Wicked Wife
Wicked Christmas (A Novella)
The Wicked Waif
The Wicked Heir
The Wicked Captain
The Wicked Sister

**Unmarriageable Series**
The Deserted Heart
The Sinister Heart
The Vulgar Heart
The Broken Heart
The Weary Heart

The Secret Heart
Christmas Heart

**The Lyon's Den Series**
Fed to the Lyon

**De Wolfe Pack: The Series**
The Wicked Wolfe
Vienna Wolfe

**Also from Mary Lancaster**
Madeleine
The Others of Ochil

# CHAPTER ONE

FOOTSTEPS ECHOED BEHIND her. They quickened and slowed when she did, and yet surely no one could see her in the thick fog that swirled off the canal and the river? She cast a quick glance over her shoulder, for it was hard to judge the distance of sounds in the muffling mist.

The indistinct shape of a male figure in a caped coat and a tall hat loomed several yards behind. She gripped her large carpetbag tighter and hurried onward. He could be anyone, though such a well-dressed man was hardly likely to live hereabouts. It was not the weather for a pleasant stroll. Even she, used to the stench of the river, was disgusted by the taste of it, which seemed to coat her lips and her nostrils, carried by the thick tendrils of fog.

With her free hand, she dug into the pocket of her cloak and grasped her house keys. They could be a weapon, if it was *him*.

Although if it was Joshua who followed her, she knew in her heart a few keys were unlikely to deter him.

She castigated herself for being so nervous of a stranger, one who walked, moreover, several yards behind, courteously keeping his distance, surely, so that she would not be alarmed. And she wouldn't have been, if only this hadn't happened before. But this was the fourth or fifth time in the last fortnight that she had suspected someone of following her along the side of the canal, and even in the more respectable streets of Kensington and Belgravia and Mayfair. Her skin had prickled, but she had refused to glance back like a hunted rabbit. It could still be coincidence, different people at different times walking in the same direction.

*I will not be cowed by my own nerves!*

The fog was so thick, she almost missed the turning into Hanson Row, her narrow street of small, terraced houses. She prayed the man behind *would* miss it, or not be looking for it in the first place... But no, by the time she reached her home, she was sure the footsteps followed, steady and measured. And suddenly, she had to know. She took the two paces that separated the street from her front step and slid her key into the lock, opening the door a mere crack before she turned and stared into the mist.

Her heart drummed. Her fingers clenched on the key. The footsteps came on without pause, and the same male figure in caped coat and hat emerged from the mist. As tall as Joshua, with the same steady, lethal grace that meant he was wary, observing...

The moment he saw her watching him was the same moment she realized with a flood of relief that he was not Joshua. He was younger, leaner, his features more refined—or at least they seemed so in that one indistinct glimpse, before he paused and met her gaze. He didn't speak or even smile. He didn't look as if he ever smiled. His face was paler than the fog, all ice and hard lines. A man to fear—no one recognized the signs better than she. But he merely touched the brim of his hat with two gloved fingers and walked on.

Weak with relief, she stared after him until he merged with the fog and vanished, his footsteps fading away.

She whisked herself inside the house and locked the door behind her. She was shaking—with more relief than fright, she assured herself. Joshua could have no idea she was back in London.

Of course, there were other dangers in the city, especially on foggy late afternoons in poor streets without lighting. The man, who knew now where she lived, could well be one of those.

There had been something menacing about him…

*Don't jump at shadows,* she scolded herself as she unfastened her cloak and hung it on the hook by the door. He was merely walking on to Commercial Road and was entitled to take any route he liked. Perhaps she would come home by Commercial Road instead of the canal next time…

Having placed her bonnet on the same hook, she took her carpetbag through to the tiny front parlor and set it on her worktable. But she really needed to get rid of the fog-borne grime on her skin before she began. She walked up the narrow staircase to the bedroom above and used water from the morning's jug to wash her hands and face. She unpinned her hair and had just begun to brush it vigorously, when, in the old, speckled mirror, she saw the foot.

She blinked. On the floor, just poking out from the far side of the bed—it was *definitely* a foot, shod in smart leather, and pointing toward her. She turned slowly from the mirror and stared at the unmoving, alien male foot.

She lived alone, without a servant of any kind. No one else should be in her house uninvited, and she rarely invited. She had never invited a man.

Swallowing, she snatched up the nail scissors from the rickety dressing table and took the two steps to the other side of the bed.

A man lay on his back. A big, powerful, well-dressed man with dirty-brown hair, a loud yellow and red paisley waistcoat, and an unfastened, rust-colored coat. His thick neck was horribly bruised. And his face…was Joshua's.

Instinctively, she raised the scissors in defense. But he didn't move. His open eyes weren't looking at her but gazing straight upward. His coarsely handsome features remained perfectly still.

Revulsion and fear almost overcame her. The scissors slipped from her grasp and fell to the floor. Her whole body shook, but somehow, she knelt and touched his wrist. She gasped, snatching back her hand, for his skin was *warm.*

She fell back on her heels, clutching at her hair. *Dear God, what do I do now?*

The thought that he was in her house, her bedroom, *alive*, terrified her. And yet, if he were dead, was that not even worse? Alive, he needed help, and though there was no one in the world she wanted to help less, she could not let him die if she could avoid it.

Could she?

*In my house! Oh dear God...*

*Dr. Tizsa!*

On that thought, she sprang to her feet and ran down the stairs. She seized her cloak and stuffed her bonnet on her head as she ran out of the front door and hurried through the fog toward Commercial Road and the direction of the clinic where she had once gone, months ago now, to consult a doctor about the headaches that blurred her vision and made it impossible to work.

He had given her a pair of spectacles that had, astonishingly enough, stopped the headaches. People said that although he was a foreigner, he was an excellent doctor and often "forgot" to charge his poorest patients. Certainly, he had charged her very little. But the chief reason his name sprang into her head was that rumor also said he could help with a variety of problems.

Whether Joshua was dead or alive, getting him out of her house was most definitely a problem.

JAMES ANDOVER HAD strolled back the way he had come and stopped on the other side of Hanson Row. Leaning against the convenient blank wall of the warehouse behind, he gazed through the fog at the house of the woman who called herself Miss Alice Gunn, but whose real name he knew to be Mrs. Joshua Jarman.

He had begun to watch her only days after his release from prison, because she very probably possessed the items that had sent him there. Contempt for her, then, had come close to hatred as he coldly plotted her downfall and that of her husband. The thinness and frailty of the figure he followed meant nothing to him. Nor did her clear exhaustion at the end of her long walks, which involved visiting respectable and often wealthy houses he supposed she was stealing from. He made notes of them all and looked forward to her punishment along with her husband's.

Until she had looked at him out of the mist just now, not in anger or challenge, but with a sort of expectant dread. To his annoyance, his contempt was becoming laced with just a shade of misplaced pity, just because she was no stranger to fear. And because she was pretty.

He should have gone home, switched attentions to Jarman himself. And yet he had come back here. Because now she *bothered* him. Intrigued him, even, and he didn't know why. For those reasons alone, he should walk away.

He didn't.

He could barely make out her front door, so he doubted she would see him if she looked out her windows. In fact, he didn't much care if she did. If he was truthful with himself, he *wanted* another glimpse of her, without the concealing bonnet. Without the fog. Perhaps he had watched her and followed her long enough that he simply wanted *something* to happen.

When it did, it took him by surprise. The front door suddenly flew open, and the young woman bolted out. She didn't stop to close, let alone lock, the door, merely tugged it behind her in a halfhearted way before rushing into the street and running up toward Commercial Road as if all the fiends of hell were after her.

James hesitated, but only for a moment. He would have liked to know where she was going in such a hurry, but he doubted he would have such a chance again. Ruthlessly, he squashed his misplaced urge to protect. As the fog closed around her vanishing form, he crossed the road and walked up to her front door. Just as he'd suspected, the door had not even closed. He pushed it open and walked in.

It smelled clean. The narrow hallway led to a kitchen at the back of the house. An even narrower staircase led up to the first floor on the left. A small parlor opened on the right, so he walked in there. She lived alone, so he didn't fear discovery by friends or servants.

A large work basket sat on the floor beside the one armchair. A quick glance showed him only reels of silk and cotton thread, sewing needles of various sizes, scissors, buttons, a few small squares of cloth. The carpetbag she usually carried—always, apparently, full—stood on the table beside the chair. This was much more interesting to him.

But when he unclipped it, he found no valuable stolen goods, only a pile of linen, a few stockings, and other garments of various children's sizes. Most had small holes or were frayed somewhere.

He frowned and closed the bag again before looking around him. He walked out of the parlor to the kitchen, which was neat and clean, the contents of the cupboards sparse, the larder half-full only of basic foodstuffs, a cheap cut of ham, bread, some vegetables, a jug of milk.

Upstairs, he glanced into the first tiny bedroom, which contained only a trunk and several bolts of cloth piled on a shelf beside ribbons and several strips of lace.

The other bedroom was clearly where she slept. It confirmed what he had already gathered with increasing consternation. This was not the home of a rich woman. No expensive art or porcelain betrayed secret wealth. Her furniture was old, rickety, and clearly secondhand. Her washing bowl and jug were chipped, and there was no obvious box of jewels for him to rifle through. There were few comforts, let alone luxuries, here. She seemed to be, in fact, exactly what she pretended—a poor seamstress.

He moved further into the room and stopped dead.

A man lay on the far side of the bed, obviously deceased, with the marks of strangulation on his thick neck. It was her husband, Joshua Jarman.

No wonder she had bolted from the house. It was past time

he did the same. First, though, he crouched beside the body. A small pair of nail scissors lay on the floorboards beside his right ankle, an odd untidiness in a neat house. He left them where they were while he went through the dead man's pockets. And then looked through the widow's bedside cabinet.

>>><<<

"DR. TIZSA!" SHE called breathlessly, catching sight of him as he walked down the street close to the clinic.

The fog wasn't quite so bad here, or perhaps it was beginning to lift, for he clearly recognized her and came to a halt with the kind of smile that told her he couldn't quite remember her name.

"Alice Gunn," she said in a rush.

"Of course. Headaches. I trust they no longer plague you?"

"I need you come with me," she blurted, ignoring this. "Please. Urgently. He might not be dead!"

Dr. Tizsa was a breathtakingly handsome man—in a dark, dashing, exotically foreign kind of a way that even she had noticed from the first. But the doctor always behaved as if no one had ever told him of his good looks. The quiet confidence of his bearing seemed to have nothing to do with the entitled smugness of so many beautiful people. His concentration seemed to be on *her* rather than on himself. Which was a danger in itself at the moment, though she didn't have time to dwell upon the fact.

"Who might not be dead?" he asked with perfect calm.

"The man in my house!" She took hold of his coat sleeve in her panic, and he didn't brush her off, merely offered her his arm properly as though she were a lady and hurried in the direction she tugged him.

"Where do you live?" he asked. "Do we need a cab?"

"Between Commercial Road and the Grosvenor Canal. I don't know about cabs. I've never taken one…"

"Tell me about the patient. Why do you think he might or

might not be dead?"

"He isn't moving. He's just lying on the floor, staring at the ceiling, but he's warm to the touch, so I thought maybe a doctor might save him."

"What happened to him?"

She shook her head. "I don't know. I just came home and found him in my house! In my...my bedroom."

"How disturbing," Dr. Tizsa murmured.

The calm understatement brought a surge of hysteria she had to choke back. "There are marks on his neck," she blurted instead.

"I see. And was there anyone else in the house?"

She stared at him in fresh alarm. "No! That is... I don't think so. I'd only just come in myself, and I didn't look..." Her blood froze upon her thought that whoever had choked Joshua to within an inch of his life might have still been lurking in the house while she was there. She swallowed convulsively. "I just went up to wash and change, and there he was. When I touched his wrist to take his pulse, he felt warm, so I ran to fetch you."

"I take it he should not have been in your house?"

"Absolutely not," she said fervently.

The doctor said nothing else, contenting himself with striding along beside her at the urgent pace she set despite her exhaustion. Only as she felt in her pocket for her keys did she realize she hadn't brought them with her. She had not even shut the front door. If the doctor noticed, he said nothing, merely touched her shoulder when she would have led the way inside and walked in before her. His head was poised as though he were listening intently.

"Upstairs?" he asked, setting his foot on the first step.

"Yes. The second door on the landing."

He preceded her into the room, while she couldn't resist sticking her head around the door of the spare room. Finding it thankfully empty, she followed Dr. Tizsa, her heart racing. It came to her that whatever he told her, whether he pronounced

Joshua dead or alive, it would be bad. There was no good whatsoever in this situation.

"He's quite dead," the doctor said matter-of-factly. He was crouching, squashed between the body and the window.

"Dear God." She closed her eyes to hide whatever it was she was feeling. Shock and cold, mainly, for she was shivering.

"He's been strangled," Dr. Tizsa observed. "Which means murder. You have to inform the police."

Her eyes flew open of their own accord. "I can't!" she exclaimed. "How would it look if a dead man was found in my bedroom? Word would spread and I'd be judged, get no work. I need to work, doctor!"

"You are a seamstress, are you not?" he asked casually, rifling through the dead man's clothing and turning out his pockets.

She nodded, trying not to look at the body.

"I'm afraid we cannot cover up murder."

At least he sounded apologetic, so she swallowed and tried, "Couldn't we move him? Even into the backyard? And then bring the police?"

He shook his head. "I'll ask them to be discreet about anything they reveal to the press. Miss Gunn, do you have any idea who this is?"

"No. None." She licked her dry lips. "Do you suppose he is a burglar? That there were two of them and they fell out over..."

His gaze flicked around the room, and she trailed off. Obviously, he could see there was nothing here to steal, let alone kill over.

"Someone told me that if I was in trouble, you might help," she blurted.

"Who told you that?" he asked, straightening.

"An acquaintance. In Covent Garden. She sells flowers."

"Ah." A faint smile flickered across his lips. He swept up his arm, urging her from the room. "I'm afraid my services do not include moving or hiding murdered bodies."

"Of course not," she whispered, swamped by shame and

humiliation. "Forgive me for asking." She would have to give up all her customers here and move away, start again. Even dead, it seemed, Joshua could hurt her. From habit, she bent to pick up the nail scissors she had dropped when she first saw the body.

"Don't touch anything," Dr. Tizsa said pleasantly. "The police will want to see everything as it was when he died."

She straightened. "But it was I who dropped the scissors when I found him."

"All the same. Do you have somewhere else you can go just now? Family? A neighbor?"

"No, there's no one," she said. No one she could trust with the information that a man's dead body was in her bedroom.

Perhaps he understood this, for he said gently, "I have to fetch the police. I'll go straight to Scotland Yard. Do you mind waiting here, with the body upstairs?"

She shook her head. If he had to be there, she would far rather he was dead.

"Do you have tea?" he asked.

She nodded, frowning.

"Make yourself a pot. Add extra sugar. It's good for shock. Let me just look in your kitchen before I go..."

Was he looking for the killer? Could the man still be here? She stared after him, not even following, until she heard the back door open and close again.

As she entered, he turned the key in the lock. "Do you always leave your back door unlocked?"

"Never," she exclaimed.

"I found it unlocked," he remarked without emphasis.

"Is that how he—they—got in?" she whispered.

"Probably."

"There was a man following me," she remembered, suddenly, then frowned. "But it couldn't have been him, could it? If he was following me, he couldn't have been breaking in."

"We'll talk about him," Dr. Tizsa said, brushing past her. "Lock the front door behind me and make that tea. I shan't be long."

THE KNOCK CAME sooner than she had expected. But then, she had been sitting in the kitchen, staring numbly into space while the tea cooled in the pot. She had lost track of time. She jumped up, almost running to the front door, because even facing the questions of the police was suddenly better than being alone.

But when she opened the door, it was not the police or Dr. Tizsa who stood on her front step. It was the man who had followed her in the fog.

# CHAPTER TWO

WITH A GASP, she tried to slam the door shut again, but he
seized the edge of the wood and held it still.

"Mrs. Jarman," he said coldly. "I need to talk to you."

Blood sang in her ears. Whatever had remained of her fragile
world fell to pieces at her feet.

*He knew.* He knew who she was. Now it truly *was* all over.
Her head spun as she stumbled back against the newel post and
the world went blessedly dark.

It didn't stay dark. She had the sensation of movement and
strong arms, which felt strangely comforting rather than
threatening. Her cheek rested against fine-quality wool, and then
the strong arms and the wool-covered shoulder vanished. She
realized she was sitting in her parlor armchair. She opened her
eyes and let the blurred edges of her vision clear.

*He* was still here. She could feel his presence, see his still
shadow across the hearth. Slowly, she turned her head and raised
her eyes.

His hair was straight and black, brushed to one side off his
forehead. He looked as deathly pale as he had in the fog, as
though he he'd been ill. But there was no hint of vulnerability, no
softness in the lean if handsome features, and certainly none in
the cold gray eyes, which were hard as slate and not comforting
at all.

And yet he had carried her into the parlor and set her down

with surprising gentleness. He must want something of her.

"Better?" he inquired with an impatience that set up her hackles once more.

"No. You're still here." Hadn't she thought any company was better than solitude? Any company, perhaps, who didn't address her as Mrs. Jarman. Or force itself uninvited into her house.

"Be grateful," he advised, without heat or mockery. "I stopped you falling and cracking your head open."

"I did not fall," she said with dignity. After all, nothing hurt.

"Only because I caught you."

In spite of everything, warmth seeped into her face.

He was still watching her with his cold, unreadable eyes. "Am I really so frightening that you faint at the sight of me? You, the lady who previously looked me in the eye without shame, who just discovered the strangled body of her dead husband and immediately set off to fetch a friend for tea?"

"Friend?" She blinked. "He isn't a friend. He's a doctor."

It was his turn to stare. "Is he, by God?"

"Yes, and he'll be back at any moment with the police," she added with relish. "So I can tell them you are the man who has been following me."

"Will you also tell them why?"

"I would if I knew."

The hard eyes bored into hers. A flicker of uncertainty took her by surprise. Then he moved aside and lowered himself to the work chair by the table. His person, his every action, was peculiarly elegant. "Do you really not know who I am?"

"I don't recall being introduced."

"We weren't, but my face was plastered around newspapers and flyers for several weeks. Three years ago. I went to prison for your husband's crime."

Her fingers tightened on the arm of the chair, and she forced them to loosen again before he noticed. "I don't know what you're talking about. I have no husband. And how do you know anything about the murdered man in my house? Was it you who broke in?"

Too late, she realized the unwisdom of accusing any associate of Joshua's, let alone this betrayed one who certainly had a motive to kill.

"No," he replied without breaking eye contact. "I walked through the front door, which you were so obliging as to leave open."

"How dare you?" she ground out as helpless fury rose over everything else. How many people had violated her home, her privacy, today? And did any of that matter beside the huge, incontrovertible fact that a man had been killed? Joshua had been *murdered*.

"It required very little daring," he said, "and I trust you'll give me credit for knocking civilly on your door this time."

Something else was distracting her from his mockery, drawing her brow into a frown. "You don't *speak* like a criminal." He spoke, in fact, with the accents of an educated gentleman. But then, so did Joshua when he wanted to.

"Neither do you."

"I am a seamstress, not a criminal. What are you?"

"Neither fish nor fowl," he said flippantly. "So, where are the diamonds?"

She blinked. "What diamonds?"

"The ones I went to prison for stealing, though the crime was your husband's."

That, she supposed, explained his unhealthy pallor. "I have never had a husband, and I know nothing of any diamonds."

He gazed into her face. "You're very good," he observed, rising gracefully to his feet. "I almost believe you."

"Are you leaving so soon?" she taunted him, rashly. "I was hoping you would stay and greet the policemen, who will surely want to know all about the dead man."

"Who knows more than a wife?" he retorted.

She couldn't help it. She laughed, a harsh, bitter sound that almost frightened her and brought a sudden frown to the pale brow of the convict. "Ask one," she muttered, pulling herself together. "Goodbye, Mr.…?"

"Goodbye," he replied pleasantly, and strolled out of her tiny parlor as though from some elegant soiree.

Her heart thudding, she strained to hear the sounds of his movements. All she heard was the opening and closing of the front door, and then she saw him through the window, his silk hat once more on his head as he stepped into the street and disappeared into the fog.

Jarman's wife confused him. What he had assumed to be act of the respectable spinster seamstress seemed, in fact, to be close to the truth. Apart from the spinster bit. She was definitely lying about that. She was Jarman's wife without doubt, though her sudden and genuine faint when he called her so was interesting. She truly *was* in hiding, and it didn't appear to be with the purpose of spending her ill-gotten gains.

More than that, there was something fragile about her. Not just in her frail physical form when he caught her in his arms to prevent her fall, but in her eyes, in her whole manner, as though she were held together only by something less substantial than the finest thread in her work basket.

She was frightened.

He knew fear well enough to recognize it and to have learned distaste for causing it. But he would not pity Jarman's wife, who was the partial cause of his disgrace and his three lost, terrible years in prison. He wouldn't. Nor would he allow this insidious, sneaking desire for her to blossom, for that was pure idiocy born no doubt of enforced celibacy. But he could adjust his thinking, for the truth was not always straightforward, and it was just possible Jarman's wife was also a victim in her own way.

James had not gone far down the narrow street before a

hackney clattered through the mist, the carriage all but brushing against him as it swept past. It halted in the region of the house he had just left, and on impulse, he walked back the way he had come. No tall-hatted, uniformed policemen spilled out of the carriage, but he recognized the handsome man Mrs. Jarman had claimed was a doctor. The other, slightly older man, upright and determined looking, he did not know at all, though the man turned back and handed out a third occupant, a fair young lady wearing a jaunty hat and spectacles. And he *did* recognize her.

As though she felt his stare, she turned and peered through the mist directly at him. And then the dark young man tugged her up to the front door and into the house.

Lady Grizelda Niven, youngest daughter of the Duke of Kelburn. He had known her once, in his youth, and rather liked her, for she was different from the other debutantes. She had been a friend of Cordelia's, which wasn't surprising. What did astonish him was that she was in any way acquainted with Elizabeth Jarman, who now called herself Alice Gunn.

DR. TIZSA, HAVING briefly introduced his companions as his wife, Lady Grizelda, and Inspector Harris, took the latter upstairs to view the body. Leaving Elizabeth—or Alice, as she must remember to think of herself, now more importantly than ever—with the unexpected Lady Grizelda.

With looks like his, she supposed it wasn't surprising that Dr. Tizsa had snagged an aristocratic wife. At any other time, she would have been flummoxed to find herself in such august company in her extremely modest front parlor, but today just seemed to keep getting stranger.

"Shall I light another lamp?" Lady Grizelda suggested. "It's getting late, and the fog makes everything so gloomy."

"Allow me," Elizabeth said, and reached for the tinderbox on the mantelpiece. She hadn't even lit the fire—no wonder she was so cold.

"I came to look after *you*," Lady Grizelda said apologetically. "This must all be such a horrible shock for you."

"Horrible," Elizabeth agreed. Large feet clomped above the ceiling, moving across the room above. Were they poking among her things? Surely there was nothing for them to see. As she lit the lamps, she was aware of her ladyship moving behind her, lighting the laid fire with a spill. With the room glowing a little brighter, Elizabeth turned and watched her guest straighten. "Please, sit."

To her surprised, Lady Grizelda took the work chair at the table, leaving Elizabeth the armchair. She perched on the edge and regarded the other woman curiously. Her hair was fair and thick and somewhat untidily pinned, but behind her spectacles, she was pretty, beautiful even, and her eyes were both sharp and intelligent.

Something thudded on the floor above, forcefully enough to shake the little parlor. Were they moving the body? Elizabeth shuddered and met her visitor's gaze.

"Do you look after all your husband's patients?" she asked bluntly.

"Lord, no, only when he asks. He said you seemed to have no family or neighbors who could be with you. And he said you were concerned for your reputation."

"I'm sure that seems odd to your ladyship," Elizabeth said defiantly, "but I depend on my reputation for survival."

"You and most other women," Lady Grizelda agreed. "I am not here to judge, pry, or gossip." A quick, rather charming smile dawned. "Well, I might pry just a little, but I am the soul of discretion."

Elizabeth's stomach twisted tighter as the men's footsteps sounded on the stairs. Inspector Harris entered first.

"Well, ma'am," he said briskly. "We know who he is."

Of course they did. She expected any policeman would have

recognized the body, although she had hoped...

"Which makes it even odder that he should be in your house," the inspector said. "Joshua Jarman is not only a criminal by career, he is very good at it, very successful and very wealthy. He is very unlikely to consider robbing a house of this size and neighborhood, and if he did, it would be his underlings, not himself, who perpetrated the crime."

"And yet there he lies," she observed.

"There he lies," the inspector agreed. "You say you didn't recognize him, had never seen him before, but is the name Joshua Jarman known to you?"

She shook her head.

"You are aware of no connection between you?"

Again, she shook her head. Two blatant lies in a few seconds. But then, she had been lying for years. Why should it bother her now? Especially when her survival was at stake once more. She was aware of Dr. Tizsa and his wife, both watching her, though without the blatancy of Inspector Harris.

"I need to ask you some questions, Miss Gunn," the inspector said. "And you will need to make a formal statement."

Lady Grizelda stood up. "With Miss Gunn's permission, I'll make some fresh tea," she said.

A titled lady was going to make tea for her. This was indeed the strangest of days. The inspector folded his bulk onto the chair Lady Grizelda had vacated and took out his notebook.

"So, tell me what happened this afternoon, Miss Gunn, beginning with when you first went out."

She began to talk, and despite being so cramped at the table, the inspector's pencil flew across the pages of his notebook.

"I went out about one o'clock, to deliver my completed work—I'm a seamstress—to my customers, and to collect more. I came home"—she glanced at the old clock on the mantlepiece—"probably just after four."

"Was your front door locked?" Harris interrupted.

"Yes, I opened it with my key."

"Did you go straight upstairs?"

"Yes." She frowned. "No, I came in here to set down my bag." She gestured to the bag still sitting at the far end of the table. "Then I went upstairs to wash and change." She shivered. "I didn't even see him at first. I'd washed my hands and face, even brushed out my hair, before I noticed his foot." She swallowed and drew in a breath. "And there he was, lying between the bed and the window."

"That must have been a shock," Harris said neutrally.

*You have no idea.* She nodded. "It was. I stared for a moment, and then I thought I should see if he was... If I could... I touched his wrist. I think I meant to take his pulse, just to be sure he was... But he felt *warm*, and I thought he might be alive. But I couldn't help him, so I ran to fetch the only doctor I knew."

"Dr. Tizsa," Harris said without emphasis. "How do you know Dr. Tizsa?"

"As a patient."

He wrote that down, too. Lady Grizelda came in, carrying a tray with her old teapot and mismatched cups and saucers. Weirdly, Elizabeth felt a little shame at that, perhaps because her mother would have been outraged. Dr. Tizsa moved from his place by the window to take the tray from his wife. Lady Grizelda removed the bag, setting it on the floor instead, while her husband deposited the tray and made way for her. It was all done with quiet, casual courtesy, almost like a practiced, well-executed dance by two people who knew each other well and acted in accord without fuss.

"Did you tell anyone else about the body?" Inspector Harris asked. "A neighbor, perhaps?"

Elizabeth shook her head.

"Why not?"

"It did not enter my head," she said defiantly. "My neighbors and I exchange good mornings or good evenings if we encounter each other, but usually, we don't. I needed a doctor, not tea and salacious curiosity."

"I see."

"Do you?" She met his gaze. "I confess it entered my head that Dr. Tizsa might be able to remove the man discreetly, either to a hospital or a morgue or to wherever he belonged. I make no apologies for that. I am an unmarried woman who scratches out a living making children's clothes and mending cloth. I have customers all over London, in Kensington, even Mayfair, respectable customers who would drop me in an instant at one whiff of scandal. I have no reason to mourn the dead man and every reason to protect my reputation."

There was silence, and then Harris's pencil moved again. "There aren't many of us who mourn this particular dead man," he said unexpectedly. "'Good riddance' would be the reaction of most of my colleagues—and probably most of his, who will now be jostling for his position. However, a man has been murdered, and we must discover by whom."

"Sugar and milk?" Lady Grizelda asked her brightly.

"A little milk, thank you," Elizabeth said automatically.

Dr. Tizsa brought the tea to her, while his wife poured three more cups without asking for preferences. It came to Elizabeth that she must know Inspector Harris quite well. Was that another threat, or a good thing?

The policeman sipped his tea. "When you came home, before you discovered the body, did you notice anything unusual in the vicinity? Was anyone else in the street when you came home?"

That was when she remembered she had already told Dr. Tizsa about the man in the mist. She couldn't pretend she had never seen him, though she really didn't want the police tracking him down and discovering her past through him. More than her reputation was at stake there.

But no one else had seen him or spoken to him. She could be selective with the truth.

"I thought a man was following me in the fog," she blurted. "For some distance—from Grosvenor Place, I thought—though it might have been more than one person going about their own business and I was just foolishly alarmed."

"Did you see his face?"

"Not until I was outside the house, when I waited to see him pass."

"Did he acknowledge you?"

"He tipped his hat to me with perfect courtesy and went on his way."

"Then he *was* just going about his own business," Harris suggested.

She didn't know far they would investigate this. If they spoke to her neighbors and one of them had seen a man at her front door...

"I might have thought so," she said in a rush, "except he came back. After Dr. Tizsa left to fetch you, someone knocked on the door. I thought it was either the doctor or the police, but it wasn't. It was this same man."

"What did he want?" Harris demanded with a frown.

"To tell me he knew there was a dead body in my house."

Harris threw down his pencil. "And how exactly did he know that?"

"That's what I wondered. When I ran for Dr. Tizsa, apparently I didn't close the door properly—it was certainly open when we returned. He—the man—said he had come in that way and had seen the body. He wanted to know if I'd found anything on him—it—the body."

"Had you?" Harris asked steadily.

She shuddered, genuinely. "Apart from one brief touch of his wrist, I didn't go near him."

"Did you get the impression he was a friend of the dead man?" Lady Grizelda asked unexpectedly.

Elizabeth shook her head. "No, he seemed to loathe him."

"Then he knew him?" Harris pounced.

"He seemed to," Elizabeth managed.

"Did he mention what in particular he was looking for?" Harris asked.

She had no time to think beyond that she should be as honest as she could be without detriment to herself. "He mentioned something about diamonds."

Harris's lip curled. "There are many who'd like to get their hands on Jarman's diamonds. What did this fellow look like?"

Elizabeth shrugged. "Ordinary. Neither tall nor short. Brown hair, I think. He might have had a beard. I was too distraught to notice much, being more concerned with getting a stranger out of my house again."

"Did he threaten you?" Harris asked.

"No, not really. He didn't stay long. I think he could see I was completely bewildered and knew nothing."

Dr. Tizsa drew the curtains. "That's the men to take the body away."

*Thank God.* Let the neighbors make of that what they wished.

"Miss Gunn, was anything stolen from your house?" the inspector asked as he rose to his feet.

"No. I have nothing worth stealing."

"It's all worth something to somebody," he said.

She shook her head. "I didn't notice that anything had gone. I suppose the cloth and the lace is saleable, but at first glance, it's all still there."

"If you discover anything missing, you'll let me know?" He put the notebook away in a pocket, and his hand emerged holding a visiting card, which he offered her.

She took the card. "I will."

As the policeman went out to deal with the removal of the body, Elizabeth faced the Tizsas.

"You won't be very...comfortable here by yourself," Lady Grizelda said. "Is there really nowhere else you can go for a few days? Or some friend or family member who would stay with you?"

"My family and I don't speak," Elizabeth said. "But I thank you for your concern. I am used to being alone, and I have plenty of work to keep me occupied." At least as long as this scandal

22

didn't get out.

Lady Grizelda handed her another card. "You can find me here or leave a message for either of us. Dragan isn't often at the clinic these days."

Elizabeth blinked. There was nothing but kindness in the lady's face or voice, and it almost undid her. "You are very kind," she said huskily, turning away to lay both cards on the mantel-piece. "But I don't anticipate any further problems."

That was before she had the house to herself again, and on impulse went upstairs to see if any of her meager possessions had, in fact, been taken. And, opening the little cupboard of her bedside cabinet, she discovered that her father's chess set was missing.

# CHAPTER THREE

T HE MORNING AFTER Joshua Jarman was killed, James Andover stepped out of his lodgings in Henrietta Street to be greeted by a cheerful "Good morning, my lord" from the young woman who fell into step beside him. A small, elegant Italian greyhound trotted along beside her on a leash.

James allowed her a haughty glance, then blinked in surprise. "Good morning, my lady." Twisting around, he could discover no gentlemen, footmen, or even maids to escort her. "I should not need to warn you that being seen with me is carrying eccentricity too far."

"Oh, nobody pays any attention to my eccentricities anymore," she said dismissively.

"If you imagine the daughter of a duke is not dogged by gossips, journalists, and fortune hunters—"

"I've grown adept at avoiding such. I wasn't sure you recognized me yesterday afternoon."

"Neither was I. You pop up in some odd places."

"So do you. Including the scene of Joshua Jarman's murder."

James said casually, "I didn't kill him. Sadly."

"I know. And it isn't sad at all that you won't go back to prison for murder."

His eyes narrowed. "You *know* that?"

"Well, you were following Alice Gunn when Jarman died. Will you come to Scotland Yard with me, and clear things up with Inspector Harris?"

He began to wonder if the duke's once charmingly eccentric daughter had evolved into clearer insanity during the three years of his "absence." "Lady Grizelda, I cannot go anywhere with you. Even were I not freshly out of Newgate—"

"Cleared of all crimes," she interrupted.

"I think you'll find that makes no odds to anyone who matters."

"I think you'll find the opposite," she replied, "though perhaps not immediately. You should know that I am married now, by the way, and not subject to quite such strict rules of propriety."

"Congratulations," he said politely. "Do I know the lucky gentleman?"

"I'd be surprised, since I only met him this year. But you might have seen him with me yesterday."

He glanced at her, feeling his lips quirk into something of the smile she had once inspired in him. "Really?" he said in blatant disbelief. "The policeman or the doctor?"

"The doctor. He's Hungarian." She took his arm companionably and tugged him south toward the river. "Why were you following Alice Gunn?"

He met her gaze with a mixture of irritation and recklessness, which seemed to be common emotions these days. "Because I heard she had the diamonds I went to prison for stealing."

Lady Grizelda's eyebrows flew up. "Who told you that?"

"An acquaintance in Newgate," he said. "He worked for Jarman."

"A reliable witness, then," she replied sardonically.

"Oh, we jailbirds tell the truth occasionally."

He thought he had kept his voice mild, with just a hint of mockery, but he felt her gaze boring into him. When he turned with a deliberately bland expression to meet that gaze, all he saw was the glint of the sun on her spectacles. It was a fresh autumn morning with no hint of yesterday's fog.

"You are understandably bitter," she observed.

"Your understanding makes it all worthwhile." His sarcasm was unforgivable, so he hoped she would simply go.

However, she didn't even release his arm. "No," she said, "but I might still be of some use to you. What exactly did you plan to do with the diamonds, once you retrieved them?"

"Travel in luxury, of course."

"Liar," she said without heat. "I think you want to rub them in the face of authority to prove that not only did you not steal them, but you succeeded in returning them when authority failed."

"Close enough." Although it wasn't *authority* so much as his family. And Cordelia.

"Then it's good enough for Inspector Harris. You'll come with me to Scotland Yard?"

"I appear to be going to Scotland Yard," he replied. "But I shall force myself to dispense with your charming company."

"There is no need," she said sunnily. "I am meeting my husband at Scotland Yard."

⇶⤜

SHE DIDN'T LIE. The handsome doctor was the first person he saw as a policeman led him along a dingy passage toward an open door at the end, from which he could hear a male voice. The doctor, leaning one negligent shoulder against the bare wall, appeared to be sketching something inside a notebook. He glanced up at their approach and smiled.

Christ, the women must just drop at his feet. No wonder Elizabeth Jarman had rushed straight to him. He had time to feel sorry for poor Grizelda Niven before she dropped his arm and went straight to her husband. The notebook vanished into his pocket.

"I brought Lord James," she said happily.

"So I see." The man's dark eyes met his with curiosity but no obvious prejudgment. James could almost believe it was how the Hungarian regarded most of the world.

"My lord, allow me to present my husband, Dragan Tizsa. Dragan, my old friend, Lord James Andover."

Tizsa offered his hand, a gesture so unexpected that James gazed at it for a moment before he took it. The doctor had a firm grip, his hands slightly rough at the fingertips, but otherwise shapely and strong.

"Are you really a doctor?" James asked.

The smile flickered again in a more rueful kind of way. "Not exactly. I did not finish my studies in Hungary before the revolution broke out. I hope to pass the necessary examinations here instead. In the meantime, while I study, I assist an English physician."

At that moment, Elizabeth Jarman, also known as Alice Gunn, walked out of the office at the end of the passage. She wore a different gown from yesterday, but it was no more prepossessing. Spotlessly clean, with a starched white collar, it might once have been blue, but had faded with age to a dull gray. Her bonnet was old, too, and had been caught in the rain several times too often.

Her step faltered when she saw him, but only for an instant before her chin came up and she walked on. Inconvenient admiration flickered again, for her courage if nothing else. Although, despite the prim dress and sad bonnet, she was not merely pretty. She was beautiful, her eyes a fine, defiant blue, her mouth curiously soft and vulnerable above that pointed, determined little chin. How could such a creature have been married to Joshua Jarman?

The police inspector he had seen yesterday emerged from the office behind her. Catching sight of James's companions, he groaned audibly. "Not you two again. What now?"

"A word?" Tizsa suggested amiably. "My wife has brought the man who followed Miss Gunn."

The inspector's glowering, perceptive gaze swept over James and widened with clear surprise. "Is it?" he threw at the seamstress, who replied clearly, "Yes."

The inspector's eyes gleamed with recognition. He opened his mouth, clearly desperate to ask a hundred questions at once.

"That word, inspector?" Lady Grizelda reminded him.

The inspector's mouth closed. He looked undecided, his gaze flying from her to James and back.

"Don't worry," James assured him. "I am prepared to wait five minutes."

The inspector swung on his heel and stomped back to his office, a Tizsa on either side of him. James couldn't hear what, if anything, was said, but there was no tension, no anger or fear in any of the three, just familiarity in the turn of the inspector's head toward Lady Grizelda, and the relaxed way Tizsa nudged the other man's elbow.

Elizabeth Jarman hovered a mere few steps from him, as though she had meant to put as much distance as possible between them and then changed her mind.

As the office door closed, he turned toward her. "Doesn't it worry you that your friends are quite so comfortable with a Scotland Yard detective?"

"Why should it? And they are not my friends. How could a seamstress be friends with a duke's daughter?"

"More easily than a master criminal's wife. Do they know?"

"Are you harping on that again? Why have you come here, anyway? To confess to breaking into my house? Or to murder?"

"Nothing so dramatic. I imagine the inspector wishes to eliminate me from his long, long list of suspects. What did he ask of you?"

"A formal statement of how I discovered the dead man."

"The statement of Miss Alice Gunn?"

Something changed in her eyes, as though she understood and fully expected the harm James would do her by revealing her true identity. But there was no gleam of fury or even fear, just…hopelessness.

"Who else?" she said dully, and walked briskly away from him.

From some instinct, he started after her, but the office door opened behind him, and he turned back instead. The inspector strode toward him, so James went forward to meet him.

"My lord," the policeman said with a curt nod. "Sorry to keep you waiting. Please come with me."

The Tizsas cast him amiable smiles as they passed, strolling down the passage as though they were at the Great Exhibition rather than the headquarters of the police.

"Please, sit," the policeman said. "I'm Inspector Harris, in charge of the investigation into Joshua Jarman's murder. I understand you would like to make a statement in connection with the case?"

"If you feel it would help."

A smile passed across Inspector Harris's harsh features. "You have been 'Tizsaed.' They are annoying but very often right. Might we begin with your name and address?"

James met his gaze. "You already know I'm James Andover. I have lodgings in Henrietta Street."

"And how did you come to be in the vicinity of Hanson Row?"

"I followed Alice Gunn."

Harris's expression gave nothing away. He was neither accusatory nor servile. "Why?"

"Because while I was still in prison, I heard a rumor that she had the diamonds I was accused of stealing."

"The accusation that sent you prison for three years and ruined your life," Harris said.

James raised one eyebrow. "There is no need to be melodramatic," he drawled. "But yes, I take a personal interest in the whereabouts of the diamonds and the arrest of the guilty."

"Did you not find it odd that your informant named a struggling seamstress in Hanson Row as the thief?"

"Oh, I always knew Jarman was the thief. I assumed she was a fence, using her trade as a cover. At any rate, I followed her a few times, to see whom she met with, and I watched her house, too. For the record, she had few visitors, none of them Jarman—until yesterday, obviously—or his lieutenants. The houses she visited were all respectable—I have the list if you're interested. My main concern was the bag she always carried, though it seems to have contained nothing more sinister than mending."

"We'll come back to that. At what time, yesterday, did you first see Miss Gunn?"

"About one o'clock. She came out of her house—with the bag—and walked along the canal to Chelsea Road, and from there to Queen's Square..." As he recited her movements, he watched Inspector's Harris. The man gave little away, interrupting only occasionally to ask about times.

At the end, James said, "Are you working out if she could have done it or if I did?"

"She thinks you couldn't have," Harris said, sitting back on his slightly unsteady chair, "since you were following her when Jarman was killed."

"You don't agree?"

"You have an excellent motive," Harris pointed out. "And while she heard footsteps behind her for most of her journey, she only *believes* they were yours. The only time she actually saw you was outside her house in Hanson Row."

James's lips twisted. "Around the time Jarman must have died."

"Close to it, certainly," Harris agreed. "On the other hand, since your list of the houses she visited aligns with hers, you do present alibis for each other."

James blinked. "You suspected *her*? Do you really think she would have had the strength? Jarman was a big man."

"He was, though you and I both know it isn't necessary to be present to cause a person's death."

James rubbed his chin thoughtfully, then let out a bark of

bitter laughter. "You don't suspect her at all, do you? You suspect me because, even without my father's support, I'm at least wealthy enough to pay an assassin."

"Correct me if I'm wrong, but you don't appear to have got far beyond the wrong that was done you. You must blame Jarman for that."

"I do," James said. "Don't you?"

"Oh, I blame Joshua Jarman for *many* things. Including the theft of the diamonds and the murder of the men transporting them. Sadly, his death prevents him from ever being tried for any of his crimes. Did you recognize Jarman when you saw his body?"

"Yes," James said evenly, as though he hadn't just walked into a stranger's empty house to do so.

"How?" Harris asked. "Three years ago, you told the police and the court that you had never seen nor heard of Joshua Jarman."

"I hadn't. But I made it my business to see him very shortly after my release."

Harris's eyes widened slightly. "You accosted him?"

"No, I hung around his known haunts, which had been thoughtfully provided for me by my Newgate informant, until an urchin identified the great Jarman for me."

Harris's gaze didn't waver from his. "I see. So, who was this helpful Newgate acquaintance who gave you all this useful information?"

"Connor," James said. "Peter Connor. He was hanged six months ago."

"He had connections to Jarman," Harris allowed. "In fact, we think he was probably Jarman's accomplice in the theft of the diamonds. Certainly, we discovered one of the stones in his possession, which is what led eventually to your release. But didn't you think it odd that Jarman would entrust such valuable loot to a poor seamstress? One, moreover, whom he never seems to have met?"

James almost laughed.

"What exactly did Connor say?" Harris asked. "That the diamonds were in the keeping of Alice Gunn?"

Now was really James's moment to tell her real name and connection to Jarman. It would come out eventually anyway. Her face, thin and brave, defiant and vulnerable, swam behind his eyes. She was not what he had expected.

"He didn't name her," James said. "Just mentioned a seamstress in Hanson Row, who held the diamonds for Jarman. Apparently, he popped in to collect one whenever he needed extra cash, as though she were his banker. Miss Gunn is the only seamstress in the street."

To Elizabeth's relief, none of the major newspapers being sold in the street made any mention of the body found in Hanson Row. The police were indeed being discreet—for now, although the death of Joshua Jarman would hardly remain a secret for long. She imagined skin and hair would be flying around St. Giles and the rougher dock areas as the criminals tussled for supremacy. Which might give her a little time, even after her identity came out.

It probably had by now, she acknowledged as she heaved the last bolt of cloth into her trunk. *He* would have told Inspector Harris. And the Tizsas. Even if no one accused her of killing Joshua, her connection to him would inevitably ruin Alice Gunn.

She wondered how far her meager savings would take her. As far as Scotland? If she kept back nothing to live on while she found work.

She trailed through to her bedroom, collecting her few clothes and her hairbrush, which she carried through to the spare room and tossed in the trunk.

A knock at the front door startled her. Her heart thudding, she crept back to her bedroom and peered through the curtains.

Whoever had knocked must have been standing too close to the front door, for she could see no one. A neighbor in search of gossip? Like Mrs. Smith, who had already accosted her in the street, asking with false sympathy about the body taken from her house yesterday. Elizabeth had muttered something about a vagrant in her garden and hurried on.

Or perhaps it was Inspector Harris, come to question her again with less sympathy than before. Or journalists.

Or Joshua's people...

A figure stepped back—a woman—and glanced up at the window. With unspeakable relief, Elizbeth recognized Lady Grizelda. Not that she wanted to face the lady's contempt, but she supposed she owed her an apology after her kindness. Lady Grizelda lifted a friendly hand in greeting, so perhaps she didn't care who Alice Gunn really was.

Elizabeth went reluctantly downstairs then unlocked and opened the front door, holding it wide by way of invitation. Whatever was said, she didn't want her neighbors to witness. Even though it was too late to matter, old habits were hard to break.

"I brought you more tea," Lady Grizelda announced, whisking herself inside and straight toward the kitchen. "Having drunk so much of yours yesterday, I was afraid you would run out." She paused, glancing around the bare shelves and the open, all-but-empty larder.

"I'm sorry," Elizabeth said. "I've packed everything away. There was no need to bring more tea, though I thank you for the kind thought. Please keep it for yourself."

"You're leaving," Lady Grizelda said. She turned to face Elizbeth. "Is that a good idea? It will make you look guilty, although no one truly suspects you at the moment. And besides, where will you go?"

"I haven't decided yet."

Lady Grizelda lowered herself into a chair, settling one arm across her abdomen. Elizabeth wondered if the lady was pregnant. *None of your business, Beth Barker.*

"May I know why?" Lady Grizelda asked.

"I think you know. He has spoken to you already."

"Who has? Inspector Harris?"

Elizabeth shook her head.

"James Andover?"

"If that's the man who followed me."

"Then yes, I spoke to him today for the first time in more than three years."

Elizabeth searched the other woman's face and found nothing but curiosity. "You don't know," she blurted. "He didn't tell you."

"Tell me what?"

"About me. About who I am."

"And who are you?" Lady Grizelda asked.

"I was born Elizabeth Barker. He—Mr. Andover—calls me Elizabeth Jarman."

"And are you?"

Elizabeth shook her head and sank onto the only other hard chair. "There was some kind of ceremony, but it wasn't legal. It's consolation, mostly, that I was never actually his wife."

"I knew there had to be a better reason he was following you." Lady Grizelda sounded slightly smug, although immediately after, she sighed. "You had better tell me."

Elizabeth stared at her. "My lady, it is not an edifying story. Did he really not tell you?"

Lady Grizelda shook her head. "Is that the reason you are planning to flee? Because you think he told us? And Inspector Harris?"

"Why would he not? He hates Jarman and everything connected with him, and he thinks I know about the wretched diamonds. I wasn't even aware of their existence until Joshua died."

"That is true. And he has cause. Do you know his story?"

"I know he went to prison for stealing the diamonds, which

I'm inclined to believe was Joshua's crime."

"James had bought the diamond and had it set in a gold ring for the lady he was going to marry. It was identified as stolen, and because the jeweler he said he bought it from denied his claim, James was charged with the theft. The importer, who had brought the diamonds legally into the country, identified the diamond in his possession as one of the stolen ones, which added murder to the charges against James. He was tried and found guilty. His family's influence ensured he did not face execution, but he went to prison for three years before another diamond was found in the possession of one Peter Connor. Another was found at a pawnbroker's. These exonerated James, who was then released. Not to a happy ending, sadly. His family and friends had already disowned him, and his betrothed married another. He is understandably bitter. Vengeful, even, and yet..."

"And yet what?" Elizabeth asked, hoarding the information to guide her tangled opinions of the man.

"And yet he never mentioned your connection to Jarman, not to my husband or me, and not to Inspector Harris."

Elizabeth stared at her, letting her breath seep slowly out. "Perhaps he prefers to handle the matter himself."

"Possibly. Or perhaps he has decided you are a good woman after all."

She closed her eyes. "I gave him no reason to think so."

"You brought a doctor to save the life of a man who, at the very least, betrayed you."

"Seduced me from my family, cheated me..." She swallowed and forced her eyes open. She would not bleat the rest like a kicked cur. "Suffice it to say, I hated him at least as much as Mr. Andover clearly does."

"Then you should not run away. You should help my husband and me discover what really happened to Jarman."

Elizabeth regarded her with fascination. The duke's daughter had a habit of saying the outrageous as if it was mere trivial common sense. "Why? Why should you bother discovering such unpleasant—"

"My husband and I share a strange compulsion to solve puzzles," Lady Grizelda informed her. "In fact, people have paid my husband to carry out such work. He's very good at it."

"I can't pay anything beyond a few shillings."

Lady Grizelda smiled. "We would never expect you to. My hope is that we can persuade James to foot the bill. Tell me, have you ever been to the Great Exhibition in Hyde Park?"

# CHAPTER FOUR

L ONDON'S GREAT EXHIBITION had largely passed Elizabeth by—apart from her staring at the huge glass building that housed it each time she took a shortcut through Hyde Park. Disparagingly dubbed the Crystal Palace, the temporary edifice suited its nickname so well that it had stuck. Despite inevitable curiosity, Elizabeth had never dared buy a ticket. She was reluctant to allow Lady Grizelda to treat her now.

"Don't worry. I have two season tickets," Lady Grizelda assured her. "And I suspect we'll find Dragan there. We need to exchange information."

"I should walk behind you as if I'm your maid," Elizabeth said nervously as they left her house.

"You're not my maid, though, are you? In fact, I rather suspect you are a gentlewoman."

"Not by your standards," Elizabeth said with the ghost of a smile. "My father is a banker."

"When did you last see your parents?" Lady Grizelda set a cracking pace toward Commercial Street.

"The day before I ran away with Joshua. They refused to come to the wedding and gave out that I had gone abroad to a school friend in France. I suppose I must still be there."

"Did you contact them again?"

"Once or twice. They never answered."

"Not even after you left Joshua?"

"I never told them I had done so. I could almost hear their *I told you so* even in utter silence. They were right. I was young, stupid, and rebellious, and I had no need to marry Joshua just to escape the dull prospective bridegrooms my father kept lining up for me."

Lady Grizelda hesitated, then said, "You don't feel it would be more *comfortable* to go home?"

"God, no," Elizabeth said with a shudder. "Besides, they wouldn't have me back. To respectable people, I am ruined several times over."

They had turned into the main road by now, and without warning, Lady Grizelda reached up and opened the door of a stationary hackney. "I asked him to wait," she said. "No point in walking the whole way and being too tired to enjoy the exhibition. There's a lot to see."

⟫⟫⟪⟪

DRAGAN TIZSA KNEW he should probably stay in his government office looking at patterns of fraud. And if he didn't, he should go home and study. And yet after he'd thrust his current work into his satchel and left the building, his feet took him not home but to Henrietta Street, where, according to Griz, resided Lord James Andover.

"Visitor, my lord!" the plump landlady yelled up the stairs, so suddenly and so loudly that Dragan almost imagined himself back on the battlefield—which was no condition in which to meet this particular man. "Just go up, sir. First door on the right."

Dragan climbed the stairs and knocked on the first door. Receiving no response, he knocked again, for the landlady had seemed sure Andover was home. Moreover, he could hear someone moving in the room beyond.

At his third knock, the door flew open and Lord James stood there in his shirt sleeves, pale, scowling, and clearly ready to excoriate whoever disturbed him so relentlessly. The sight of Dragan appeared to take him by surprise, for his mouth closed without his uttering a word. On the other hand, there was no softening of his expression. The alteration of his demeanor was subtle, but it was neither welcoming nor comforting. The man's very stillness was threatening. Something learned in prison, perhaps—how to intimidate without violence. And yet Dragan was left in no doubt that resorting to violence would not trouble his lordship either.

"Forgive the intrusion," Dragan said mildly. "I felt we should talk."

"What about?" Andover asked. He neither stood aside nor invited Dragan in.

"Jarman."

The slate-gray gaze seemed to be trying to pierce through Dragan's eyes to his brain. Then, impatiently, Andover spun around and walked away, leaving the door open. Dragan took it as invitation and stepped inside a drafty, untidy sitting room.

The reason for the draft was immediately clear—the windows were wide open. Andover waved at a sofa cluttered with books, papers, and a carelessly discarded coat. Dragan moved the coat and sat. A desk at the window was piled high with more paper. Two cups sat on top of the piles. A used glass and a brandy bottle stood on top of a bookcase. A pair of boots graced the middle of the floor. A second door to an equally untidy bedchamber stood half-open—a curtain flapped in the breeze as though the windows in there were open too. Dragan supposed a man just out of prison would appreciate even what passed in London for fresh air.

"What about Jarman?" Andover snapped.

"Do you want to know who killed him?"

"Apparently, my motive is greatest, as it was greatest in the crime of diamond stealing and accompanying murder, despite my family's wealth. So yes, given the alternative of a return to Newgate prior to execution, I *would* like to know who killed the bastard."

"So would I," Dragan said.

Andover stood gazing at him. "Why? What does some underworld killing matter to you? Did you know Jarman?"

Dragan shook his head.

"Or do you want to exonerate *her*? Alice Gunn, who found herself in something of a pickle with a dead man in her chaste spinster's bedchamber?"

"I feel for her plight, yes," Dragan allowed.

"Why? Because she's more than a patient to you? I hope not. I always rather liked Lady Grizelda."

"Good. Though I would like to point out that your suggestion insults her as well as Miss Gunn and myself."

Andover thought about that. "I suppose it does. Sorry."

For the first time, Dragan found him mildly endearing.

Andover kicked his boots aside and swung the desk chair around to face Dragan before he sat. "Why *do* you want to discover Jarman's killer? And why are you sure it isn't me?"

"Griz and I like puzzles," Dragan said vaguely. "I don't think Miss Gunn killed that brute of a man, and Griz doesn't think either of you did."

"And your friend Inspector Harris?"

"He will decide by the evidence, of which there is remarkably little. I don't suppose you removed a set of chess pieces from Alice Gunn's bedside cabinet."

The scowl reappeared. "Of course I did not."

"Well, someone did, and it was probably whoever killed Jarman. Only, it seems an odd thing to steal."

"There didn't seem to be much else of value," Andover pointed out. "But I return to the original point. Will your friend the inspector not object to your blundering about on his case?"

"Frequently. But he is not an unreasonable man."

"And how is it you have time to indulge such curiosity, if you assist this doctor and study for your medical examinations at the same time?"

"I also do a little work for a government department, and

people pay me sometimes to solve their puzzles."

Andover's lips twisted. "You want me to *pay* you?"

"I wouldn't object. You can pay me if I produce results, if you like. Or not pay me at all. I imagine I'll keep working on this in any case. But I feel strongly that you and I need to work together, along with Griz. You need to be honest with us and tell us what you know."

"I don't know anything. That's the trouble."

"You told Harris that Connor, a member of the gang who stole the diamonds, told you Alice Gunn had them. Is that true?"

"It's what he told me, though I wouldn't say Miss Gunn lives high on the proceeds."

"It doesn't make much sense to me. You've been looking for the diamonds since you were released from prison. You've spent a lot of that time following her, as though you find this accusation a lot more credible than I do."

Andover shrugged. "Connor had no reason to lie."

"We need a conference," Dragan said abruptly. "With Griz. We can all lay our cards on the table and plan out the investigation properly. Can you come now?"

"Where?"

"Our house. Well, via the Exhibition. Griz and I were going this afternoon. I've to meet her there in…just under an hour."

Andover regarded him for a moment, a hint of bewildered amusement amongst the suspicion. Then he stood and reached for his coat from the sofa. "Very well."

ELIZABETH'S FIRST IMPRESSION of the Exhibition was of noise—a roar of mingled human voices, clomping footsteps, and mechanical hums, all echoing around the huge glass and metal barn of a building.

She was relieved to be able stand still for a little, close to the entrance where Lady Grizelda had arranged to meet Dr. Tizsa, and just get used to being there.

"So many people," she murmured.

"I know, but once we start moving, you'll find the crowds a bit more spread out and bearable! Besides, there is so much of interest to see that you forget about the milling throngs. There are a few sewing machines I'm sure would fascinate you. You could speed through your work with one of those. Ah, is that Dragan?"

Elizabeth followed her ladyship's eager gaze, but not to Dr. Tizsa. Her heart gave a huge thud at the unexpected sight of James Andover. He saw her at the same time, and immediately frowned. His lips moved, saying something curt to the man beside him—and *there* was Dr. Tizsa.

The doctor didn't reply, for Lady Grizelda had rushed on him like a whirlwind. His handsome face softened into a smile, and just for a moment, his arm crept around his wife's waist. Understated marital affection was much easier to watch than Andover's suspicion and frank dislike.

Elizabeth stayed where she was, though inevitably Lady Grizelda towed the two men to join her.

"Look whom Dragan has brought," Lady Grizelda said cheerfully. "Now we can have a more constructive conference. But first, I promised to show Miss Gunn the sewing machines..." She set off at her usual brisk pace, holding her husband's arm and leaving the other two to follow.

Mr. Andover did not offer his arm, although he made a polite inclination of the head as he and Elizabeth walked together. "They are a force of nature, are they not?" he said wryly. "Like a hurricane or a whirlwind."

"Or high tide in a storm." She flicked a wary glance. "Are you angry?"

He sighed. "No. I feel I should be. I just can't remember why."

A breath of laughter escaped her, and she risked another

glance, only to find his gaze strangely steady on her face, a sardonic almost-smile fading from his lips. For no reason, her stomach fluttered—or was it her heart? Then he blinked and looked ahead at the other two. Elizabeth hurried along at his side, unspeaking.

She poked around the sewing machines with interest, investigating their ingenious stitches and hand and foot treadles. The others lost interest more quickly, although she found she was a little too aware of Andover's still person beside her, distracting her from the machine's perfect row of loop stitches.

A woman's voice broke through her abstraction. "All very well, Arthur, but I deny it could challenge my embroidery skills!"

And abruptly, something changed. The hand she could see hanging at Mr. Andover's side suddenly clenched, and although it loosened again almost immediately, something had changed in his posture. It was no longer casual but almost frighteningly tense. And the silence stretched, not even broken by Lady Grizelda.

Surreptitiously, without straightening, Elizabeth glanced up and saw a group of newcomers, two fashionably dressed young ladies with wide crinolines, escorted by two well-to-do gentlemen.

One of the ladies appeared half embarrassed, half irritated.

The other looked...stricken. "My lord," she got out, and despite the huskiness, it was the same voice that had already spoken. And she was staring at Andover.

*My lord?*

"Lady Hampton," he said distantly. He even bowed slightly, and yet Elizabeth had the odd notion there was more mockery than courtesy in the gesture.

"Why, Lady Grizelda," the other woman said, stepping forward and extending her hand. "What a pleasant surprise to see you here."

"Lady Helen," Grizelda murmured, taking the offered hand. "Do you know my husband, Mr. Tizsa?"

"I have not had that pleasure. How do you, Mr. Tizsa?" The woman looked slightly dazzled, as most women probably were at first sight of the good doctor, but only for an instant. "And I doubt you know my husband, Mr. Front. Earnest, Mr. and Mrs. Tizsa."

Under cover of the introductions, which had not included Andover, the woman called Lady Hampton had taken a step nearer to him.

"How are you?" she murmured, all but devouring him with her eyes. "Are you well? You look pale."

"The pleasures of Newgate do that to a man," he replied brazenly, not troubling to lower his voice as she had. Lady Helen—Mrs. Front—looked pained. Lady Hampton whitened and stepped back as though struck.

"Are you acquainted with Sir Arthur and Lady Hampton?" Mrs. Front said to Grizelda, with just a hint of panic.

Andover stuck out his hand. "How do you do, Hampton? It's been a long time, has it not?"

Sir Arthur Hampton looked appalled. So did Mrs. Front. An unpleasant half-smile played on Andover's lips as he held the other man's gaze. He didn't drop his hand.

"Arthur," Lady Hampton whispered, almost pleading.

Sir Arthur barely touched the outstretched hand. "How do you do," he said. "Lady Grizelda, Tizsa, a pleasure to meet you. Best get on, eh, my dear?" Taking his wife's arm, he tugged her with him.

"Goodbye, Helen, Front," Andover drawled. "I know you'll pass on my best wishes."

Elizabeth straightened at last, looking from Andover to Grizelda and back. *"My lord?"*

Unexpected laughter hissed between Andover's teeth.

"Lord James Andover," Grizelda said. "I thought you knew? He's the younger son of the Marquis of Gartside. Lady Helen is his sister."

"There's no need to spare the rest," Lord James said sardonically. "Cordelia, Lady Hampton was formerly my betrothed. Do you know, I think I have had enough of…sewing machines for one day? Why don't I call upon you this evening?"

Dr. Tizsa passed him a card without a word. Lord James nodded curtly and walked off in the opposite direction to his sister and his once-affianced bride.

JAMES HAD NO desire to go back to his cramped rooms in Henrietta Street. He just needed to be away from the Crystal Palace, which echoed like a prison, and away from all these *people*. Especially people from his old world, from his past. Helen couldn't even look at him. And as for Hampton, the jumped-up fop Cordelia had married in preference to him…

And Cordelia herself, a little more mature and poised, but just as pretty as ever. And with more than fear in her eyes when she looked at him. There had been memory, even an echo of old love, and that he could bear less than anything else.

So he strode out of the Crystal Palace as though all the fiends in hell were after him and kept going until he was clear of the crowds. Eventually, he found himself by the Serpentine and kept walking, making sure he kept away from other strollers—children with their mothers or nannies, young women in pairs and huddles of all ranks, young lovers casting anxious eyes at the unreliable sky.

He knew he was being unfair to Cordelia. Even if she had believed in his innocence, he could not blame her for moving on with her life. Everyone had expected him to spend the rest of his days in prison. Even he had not expected to get out in three years. It had taken Cordelia something less than two to marry her faithful baronet, and he knew she would have faced pressure. He didn't blame her. What he couldn't bear, he thought ruefully, was that other people's lives had progressed while his stood still.

Or had it? He doubted he was still the same man who had gone, bewildered and outraged, from the Old Bailey to Newgate. Injustice changed a man. The brutality of Newgate would alter anyone. He didn't mind being bitter, though it got tedious now and then, but he didn't want to degenerate into a *whiner*.

He thought of Cordelia's beautiful, anxious face so close to his, and with odd dispassion wondered how he would feel should Hampton die tomorrow. Would she consider James's courtship again? Would he?

He doubted it. A world of hurt and betrayal that he doubted either of them could get beyond lay between them. Worse, he wasn't sure he minded. Despite his reaction to the unexpected meeting at the Exhibition, his sense of betrayal by Cordelia, by his family, had, in fact, receded. It now took second place to his determination to find the diamonds and prove his innocence beyond anyone's doubt. Which now appeared to involve finding Jarman's murderer. And somehow, he had acquired unexpected allies, which he didn't seem to mind at all. In fact, if anything, the intrusion of Lady Grizelda and her equally eccentric husband into his affairs seemed to lend a touch of fresh excitement to his purpose.

Breathing normally once again, he realized he had sped beyond Hyde Park into Kensington Gardens. He decided to walk back to the bridge over the Serpentine and cross Hyde Park to the Cumberland Gate and home.

But all the instincts for trouble that helped keep a fellow alive in Newgate were still with him. As he approached the bridge, he was aware of a woman and two men hurrying toward a group of trees on the same side of the river. Something was not right about the picture they presented. They were all too close together, almost as though drunk and holding each other up. But the woman's feet didn't quite touch the ground, and she was twisting in their hold.

This was an abduction.

He could never have looked the other way. And in this case,

the female was ill-dressed and thin and reminded him far too much of Elizabeth Jarman. He spun away from the bridge and sprinted after them. Calling out might have attracted attention and help, but it would also warn the abductors to run faster. So, he pounded after them at full tilt until he got close enough to be heard.

Both men jerked their heads around—a villainous-looking pair, none too clean, but not ill-dressed or undernourished. He would lay odds they were the henchmen of someone like Jarman.

Their captive used their moment of inattention to hurl herself backward, twisting her head around frantically. Her mouth opened wide to cry out. It was indeed Elizabeth Jarman.

# CHAPTER FIVE

HER CAPTORS WERE too strong for her. One shoved his arm further around her shoulders and clapped a hand over her mouth. The other man yanked her straight between them once more.

But they had all seen James now. He was gaining on them, and they knew it. They halted just inside the group of trees, far enough away not to be seen by anyone wandering the paths. As James slowed, one of the men released her and whirled to face him, while the second man clamped both arms around Elizabeth, holding her hard against him. Above his grubby hand, which James was viciously glad to see bleeding, her eyes were wide and terrified. And furious, which made him unreasonably proud.

"Not your business, mister," the first man snarled, slashing a knife before him.

"Wrong again," James said, and snatched a long-bladed dagger from his boot. "Mine's bigger."

The man holding Elizabeth sniggered, presumably at the very idea of a toff being able to fight with a knife, which was generally the preserve of the gutter. Newgate, of course, was one big gutter, and James had learned how to be the rat that survived.

"Better run away, rich boy," the knife man taunted him.

"Better let the lady go, then."

"Get it over," growled the man holding Elizabeth, who stamped hard on his instep and tried to break free.

James had no time to observe more, for the knife man lunged at him. He sidestepped and aimed a vicious stab that would have paralyzed his opponent had the man not made a last-second parry and rolled. James was on him in a flash, not falling on top of him and risking the knife but swinging his boot hard against the knife hand.

The man cried out in agony, but while James snatched up the knife, his opponent leapt to his feet and charged him with fury, head down. James barely had time to sidestep him this time, but he did manage to seize the man by his belt and hurl him headfirst into the tree. He dropped like a stone among the roots, and James swung on Elizabeth's captor.

The thug, clearly, knew that he couldn't hold the twisting, scratching termagant that Elizabeth had become and still fight off James without his comrade. His arm was already up, his meaty fist clenched and ready to punch her in the jaw. James couldn't wait. He took a flying leap, kicking out, and struck the man full in his stomach.

His fist fell and Elizabeth broke free with a sob. The man dropped to his knee, clutching his stomach, and Elizabeth ran to James, who had landed heavily on the ground.

He was so relieved he hadn't misjudged and kicked her instead that he lay there for a moment longer than he should. She fell on her knees beside him, distress written all over her face. Somewhere, she had lost her prim bonnet, and her hair was mostly loose from its pins. The combined effect was like a blow to his own stomach. He tried to grin, to stop her immediate worry.

Her eyes widened. "You *can* smile."

Laughter shook him. "Only after a fight." He hauled himself to his feet, hastily glancing around their immediate surroundings. The unconscious man still lay groaning at the foot of the tree. There was no sign of the other.

He flung one arm around the girl's waist, hurrying her away from the trees and back toward the Exhibition building. "Are you hurt?" he demanded. "What happened?"

She wiped her eyes almost angrily but didn't pull away from him. For some reason, he was glad of that. She felt as tiny and delicate as a bird, and she was shaking uncontrollably.

"I'm fine," she managed. "Are you?"

"Of course."

She swallowed. "I left the Tizsas at the Exhibition, since I have work to do before tomorrow. I didn't see the men. I didn't look, even though I *felt* them following, as I did when *you*... I thought I had grown too nervous, was just imagining things. I reminded myself you weren't following me anymore, and then they just swept up on either side of me and dragged me toward the trees. I struggled, tried to cry out for help, but one had his arm around my shoulders and his hand over my mouth. I bit him," she added with satisfaction.

James's lips quirked. "I know. I congratulate you, although you might want to wash out your mouth when you get home. Is this yours?" Releasing her with reluctance, he swiped a familiar, tired bonnet off the ground and gave it a shake.

"Oh, yes," she said with relief. "It's the only one I have, and I was annoyed to lose it."

Anyone should be glad to lose such an ugly hat. It annoyed him that she was poor enough to value it.

She plonked it on her head and tried to tie the ribbons, which were still knotted from before it had been knocked off. And her hands still trembled. He caught her arm to make her stop and turned her toward him. Wordlessly, he brushed her hands aside and unknotted the clean but faded ribbons. She let him. She even let him catch her hair and twist it beneath the bonnet, although she held her breath. As he tied the ribbons for her, he didn't look at her just because he wanted to so much.

His gaze was never still, though, as he sought any further threats or even people who looked too interested in them. No one paid them any attention, so when the bonnet was tied, he offered her his arm.

She took it gingerly, as though she were not used to such courtesies. "I'm still shaking," she said. "You must think me a very poor creature."

"I think you're magnificent. Shall we go back into the Crystal Palace and see if Lady Griz is still there?"

She shook her head almost violently. "I don't want to go back in there. I want to go home and work."

"Then we'll take a cab."

She looked up and met his gaze.

"We will," he insisted. "But if you wish it, I'll merely drop you off. I would rather go into the house with you and accompany you to the Tizsas' house afterward."

"There is no need," she protested. "I don't *want* to be so afraid I can't go out alone."

"And you won't be. This is just until we sort out the problem."

"Problem?" She stared. "You think this attack was related to the murder?"

"It's a bit of a coincidence, otherwise. Why else risk abducting an obviously poor young woman from a busy public park?"

"He's dead," she said.

"Jarman is. Did you recognize those fellows?"

She shook her head. "No. You think they are—were—his underlings?"

"Possibly. Or they belong to some rival."

She appeared to mull that over as they left the park by the Albert Gate, and he handed her into the first available hackney. He told himself he sat beside her, their shoulders touching, because she needed the comfort of friendly human contact.

Friendly. He had followed her more than once. He hadn't meant to be seen, to frighten her, but he hadn't much cared if he did, either. Shame at his own behavior mingled with admiration of her, of a new, intense interest he had not bargained for.

"Do you trust the Tizsas?" she asked abruptly as the cab set off.

"Yes. With less reservations than with most. Do you?" *Do you trust me?*

She nodded. Then, after taking a deep breath, she said, "You didn't tell them about me. You didn't tell the police either, according to Lady Grizelda."

He shifted on the bench. "It must have slipped my mind."

"Thank you."

He dragged his gaze free. "It's your secret. But I think you have to tell them if we're to get to the bottom of all this. Tizsa at least suspects there's more to my following you than the word of a fellow jailbird."

"I told Lady Grizelda, so I expect Dr. Tizsa knows by now, too. You shouldn't do that, you know."

"Do what?"

"Refer to yourself like that. You were wrongfully imprisoned. The blame for that lies with those who did commit the crime, and with those who misjudged you. You are blameless."

It wasn't easy to deprive James Andover of words, but the seamstress managed it. Moreover, she had stopped trembling. Some warmth seeped from her fragile frame against his shoulder, bringing with it gratitude and protectiveness and something stronger—that was almost hope.

»»«««

As SHE WAITED for James Andover's return that evening, she wished she had asked him to stay with her. It had made no sense sending him away for a mere two or three hours, most of which he had to spend rattling around London in hackneys.

She had spent the time sewing and mending and thinking. She tried not to dwell on the awfulness of her attempted abduction, when she had been terrified she would be dragged back into the world she had escaped three years ago. She had been saved, and by the unlikeliest hero.

Lord James Andover. He looked so pale, so refined and elegant, that it had never entered her head that he could, let alone would, take on such a pair of thugs, and certainly not for her. But he had raced after them, attacked, kicked, and punched without losing one iota of grace. And without showing any fear.

Had she even said thank you? Or had she been too dazed by her experience, and by the novelty of the "white knight" who had flown so improbably to her rescue? No one had ever defended her before. That *he* had risked himself for her melted the layer of ice that had formed around her heart. And now his visage, his quick, confident violence, seemed to be etched behind her eyelids. Everything about him had a strange, frightening beauty she had never imagined or acknowledged before.

She had no idea what it meant, but she felt almost embarrassed as she changed into her Sunday gown, a modest dove gray that was little brighter than her everyday dress but less worn. Normally, she wore it with a rather puritanical white collar. This evening, self-consciously, she substituted a short red paisley shawl that she had once made for a customer who had never claimed it. Then she sat by the window of her parlor and continued calmly to sew.

But inside, she was not calm at all. She looked forward to finally fighting back, to joining her unexpected allies in the seeking of the killer and the stolen diamonds. And yet it was James Andover's face that still kept intruding on her work. *Lord* James Andover, a marquis's son who would not have looked at her even in her old life as a banker's respectable daughter. So he had gallantly saved her from abduction this afternoon. His violence had both shocked and gladdened her. His kindness when she had been so shaken by her ordeal had surprised her even more. But she suspected he would do the same for anyone. Newgate might have embittered him, but at heart, surely, it had not changed him. She found herself wishing she had known him when he had been young and carefree and trusting.

He hadn't spoken in the carriage, after she had told him he was blameless. As the hackney had turned carefully into Hanson

Row, she had wanted to blurt out that there was more to him than three years in Newgate, but she had neither the courage nor the right. For it had taken until then for her to realize that there was more to her too than a series of mistakes and a year as the supposed wife of Joshua Jarman.

Only when the hackney had halted at her door did he speak again, promising in his old curt, yet casual, style to return for her just before seven. Acceding to her wishes, he had not handed her down, but she knew he waited until she appeared at her parlor window before he gave the signal to the hackney driver to move on.

And now her heart beat too fast as she waited for him to return. Her original fear of him seemed to have vanished altogether. Now he intrigued her too much. But she was also looking forward to the whole evening, to seeing the Tizsas in their own home, to the first social occasion she had enjoyed for years, even if it was inspired by such strange and brutal events.

And wouldn't her parents goggle to know that her companions included a duke's daughter and a marquis's son?

The thought made her smile ruefully, just as she heard the clop of a horse's hooves and the rumble of carriage wheels in the road. She forced herself not to look up until they halted. A hackney stood outside her door. She set down her work and rose, calmly blowing out the candle before swinging her cloak around her shoulders, drawing up the hood, and leaving the house.

Only as she locked the front door did it enter her head that she had not seen Lord James in the coach. She had asked him not to show himself to her neighbors for the sake of her reputation, but what if it was not he who sat inside waiting for her? A few hours ago, she had been the victim of an attempted abduction...

As she walked up to the carriage, the driver touched his whip to his hat by way of greeting. The carriage door swung open.

Just for an instant, Lord James's face loomed from the darkness, pale and gaunt and absurdly elegant for the neighborhood. His hand caught hers, helping her inside. He reached past her to close the door, and she forgot to breathe. The horse trotted on, rolling them to the end of the street to turn.

"Were you afraid it wasn't me? Or that it was?" he asked sardonically.

"I am not such a fearful creature," she retorted, although she was.

"On the contrary, I suspect you are one of the bravest creatures I ever met."

Her whole being flushed with embarrassment or pleasure—she couldn't tell which. "I don't know why you should think so."

"You stood up to me, and to those villains in the park. I can guess what your life with Jarman was like. Even the last straw of his death in such circumstances has not crushed you."

"He has not crushed either of us." She turned to meet his rather hard gaze. "I don't think we should let him."

"Hear, hear," Lord James murmured.

The Tizsas had a half-hidden house in a lane off Half Moon Street. By the standards of Mayfair mansions, it was small and quirky, and it suited them perfectly. A cheerful maid admitted Elizabeth and Lord James and led them to a surprisingly spacious drawing room that seemed to be part study. There, their host and hostess were arguing animatedly over something.

They broke off without heat to welcome their guests. In something of a daze, Elizabeth curtseyed and accepted a glass of sherry. The crystal was cool and fine in her fingers, reminding her how long it had been since she had been a guest anywhere. For the Tizsas treated her no differently to the marquis's son, friendly and not remotely condescending.

"What happened to your lip?" Lady Grizelda asked, sitting beside her on the comfortable sofa. "Did you bite it?"

Elizabeth touched it self-consciously and glanced at Lord James. "Yes, but not as hard as the hand I was aiming for." And she spilled out the story of her attempted abduction and Lord James's rescue.

The Tizsas listened, alternately wide-eyed and frowning with concern. And then the same maid appeared and announced that dinner was served.

"This changes everything," Dr. Tizsa said as they walked in a casual huddle into a cozy yet elegant dining room. An oval table had been set with four places, and Lady Grizelda indicated they should sit anywhere.

"In what way?" she asked.

"To begin with, Miss Gunn is in danger, which we never imagined."

The maid left them. Dr. Tizsa poured the wine, and Lady Grizelda ladled clear soup into bowls.

"I think," Elizabeth said, "that you should probably call me by my real name, which is Elizabeth Barker. When I was barely seventeen years old, I allowed Joshua Jarman to lure me from my respectable home into what I thought was marriage. It wasn't, though I didn't discover this for months. By then I was already utterly disillusioned. I had thought him a decent, charming gentleman who cared nothing for established wealth or Society's silly rules. He was different from anyone else I had ever met, and he claimed to love me. Of course." Her lips twisted.

"But I very quickly discovered he was no more a gentleman than the dogs that fawned over him from fear. I realized he was an important figure in the underworld he haunted, a thief, a man of violence, exploitation, and..." She broke off and took a deep breath. "I planned carefully before I left him. He gave me no money except for the food and ale he demanded at his table, but I knew where he kept it. I stole enough to get me to France and live for a little, and then, instead of going to the market one day, I kept going, with nothing but the money in my pocket, a change of clothes, and the chess set my father had given me."

"Did you make it to France?" Lady Grizelda asked.

Elizabeth nodded. "I did. I changed my name to Alice Gunn and took a job as a temporary nursery maid with a couple in Normandy, and then with an English couple in Paris. It was they who got me the requisite papers in my new name, and then, after almost a year, I returned to England."

"Why?" Lord James asked.

"Because he would have found out I had gone to France and would not expect me to return to London."

"Then he pursued you?" Dr. Tizsa asked.

"I knew he would. Oh, not that he wanted me back in any capacity. That joke had already run to its end for him. But I had stolen from him. Not a large amount by his standards, but the principle was the same. He killed anyone who cheated him. And in his eyes, he was never the cheat."

Lord James muttered something under his breath.

Elizabeth remembered to eat her soup.

"It's a long time to live with fear," Dr. Tizsa said.

She shrugged. "I grew used to it. I used the last of his money to rent the little house in Hanson Row, and I took in mending and sewing work. Needlework was my one ladylike skill. I expanded into making clothes for babies and young children and was able to put a little money away. Eventually, I wanted to be able to move out of London, to some quiet village and maybe teach children..." She gave a quick, embarrassed smile. "Everyone must have a daydream. But then I found Joshua's body in my house. He had found me. And if he hadn't been dead, I would be."

Lady Grizelda rose and collected the soup plates. After laying them in a neat pile on the sideboard, she uncovered the other steaming dishes waiting there and brought them to the table. Dr. Tizsa helped Elizabeth to fish with a tarragon sauce.

"I'm not sure," Lord James said, performing a similar service for Lady Grizelda, "that that is true. Jarman must have known where you were for several months. According to Connor, his one-time henchman, Jarman called on you and helped himself to the odd diamond when he needed to."

"*What?*" Elizabeth dropped her fork onto the plate with a clatter. "Dear God," she whispered. Dr. Tizsa reached over and pushed her wine glass closer to her. She took a sizeable gulp.

"I suspect now that he came while you were out," Lord James said. "And he didn't stay long."

"How did he get in?" Lady Grizelda demanded.

"I don't know, but I suspect he picked the lock on the back door."

Dr. Tizsa nodded. "That explains the unlocked door when I first went there."

"Yes, but I never *had* the diamonds!" Elizabeth exclaimed. "So why was he there?"

Lady Grizelda exchanged a glance with her husband. "We think you did have them and never knew. What was the only thing missing after you found Jarman's body?"

"The chess set," Elizabeth replied, frowning.

"Exactly." Dr. Tizsa leaned forward. "He pursued you for the diamonds, not for whatever else you took from him. He must have hidden the diamonds inside the chess pieces. It's perfectly possible to do so. He would have been livid when you ran away, and he probably knew as soon as you returned to the country."

"And then," Lady Grizelda added, "he must have decided it was much more convenient to keep you ignorant. No one would even think of looking for the diamonds in a house occupied by a poor, respectable seamstress. So, he just helped himself when he needed the funds."

"But he couldn't hide it forever," Lord James mused. "Pete Connor knew. He even traced the location down to a seamstress's house in Hanson Row. Jarman possibly gave him the diamond he was caught with to shut him up."

"He might even have pointed the police in his direction," Elizabeth offered. "It's the sort of thing he would have done to prove no one got the better of him."

"But Connor could then have pointed the police to Jarman," Lady Grizelda argued. "And to Elizabeth."

"Not if he valued the lives of his family," Elizabeth said in a small, hard voice.

"So, he told me instead," Lord James said slowly.

"Then Jarman was murdered for the diamonds by whoever stole the chess set." Dr. Tizsa forked the last mouthful of fish and ate with evident enjoyment.

"So all we have to do," Lady Grizelda said, equally pleased, "is find the missing chess set."

"I don't think it's quite as simple as that," Lord James said. He laid down his knife and fork. "Because I don't think whoever killed him *has* the chess set. If they had, why would they try to abduct Elizabeth?"

They all regarded each other as the implications began to dawn.

"Andover's right," Dr. Tizsa said at last. "Whatever happened in the house that day, Jarman was killed too quickly, before the murderer found the diamonds."

"If Joshua saw him," Elizabeth said, "he would have to kill or be killed." She shuddered.

There was silence in the dining room.

"After dinner," Lady Grizelda said, "we need to make a list of all the people who would or could have done this. Dragan, will you slice the beef?"

# CHAPTER SIX

T HE TIZSAS DID not appear to bother with the tradition of the ladies leaving the gentlemen to their port, for after the meal was finished, they all trooped together back to the drawing room, where the maid served coffee and Dr. Tizsa poured brandy for any who wanted it. Elizabeth, whose head felt fuzzy enough, refused, and Lady Grizelda wrinkled her nose.

"Then I'll drink for two," Dr. Tizsa said with a quick smile that was immediately reflected on his wife's face.

Oh yes, Lady Grizelda was expecting a baby, Elizabeth thought, accepting her cup and saucer from the maid.

"Would you prefer tea?" Lady Grizelda asked, catching her observation. "We've got into the habit of coffee, but…"

"No, coffee is perfect," Elizabeth assured her. "I need to stay awake, and so far, very little is making sense for me. If the murderer doesn't have the diamonds and was scared off by my return so soon after he killed Joshua, why attack me now? Why have they not torn the house apart already? Why did he not wait for me and try to get the information out of me as soon as I came home that afternoon?"

"Perhaps he was too appalled at what he had done for nothing," Lady Grizelda suggested. "Perhaps he saw James following you. In the mist, he wouldn't be very recognizable, so the killer might have imagined he was police."

"You mean he was watching me walk toward the house?"

Elizabeth exclaimed in fresh horror.

Grizelda cast her an almost apologetic glance. "We think he probably escaped via the back door almost as you entered by the front. The fog will have obscured vision, muffled sounds, and you were more worried about James than anyone inside the house. Probably just as well."

"God yes," Lord James said, though a sardonic curl of the lip dawned almost immediately. "By all means, let us pretend I am the hero who saved Miss Elizabeth's life."

"You are," Elizabeth said. "Twice, it would appear. But how did these men know I was at the park, at the Exhibition? Did they follow Lady Grizelda and me from the house?"

Lady Grizelda glanced up from her coffee. "I didn't see anyone, did you?"

Elizabeth shook her head. "But if they are watching the house, it makes no sense for them to try to abduct me from a public park rather than scare me to death in the privacy of the house. I don't imagine locked doors would be any more challenge for them than for Joshua."

"Perhaps they've been waiting for some announcement about diamonds being found along with Jarman's body," Dr. Tizsa speculated. "His murder was reported in the newspapers this morning."

"But not the place he was found," Lady Grizelda said. "Inspector Harris kept that information quiet—as much to catch the killer out in knowledge he shouldn't have as to protect you, I'm afraid, but it still works in your favor."

"All the same, she can't go home now," Lord James said. "It is much too dangerous."

Elizabeth felt torn between a jolt of pleasure at his care and annoyance at his impertinence.

"Of course, you must stay here," Lady Grizelda said as though it were a matter of course, and then she turned her head toward her husband. "Unless…"

His lips quirked upward. "Unless Andover and I wait there

instead."

"I was thinking more that you join us there," Lady Grizelda said airily.

"No," Dr. Tizsa said. "You need your rest."

"These people are ruthless," Lord James added. "Killing a duke's daughter after Jarman will make no difference to the murderer's sentence. I'm happy to take them on, but the ladies should not be present."

"I doubt they'll arrive en masse," Elizabeth said, frowning. "If Joshua was killed as part of some underworld coup, there won't be many people who know who did it or why, and the murderer will need to keep it that way to maintain old loyalties. Surely they'd risk no more than two people breaking into my house? And Lord James dealt with both my attackers this afternoon. With Dr. Tizsa present as well, I cannot imagine I'll be in any danger whatsoever."

"Nor I," Lady Grizelda added. "And Elizabeth will need a chaperone."

Elizabeth laughed, just because she had stopped thinking about her once-precious reputation. When had that happened? When she'd realized she would have to leave Hanson Row behind and make a new life somewhere else? When these people accepted her and helped her despite her being no more than the mistress of an underworld villain? She became aware of Lord James watching her mirth, the faintest of smiles playing on his own lips, lightening his hard eyes. Her stomach fluttered because he looked so...

Sudden lack of breath forced her to sobriety. "Lady Grizelda could have my bed."

Dr. Tizsa opened his mouth to object, then closed it as his wife took his hand.

"You mentioned lists," Lord James said. "Of possible suspects. Do we need to bother with such if we're just going to wait at Hanson Row to catch whoever it is?"

"Definitely," Lady Grizelda said, jumping to her feet and

going to one of the desks behind the sofa. She collected two notebooks and pencils and dropped one of each into her husband's lap, before resuming her place beside him. "So, we think the likeliest reason is an underworld coup against Jarman, either from his own underlings, or a rival gang. Do we know anything about Jarman's people?"

"I've discovered a little," Lord James said, "during investigations of my own. Jarman's lieutenant is a nasty piece of work called Porter."

Elizabeth shivered. "He would turn on his own mother. Brutal does not begin to describe him."

"But would he turn on Jarman?" Dr. Tizsa asked, his pencil moving across the page.

"I wouldn't put it past him," Elizabeth said. "Though he seemed devoted enough...and I wouldn't have said he had the intelligence to manage such an organization. He carried out orders, scared people into compliance. Bertie Sandman, whom he called his nephew, was brighter and younger, though his mother, Joshua's sister-in-law, seemed too loyal to turn on him."

"Barb Sandman?" Lord James said. "She and her son were living with Jarman."

Elizabeth shrugged. "Even in my day, she wanted to. She's young and comely enough, despite having a grownup son." She frowned. "Bertie's loyalty might well be questionable. When I knew him, he was too frightened of Joshua to do anything about it, but he used to *look* at me." She stopped, feeling all the old revulsion at that life she had so stupidly and happily walked into. Even now, it chilled her bones.

"They would be the likeliest of his inner circle," Lord James opined, dragging his gaze from her face, though he could not hide his distaste. That was worse. "Although there were others who worked for him with reluctance and might well have found the courage and the means to turn on him."

"Mrs. Silver," Elizabeth said at once. "Constance Silver."

"What do you know of Madam Silver?" Lord James asked,

staring.

"I think she ran a house of ill repute," Elizabeth said. "She came to the house occasionally, often with ledgers. She seemed to actually produce accounts for Joshua, which amused me in a shocking kind of way. But I caught a look in her eye once or twice... She didn't like him. She didn't like him at all." Another memory jolted her. "She even told me her address once, just as she was leaving and Joshua couldn't hear. Almost as though..."

"She was offering you work?" Lord James said with distaste.

Elizabeth shook herself. "Or sanctuary. At any rate, she is not a weak woman and did not like her situation."

"Interesting," Dr. Tizsa commented.

Lady Grizelda looked up from her notebook. "What about rival gangs who might have wanted the diamonds for themselves, as well as Jarman out of their way?"

"Zeb Fisher is likeliest," Lord James said, as though he had been considering this for some time. "I spoke to him not long after I came out of prison, and he would certainly have been happy to do Jarman any bad turn he could. And he definitely envied some of his—er...businesses. But there were other people who have major grudges against Jarman. Respectable people he has cheated or stolen from, or whose reputations or lives he has threatened. And some of those have connections to the diamond theft."

"Such as?" Dr. Tizsa asked, his pencil so busy that Elizabeth thought he was no longer writing but drawing. Or perhaps just scribbling. After all, Lady Grizelda was clearly taking copious notes.

"Such as Solomon Grey, the shipper who imported the diamonds. It was his employees Jarman murdered to steal the gems. Plus, around the time I was arrested, rumors sprang up that Grey had connived at the theft by telling the thieves where and when the diamonds were being transported. The gossip must have affected his business. And apparently, he is an ill man to cross. Having met him, I would agree."

"We have a friend involved in shipping," Lady Grizelda said, making another note. "I can make inquiries about this Grey. Who else? What about the jeweler you bought the ring from? Who denied ever selling you the ring?"

James shrugged. "Mason? I think he denied it through fear of Jarman, and you're right. His business did suffer from the notoriety. On the other hand, my sympathy is limited, since he also claimed my purposes in his shop had been to *sell* him diamonds for a song."

"But that's bizarre," Elizabeth said. "A reputable jeweler would never buy goods in such a way, and someone like Lord James would know it."

"Besides," said Dr. Tizsa, "none of the other stolen diamonds were ever found in Andover's possession. Yet Mason had no obvious reason to lie."

"Good points," Lord James replied. "Unfortunately, we can't ask Mason about them because he died in a carriage accident while I was in Newgate."

Dr. Tizsa glanced up sharply. "Accident?"

"I would doubt it," Lord James said. "Mown down, apparently by a coach and four out of control. They found the coach and horses, but not the driver."

"It sounds like Joshua," Elizabeth said, twisting in her chair. "I once overheard him giving such an order."

"When exactly did you leave him?" Dr. Tizsa asked.

"Monday the twenty-eighth of August, 1848," she replied.

"Five days after the robbery," Dr. Tizsa observed. "Which certainly gave Jarman time to hide the diamonds in the chess pieces. Though I suppose we're only guessing about that. Did you notice nothing odd about the pieces? Any change in them."

"I never took them out the box," Elizabeth admitted. "I took them in a moment of sentiment, a last-minute decision when I saw them on the desk in Joshua's room. The drawer where he kept his reserves of money was underneath. He did play chess sometimes, though, with Bertie Sandman among other people.

So it might have given him the idea."

"I think we have enough to begin with," Lady Grizelda said. "We have some likely suspects—Porter, his lieutenant; Bertie and Barb Sandman; Zeb Fisher, the rival villain. Then we have Constance Silver and Solomon Grey. And Mason the jeweler, though obviously we can't interview him in person. Which of these would have been strong enough to strangle Jarman with so little damage to Elizabeth's bedroom? I understand he was a large, strong man. Which probably eliminates the women."

"Unless they had help," Lord James pointed out. "And the murderer clearly does, because the thugs who attacked Miss Elizabeth were mere henchmen."

"Yes, but would you trust mere henchmen to kill a man of Jarman's importance in the underworld?" Dr. Tizsa asked. "For one thing, it would have to be a very loyal thug to be prepared to take it on such an enterprise."

"Fisher, then, maybe?" Lady Grizelda suggested. "At any rate, we need to find out what all our major suspects were doing and where on the afternoon that Jarman died."

Dr. Tizsa closed his notebook. "Then why don't we pack up and find a cab to take us to Hanson Row? We can divide up tasks on the way."

⤜⤛⤚⤙

THE APPORTIONING OF tasks proved not to be straightforward. Although it made sense to make use of everyone, Elizabeth's lack of safety bothered everyone.

"There's little sense in us all piling into your house to protect you, if we then all abandon you as soon as it's daylight," Lady Grizelda said. "After all, you were attacked in daylight today."

"The house needs to be searched from top to bottom to find the chess set," Lord James pointed out. "Supposing Jarman did hide it somewhere else. I could help Miss Elizabeth with that."

"Though if Griz and I are searching out suspects, it leaves Elizabeth with only one guard," Dr. Tizsa added.

"Well, the alternative seems to be that we all huddle in my house and never go out at all," Elizabeth said tartly, "which would get *nothing* done. It seems to me that the most important thing is to find the diamonds as quickly as possible. So, I will happily search the house, and then go out in search of our suspects. If we go in pairs, I will have a guard."

Flashes of light from street lamps and other carriages flickered over Lord James's pale face. "And if you're walking straight into the lion's den?" he asked quietly.

"Then we'll just have to appear as unthreatening as possible," Elizabeth said.

"Or keep Inspector Harris informed of our whereabouts," Tizsa suggested.

Lady Grizelda smiled. "Or Elizabeth pretends that she has."

Elizabeth could almost feel the curtains twitching and the eyes glued to the hackney as she and her allies alighted. They must already be fascinated by the number of carriages and strangers seen outside her house these last few days.

Ignoring them, Elizabeth marched up to her front door. Lord James's hand closed over hers. She jumped in the darkness, suddenly aware of his nearness, of the intimacy of the moment, even though he was only taking the keys from her hand.

"Your pardon," he murmured.

Lady Grizelda drew her back to let the men enter the house first, although she clutched her umbrella like a sword before her. Elizabeth peered into the street, following the lights of the carriage. Hanson Row appeared to be empty of everyone and everything else.

A light glowed from the hall, and she turned to see that Lord James had lit the lamp there. Holding it high, he looked into the parlor, nodded, then made his way to the kitchen. Dr. Tizsa came downstairs, carrying a candle and pronouncing all well.

They all repaired to the kitchen and lit some more candles,

which Dr. Tizsa had taken from his pocket.

"Unfair to use up all of yours," Lady Grizelda said, "when we'll be occupying all your rooms."

Elizabeth threw her cloak over the back of the nearest chair. "I'll make up the beds and find some old blankets."

"I'll help you," Lady Grizelda said at once.

Elizabeth was surprised to find her ladyship was not more of an observer than a helper.

"Are duke's daughters normally so at ease with bedmaking?" Elizabeth asked as she shook the pillow into its linen case and placed it on the bed.

"Probably not. But I did not marry a rich man, and we only have one maid."

"Does your family not support you?"

"My father gave us the house as a wedding present. Beyond that, Dragan and I would rather support ourselves." She cast Elizabeth a quick, rather endearing smile. "Yes, I know. I have always been eccentric."

"You are free spirits," Elizabeth said, placing the pillow on the bed. "I admire that."

"Well, independent spirits, so far as we can be with the exigencies of life!" Lady Grizelda sank down on the bed, as though suddenly exhausted.

"You should sleep," Elizabeth said. "When is the baby due?"

"Oh, not until the spring. But I don't like putting you out of your bed."

"It's the least I can do," Elizabeth assured her. "I shall be perfectly comfortable in the other room, where I have a ready-made mattress of new fabric and old clothes." She hefted the washing jug. "Let me bring you fresh water."

An hour later, she folded herself onto that makeshift mattress and pulled the sheet and blanket up to her chin. The house was quiet. Dr. Tizsa was reading—studying, Elizabeth suspected—by the light of a single candle in the parlor, a slightly moth-eaten blanket around his shoulders. Lord James sat in the kitchen, in darkness.

It didn't seem right. She suspected Dr. Tizsa had suffered considerably in the late revolution and war in Hungary. Lord James had definitely suffered in Newgate. And yet both were enduring more discomfort for her. Of course, Lord James was on a mission of mingled self-exoneration and revenge, and he probably felt guilty about frightening someone who had been yet another of Jarman's victims. But he had had no need to risk himself for her this afternoon in Hyde Park.

Her mind drifted to the confrontation inside the Crystal Palace, when Lord James's sister had blatantly ignored him, and the woman he had surely once loved, Lady Hampton, had stared at him as though she had seen a ghost. There had been *feeling* in the lady's stare. Guilt, shame, or just love, Elizabeth didn't know her well enough to say, but the tension between them could certainly have been cut with a knife.

Did Lord James still love her? At the very least, he must have felt her betrayal. And yet his own sister consorted with his betrayer while cutting James who was innocent. Elizabeth felt indignant on his behalf. And sorry. For there was an intense, corroding loneliness to the man that she recognized only too well. Perhaps it was that which spoke to her. Not just his touch. Or the unconscious elegance of his every movement. Or his pale, refined face and long, graceful mouth, so touched by sadness.

He disturbed her, this aristocratic jailbird with the violent hands and the gentle touch... Lord James, the marquis's son, who was so much *not* for her that it was surely safe to think about him just a little...

# CHAPTER SEVEN

G RIZ WOKE TO her husband's gentle kiss, daylight, and a cup of tea.

"That's better," she sighed, returning his embrace and using him as a lever to haul herself into a sitting position. He wrapped her fingers around the teacup, and she sipped, settling the tingly, sick feeling that still troubled her occasionally first thing in the morning. "Quiet night?"

"As the grave. They may be waiting to see what if anything happens after their botched abduction yesterday. Too soon, perhaps, to try again."

She reached up to brush his tousled hair off his forehead. "Did you get any sleep?"

"I did. The chair is quite comfortable."

"What about James?"

"I found him asleep with his head on the table. Like me, he wakes at the first sound—I expect prison works as well as war to that end. He's drinking coffee while our hostess makes breakfast. Toast and eggs."

Griz rubbed her tummy in anticipation. Dragan laughed and kissed her once more before rising and going to the washing bowl.

An hour later, duly washed, dressed, and breakfasted, they left Elizabeth and James to search the house and set off in search of a hackney to take them to the London Docks.

"Our hostess appears to have abandoned her insistence on propriety," Dragan observed.

"I think she's resigned to moving on. And after yesterday, she seems to trust James."

"Do you?" Dragan asked.

She turned her face up to his, frowning. "Mostly. He's...tougher than the man I knew, and much more secretive, but yes, I trust him with Elizbeth."

"But not that he didn't kill Jarman?"

Griz had been thinking about that a good deal. "He's capable of it," she said ruefully. "And before he knew her, he might well have left the body there to punish her. But I don't think he did. As Harris said, he could have done it and stepped out of the back lane in time to greet Elizabeth in the fog, but I don't think he did. He only found the body when she ran out to fetch you and he walked into the empty house."

"Or says he did."

Griz said uneasily, "*You* don't trust him."

"He isn't an easy man to trust. He has too many...layers. I suspect he didn't kill Jarman, but he could still have taken the chess set."

"Compensation for three years in Newgate?" Griz said. "I don't think that's his way. He's more likely to throw the pieces in front of the police, the courts, and his family, and stalk away."

"Probably."

"You don't like him," Griz observed.

"Actually, I do. But I like a lot of people who don't adhere closely to the law."

She squeezed his arm. "And Elizabeth. Do you suspect her, too? She could have knowingly stolen the diamonds from Jarman three years ago."

"She could, but wouldn't she have sold them abroad in that case?"

"We have no proof she didn't. Except that she's hardly living like a princess on the proceeds, and she could never have killed

Jarman without an ally. On the whole, I retain an open mind, but I believe I do trust both Elizabeth and James."

Dragan nodded.

She waited a moment, then said, "Something still bothers you. About either of them?"

He sighed. "No, I tend to agree with you. But something isn't right about the original theft. If Andover is telling the truth about where he acquired the diamond, why would a reputable jeweler buy from an unknown source like Jarman?"

"Shall we visit his widow after we've investigated the underworld for a little?"

"Why not?" Dragan said amiably. "Though I do have to be at the clinic by four o'clock."

"I MIGHT AS well start in here and tidy as I go," Elizabeth said in the kitchen. She imagined Lord James would take himself to the parlor or to one of the other rooms to search, but, in fact, while she cleared the table and washed the used dishes, he went to the kitchen cupboards, checking inside pots and pans as well as the backs of shelves.

It should have been uncomfortable at the least to have a relative stranger poking about her meager possessions, most of which weren't even hers but had been left by the previous tenants. Instead, it felt oddly companionable.

Which was probably why she was emboldened enough to ask, "Why do your family not acknowledge you now that you are proved innocent?"

He straightened and opened the larder door. "Habit, probably. And the fact that I don't acknowledge them."

"Because they didn't support you at your trial?"

"Yes, I am that petulant."

"It isn't petulance," she argued, lifting the pile of clean dishes and carrying them to the cupboard he had just searched through. "I imagine it was very...hurtful."

He was silent, and she thought he would never admit to that, even now. Then, running his hands down the back of the larder, he said, "No one had ever disbelieved me before. Even as a child, I always owned up to misdemeanors, even when my siblings didn't. Not to be righteous, you understand, just because I always knew we were found out and wanted the punishment over with as fast as possible. I presume my father thought I was so afraid of the noose that I changed my habits and lied. But I should not whine. I understand his influence made sure I did not hang."

"Even your siblings did not believe you?"

"I'm not sure anyone cared that much whether I lied or not." His lips curled. "It was the scandal that horrified them most. Helen was furious with me because the earl she was all but engaged to stepped back and she had to resort to the devoted but very un-noble Earnest Front."

"It's hardly your fault if her suitor has no honor."

"I may have pointed that out in my own head. At any rate, we don't talk, and I am more comfortable that way."

She closed the cupboard under the sink and turned to the kitchen table drawers. Remembering how Joshua had often hidden things he didn't want her to find—like bank drafts, coins, and jewels—she felt above and below each drawer in case anything had been stuck there. Lord James was moving things around on the larder shelves.

"And Lady Hampton?" she asked casually. "Did she not believe you either?"

He shrugged. "She never said either way. In fact, she never said anything at all until the unfortunate encounter at the Exhibition."

"I'm sorry," Elizabeth murmured, distressed on his behalf.

"Don't be." He shut the larder door and walked toward her. "I've just realized I'm not."

"And yet it hurt you to see her." Her breath caught as he

came close to her, but he only crouched down beside her and crawled under the table.

"A lot of things hurt. I don't need to pay attention to them."

"Newgate does not define you," she blurted.

He emerged on the other side of the table and rose to his feet. There may have been a faint hint of color along the ridge of his cheekbones, but he didn't avoid her gaze. "As Jarman does not define you."

It was her gaze that dropped. She closed the drawer.

"Did he hurt you?" Lord James asked. "Physically."

She swallowed. "Sometimes. Often enough that I regretted the dull bankers my father picked out for me."

"Did it have to be one or the other?"

"Perhaps, when one is seventeen. After I left, I came to like relying on myself."

"Working constantly, with no friends? Weren't you lonely?"

She didn't answer directly, merely smiled faintly. "It was better than the alternative. Have you not resumed your old friendships?"

He shook his head. "I've been too focused on making Jarman face the law."

"I suppose a higher power judges him now. What will you do once we prove his guilt?"

Something very close to a smile flickered across his face and vanished, perhaps because of her unreasonable certainty. And then the light faded from his eyes, leaving them hard and desolate as a winter moor. "I don't know. Go abroad, maybe. I think we've looked all over the kitchen. Where next?"

"The backyard," she said, aching for him. "It struck me last night, perhaps he threw the pieces out the window in panic."

He went to the back door and turned the key. "I'll watch from in here, to preserve your reputation."

She brushed past him into the tiny yard. Her washing line stretched from a hook in the house wall to the back fence—barely enough hang a sheet. She had planted a few vegetables and herbs in the spring, but they hadn't grown. Only weeds and brambles seemed to thrive in this soil. She poked halfheartedly among the few overhanging branches, but it was clear from the beginning that unless Joshua had buried the chess pieces, they weren't here.

"Morning, Miss Gunn," screeched her neighbor in the next garden.

"Good morning, Mrs. Moore," she replied to the woman who was all but hanging over the garden wall.

"Got some visitors, then?" Mrs. Moore asked, her eyes gleaming avidly.

"That's right. Family," Elizabeth lied without a qualm. "From the north."

"Lovely company for you, especially with you working so hard. Staying long, are they?"

"Just a few days, Mrs. Moore. How is your husband?"

She scowled darkly. "Malingering, if you ask me. Now I got to take in washing or we can't pay the rent. Got any for me, dearie?"

"Sorry, I haven't, but I'll spread the word, if you like."

"Thanks, love."

With what she hoped was a cheerful wave, Elizabeth turned to go back inside. The sight of Lord James's shadow behind the door brought another thought to mind, and she paused. "Mrs. Moore? There hasn't been anyone lurking around the row asking questions about me, has there? We're expecting another cousin," she added inventively, "and he hasn't turned up yet."

"No, no one's asked me anything, but you know how I keep myself to myself."

Elizabeth refrained from snorting.

"I did see someone lurking across the street a day or so ago, mind. When it was foggy? Probably that same man what turned up dead in your garden. Nice for you to have family here at such an upsetting time."

"It is," Elizabeth agreed, and walked inside before firmly closing and locking the door. "Do you think she saw Joshua?" she asked Lord James, who was lifting one of the hard chairs and examining its underside.

He set it down and upended another. "Maybe. She might have seen me. Or whoever killed Joshua. I expect the police have already asked the neighbors about strangers. And Harris must have told them the body was in your garden."

"I didn't think he would be that kind. Of course, he doesn't know who I am, does he?"

"I think he knows Jarman well enough that he would still be kind."

"I'll make a start on the parlor."

By the time they had fruitlessly searched the parlor and the cubbyhole under the stairs, her frustration had mounted. "This is impossible!"

"You'll never find the treasure with that attitude," he said sardonically. "Where *would* a pirate bury his treasure?"

"In the house of his estranged not-quite-wife, apparently."

"No, you put it there, and he found it." He brushed past her to the stairs. "Up the rigging, me hearties," he murmured. "That's why he was in your bedroom. And from there, he could have seen—or heard—anyone coming to the house."

Without apology or permission, he walked into her bedroom—currently Lady Grizelda's—and stood by the window. Fortunately, the curtains were shut. He peered through a crack down to the street, then swung back to her.

"Here I stand, the treasure in my hand, and I see someone coming through the fog. Or perhaps someone else has come in the back way and I hear a voice I recognize downstairs. Someone I don't want to find the treasure. What do I do? Throw it back in the cabinet?"

"Too easy to find," Elizabeth said. "Shove it under the mattress?" As one, they stepped to either side of the bed and heaved the mattress up.

"No," Lord James said regretfully, and they let it fall again. Dropping to his knees, he peered under the bedframe, feeling with his hands as far as he could stretch. On her side of the bed, Elizabeth did the same, but could feel nothing.

Re-emerging from under the bed, she sneezed. Across the mattress, Lord James was standing gazing across the room and through the open door. He moved suddenly, striding around the bed and seizing her hands to draw her to her feet.

"From the window, he would have seen straight through to the spare room. You don't keep the door closed."

"There's no furniture, no cupboards there," she protested, but allowed herself to be towed along with him. He hadn't released her hand, and although she blushed, she didn't mind. Inside the small spare room, he looked about him.

"The trunk?"

"It's empty."

"You could hide chess pieces among the lace."

"You could," she agreed, going to the pile and rifling through it. Nothing felt hard or lumpy.

He crouched by her makeshift bed, kneading the soft fabrics she had been lying on. A caustic remark rose to her lips but was never spoken. She was distracted by his hands—long and slender and as graceful as the rest of him, even though his knuckles were still grazed from yesterday's fight. His fingers rifled the sheets, at once strong and gentle and, she suspected, sensitive. They touched where she had lain, and for an instant, her whole body tingled as though they stroked her person.

Heat swept through her, and she dragged her gaze away to the bolts of cloth piled against the wall. Needing desperately to do something rather than stare at those mesmerizing hands, she stumbled past him, raking through the bales.

And then she saw it.

A silk cord hung around the innermost fold at one end. A cord she recognized.

"James," she breathed.

>>>><<<<

GRIZ AND DRAGAN'S first port of call was a surprisingly pleasant square between the London Docks and Whitechapel.

"Crippled soldiers or orphans?" Dragan murmured as he handed her down from the hackney a couple of streets away from their goal.

She cast him an assessing look as he paid the driver. "Orphans are less threatening."

Dragan offered her his arm, which she took delicately and rather coyly, blinking at him through her spectacles. His lips twitched minutely and his eyes gleamed, but he limped when he walked, leaning on his cane as though it were a walking stick rather than a weapon.

They made their way toward the square, examining the houses and shops they passed on the way. To any observers, they would have appeared to be searching out the most likely dwellings to provide charitable donations. A light, continuous drizzle served their purpose by dampening their cloaks and hats and adding to the impression they were trying to create, of good, downtrodden people doing their best to help those even more downtrodden.

The house where Elizabeth had lived as Joshua Jarman's wife was the largest in the square. Its iron gates were painted with gilt at the tips of each spar, and large pots of flowers flanked the impressive porticoed front door.

"Good God," Griz murmured. "He didn't hide his wealth, did he?"

"No wonder Harris wanted to bring him down. And Andover. Let's try this one first."

At the first front door they knocked upon, a man swore at them and told them to "shab off!" At the second, a slovenly maid let them wait in the dark front hall while her aged mistress hirpled slowly down the stairs to bestow a pound upon them. At the third, a blowsy woman tossed her head and claimed to have nothing left over to give anyone else.

"Go and try the big house over there," she advised with a hint of malice that might have been aimed at them or at the Jarmans. "They got loads to spare."

"Thank you and God bless you," Griz twittered, and was surprised as she turned away when the woman shoved a coin into her hand. The door slammed before she could utter a word of thanks. She didn't feel bad. The money really would go to one of her charities.

With the advice they wanted, they made straight for the Jarman house. Dragan rapped on the door with his cane. A large bruiser of a man in a plain black coat glared out at them.

"What d'you want?" he demanded.

"Sir, we are collecting charitable donations for the poor orphans of the East End," Griz began.

"Do it somewhere else," the bruiser recommended.

"Perhaps I might speak to the lady of the house?" Griz said with an ingratiating smile, while Dragan stretched his "bad" leg and replaced his foot in the way of the door. "I know she'll want to hear what we have to say."

Something in her words, combined with the sight of Dragan's large foot, must have caught the man's attention, for he paused in his clear intention to eject them. Before he could decide, the door was snatched from his hand and a buxom woman in a wide black and gray silk gown stood there. Gold and jet earrings swayed with her every move, and a matching necklace drew attention to her generous and well-displayed bosom.

"Who's this, then?" she demanded.

"I was just telling this gentleman," Griz said before the doorman could open his mouth, "that such a prominent lady, as you clearly are in the neighborhood, would surely want to hear about my church's charitable work with poor orphan children."

The woman looked Griz up and down and curled her lip. Then her gaze moved on to Dragan and she smiled. "Well...!"

"You are the lady of the house, ma'am?" he asked, removing his hat and allowing her the full effect of his visage.

Griz had always thought Dragan endearingly unaware of his breathtaking good looks. Now she began to suspect that he merely chose to ignore them until they were necessary. There was always a new layer to be discovered in one's husband.

The woman all but goggled. "I'm Barb Jarman," she said at last. "Of course you must come in and tell me about your charity, but you must know this is a house of mourning."

"I'm so sorry to hear that, Mrs. Jarman," Dragan said, ushering Griz over the threshold. "Who is it you mourn? Your grandfather, perhaps?"

Barb preened. "My husband," she said tragically, raising a black lace handkerchief to her eyes. "Gone to his rest too soon."

"You should bring your mistress a cup of tea," Dragan said sternly to the gaping doorman, who might, in fact, have been her son or Jarman's fearsome lieutenant, Jack Porter. "You must see how upset she is. Ma'am, will you allow us to distract your grief with those of others even less fortunate?"

Barb nodded bravely and seized Dragan's arm in a viselike grip, leaving Griz to trot after them and swallow back her entirely inappropriate mirth.

Ten minutes later, they were interrupted not by tea but by the precipitate arrival of a stocky dandy in a dazzling flowered waistcoat.

"Who's this?" he asked.

"They're from the church," Barb said in clear annoyance. "Collecting for charity."

"Outrageous," the dandy declared with relish. "The only business of the church in this house should be arrangements to bury my poor, deceased stepfather! Not cozening my grief-stricken mother out of her widow's mite!"

"Now, now, Bertie, there's no need o' that," Barb chided. "Where's your Christian manners?"

Bertie stared, and Dragan used the brief advantage of his

silence to take out his notebook and scribble.

Catching on, Griz said, "No, no, ma'am, your son is quite right. Why don't you think about what we have said, and when you are feeling more the things, perhaps you would consider leaving any donation you'd care to make with our charity's treasurer? This is her address."

Dragan tore the page from his notebook and rose to present it to Barb with a bow. Then, under the glower of Bertie and the doorman, they walked sedately out of the lion's den.

# CHAPTER EIGHT

"JAMES."

The breathy way she spoke his name vibrated through his whole body, inspiring a sudden surge of lust and quite inappropriate fantasy—perhaps because he had just been somewhat intimately handling the makeshift bed she had slept on only a few hours before. He let it fall a little too quickly and schooled his expression to polite interest before he glanced up.

He needn't have worried. She was not looking at him at all. She stood perfectly still with her back to him, one hand on a bolt of printed calico. Had he noticed her shape before? Beyond remarking that she was too thin. He supposed she still was, but she curved in all the most alluring places, and the slender column of her neck, her nape vulnerable to his eyes and hands, suddenly moved him unbearably.

*What is the matter with you, man?* he demanded of himself, forcing himself to step over the mattress and approach her with his hands hanging by his sides. By some effort of will, he remembered what it was they were looking for and forced himself to look at the bolt of cloth she was touching—and the silk string at its center.

As though she felt his approach, she cast him a quick glance, then slipped the cord off the cloth and tugged. The top of a small bag emerged. She grasped it and wriggled it out from its surrounding roll.

"It's them," she said in clear delight. "The chess pieces. I can feel them."

Brushing past him, she fell on her knees on the makeshift mattress and emptied a pile of smallish wooden figures from the bag. James followed more slowly, crushing the tangle of emotions that threatened him. He had been doing this for so long, it was second nature to him now. And yet it was more than likely that inside these elegantly carved but unassuming chess pieces was the reason for his three nightmare years in Newgate, and the ruin of his life.

He took the knife from his boot and knelt on the edge of the bed. Elizabeth's eyes widened. He picked up the white king. "May I?"

She nodded wordlessly, and he inserted his knife beneath the green baize at the king's base. It came away easily enough to reveal a disk of a different shade to the rest of the wood. He used the fine tip of the blade to pry that out, too, and turned the king the right way up. A hail of small, glinting jewels poured out onto the blanket.

Slowly, she reached out, her hand almost brushing his, and picked up the largest of the stones. She held it between her fingers, almost level with her face, to let the light from the window reflect off the diamond's multifaceted surface. She smiled, excitement gleaming in her fine blue eyes. And suddenly, beside her, the diamond was dull. A small piece of rock cut and polished by men and declared by them to be of surpassing value. But she, a young woman of character and courage who must have faced most of the ills the world could throw at her, and yet come through it, alone, with her sweetness and humor intact...

Still smiling, she moved her gaze to his. "Isn't it beautiful?"

"Not beside you."

Soft color seeped into her cheeks, but though she seemed surprised, she did not look away. "Are you being gallant?" she asked.

He pulled himself together. "Lord, no. I'm merely having a

Road-to-Damascus moment. How many people have died, how many lives have been ruined, for these crumbs of stone? And yet what do they actually matter beside your life or mine or even Jarman's? I find my obsession to find them somewhat pathetic. They change nothing that matters."

She searched his eyes, her smile fading. "Because it was you and I who found them in my house? And that will not take either of us off Inspector Harris's list of suspects?"

"There is that, too," James allowed. For the first time in years, his lips quirked upward involuntarily. "You were more right than I understood. We are not defined by our past misfortunes but by how we deal with them. You impress me. I do not impress myself."

She dropped the diamond among its fellows and took him by surprise, closing her hand over his where it lay on the white king. "Your choices were taken away, while mine were not. Yet you came back into your world, fighting, while I hide from mine."

A frown tugged at his brow, while warmth spread through his veins from her hand on his. "Is that truly how you see me?"

Another, gentler smile flickered in her eyes, but she didn't answer. He turned his hand, twining his fingers with hers. Her breath quickened but not, he thought, with fear. Embarrassment, perhaps, at the clasp of his hand when she had only intended a brief brush of comfort. Or did his touch move her? As it was moving him. He couldn't help the soft caress of his thumb against her skin.

"You and I," he began, with something approaching wonder, and then abruptly broke off at the sound of the front door opening. He snatched his hand from hers and seized his dagger once more.

"Andover?" came Tizsa's distinctive voice. "Elizabeth?"

James's shoulder dropped with relief.

"I gave them my spare key," Elizabeth said.

Was there a tremble to her voice? Had he frightened her after all? Or... *Stop being such a coxcomb!*

"Up here!" he called.

In moments, Tizsa appeared at the top of the stairs with Grizelda at his heels.

"We found them," Elizabeth said happily.

ELIZABETH WASN'T QUITE sure what, if anything, had happened between her and Lord James. Awareness of him, something that had always been there, had turned more pleasurable with each moment spent in his company. But that was a distant thing, something foolish she could hide while going about her life. Those last moments had suddenly felt intensely, almost unbearably intimate. He had understood her, touched her, and not only with his elegant fingers, skin to skin, but something deep inside her, barely acknowledged.

The arrival of the Tizsas granted her a moment of respite and relief, and yet she was honest enough with herself to recognize disappointment as well. If they hadn't come at precisely that moment, what would Lord James have said? What would he have done? Would his thumb have caressed her again, butterfly light and sweetly arousing? Would he have raised her hand to his lips? To that hard, sculpted mouth... Because she had the odd, unbalancing notion now that he wasn't hard or cold at all. Not remotely.

While the Tizsas exclaimed over their discovery and they all set about investigating the rest of the pieces, she kept her expression pleased and tried to pull herself together.

*"You and I..."*

"How was your morning?" Lord James asked, adding to the little pile of diamonds from a pawn's innards. "Constructive?"

"Interesting," Dr. Tizsa said. "We called on the delectable Barbara Sandman—who calls herself Mrs. Jarman, by the way—and met her son Bertie, too."

"It was not," Lady Grizelda said, running an idle hand

through the growing pile of diamonds, "a house of mourning, whatever she told us. She *is* wearing black, but it's gorgeous silk and low cut as an evening gown. Even her jewelry is black. But she could barely keep her hands off Dragan. She'd have eaten him alive if she could. Of course, we all face grief in our own way, but I'll lay you any odds you like that she doesn't feel much of it for Joshua Jarman's passing."

"And the son?" Lord James asked.

"Strutting like a peacock," Dr. Tizsa said, "with absolutely no concession to mourning. He thinks Jarman's little empire has fallen into his lap."

"Has it?" Elizabeth asked.

"Not if that doorman has anything to do with it." Lady Grizelda glanced at her husband, who abandoned the black knight in order to draw his ubiquitous notebook from his pocket and flip through the pages.

"Him," he said, setting the notebook down. "Do either of you recognize him?"

"Jack Porter," Elizabeth said at once. "Are he and Bertie at daggers drawn?"

"Griz caught a pretty filthy look between them as we were leaving," Dr. Tizsa said. "Certainly, it will be interesting to see which of them turns up here."

"Here?" Lord James said sharply. "Then you're sure one of them killed Jarman?"

"No," Lady Grizelda said, "but I'm afraid we gave them your address, Elizabeth. As the treasurer of my church's orphan charity."

Elizabeth let out a breath of laughter. "I wish I had been there to see Barb's charitable face."

"She'd have handed over hundreds for Dragan," Grizelda said with a mischievous grin.

"Only if she was sure of stealing it back again," Tizsa said. "We also called on the widowed Mrs. Mason, who still lives above the jeweler's shop in Ludgate Hill."

Lord James curled his elegant lips. "Mason, who denied I had bought the ring from him and yet swore I had instead tried to sell him several diamonds at a bargain price? Me being, apparently, an impoverished gentleman."

"Were you?" Lady Grizelda asked.

Lord James shrugged. "Not by most standards. But I couldn't afford too much expensive jewelry if I planned to refurbish my house in Kent for my wife. To that extent, Mason's lies were believable."

"He didn't lie," Dr. Tizsa said, meeting and holding James's gaze. "His wife was present throughout the transaction, was even introduced to the gentleman concerned—one Lord James Andover. Mason, she said, agreed to buy the diamonds only because the name of Andover was above reproach."

*No. No, that cannot be right!* Elizabeth's stomach twisted with denial, with anger that he was still being accused.

James's lips had thinned and whitened. He sprang to his feet, his very presence transformed. No longer the comfortable companion, he stood now as contemptuous and downright dangerous as Elizabeth had ever seen him. And yet she ached for him because she understood his hurt. Even these unexpected new friends and allies had turned against him.

"They both lied," he said haughtily. "Since you choose to believe—"

"Not deliberately," Dr. Tizsa interrupted. He flipped over a page in his notebook to show an alarmingly accurate sketch of Lord James. The portrait—astonishingly good—caught the supreme poise of the man, from the movement of his perfectly arched eyebrows, to the lean, fine-boned contours of his jaw and the firm, graceful lines of his mouth. Elizabeth could almost see a hand sweep up to push back the lock of hair fallen across his high forehead.

"She identified me from that?" Lord James said between his teeth. "Then she lies."

"On the contrary," Dr. Tizsa said. "She had never seen you

before in her life. She said this"—he waved a hand toward the portrait on the floor—"was not Lord James Andover, that she could not recall ever seeing such a man. The man who was introduced to her as Andover was several years older than you, and though distinguished and aristocratic in both appearance and manners, he had blond hair, long sideburns, and a neat mustache. He seems also to have been some three or four inches shorter than you."

Lord James sank back down beside the mattress, his physical threat vanishing into thought. "Mason never testified in person at my trial. They merely read his signed statement, naming me as the man who had sold him the diamonds. How did he pay this fellow?"

"He didn't, in the end. He heard about the robbery and realized what he was being offered."

"Mrs. Mason's description sounds nothing like Joshua, either," Elizabeth observed, frowning, "or any of his associates that I ever met. Is it possible rumor is wrong, and Joshua didn't steal them in the first place?" She scowled. "Then how would they have got into my chess set?" she said, answering herself.

"An ally of Jarman that we know nothing of?" Lord James suggested. "A genuine gentleman, even, whom he used to sell the diamonds to Mason quite plausibly at a low enough price to entice the jeweler, but still more than he would have got fencing them so soon after the theft. But Mason heard the news about the theft too soon and informed the police *I* tried to sell them to him. And then Mason conveniently died to prevent the truth coming out."

"That's what we were thinking," Dr. Tizsa said.

"But how did the diamond end up with James?" Elizabeth demanded, then blushed. "*Lord* James."

"Oh, I think we're all beyond the foolish formality of titles," James said.

"Probably," Lady Grizelda said, sticking with the question, "because Mason was given a sample as proof of quality. Was it

Mason himself you dealt with, James?"

He frowned. "Actually, I don't know. I assumed it was, but Mason was not the jeweler frequented by my family, which was why I went there, determined to do things my own way. But the man was quite young. I suppose it could have been his son, or a trusted employee." He shook his head. "I probably bought the wretched ring the very afternoon Mason went to the police."

"The Masons didn't have any sons," Lady Grizelda said, "but they did have an assistant. And the assistant shouldn't have sold the diamond or set it in the ring for you. I expect that was why he kept it from his employers."

"Or the assistant was one of Jarman's men," Dr. Tizsa speculated. "Either way, rather extraordinarily coincidental, wouldn't you say?"

James met his gaze. "I would," he agreed. "Can we speak to the assistant?"

"If we're prepared to travel to the United States," Dr. Tizsa said wryly. "He emigrated."

"Conveniently," Griz said.

"Why *did* you choose Mason's?" Elizabeth asked James. "Out of all the jewelers on Ludgate Hill your family does not frequent?"

He let out a frustrated sigh. "I can't really remember now. Someone recommended Mason, though I've forgotten who." His lips twisted. "I celebrated my engagement the night before. A rather wild party—I recall that much, though very little of what passed after midnight. And in the morning, I found a note in my pocket with the name and address of Mason's, scrawled untidily but in my own hand, though I don't recall writing it."

Dr. Tizsa sat forward. "I don't suppose you still have that note?"

"Lord, no, I threw it away before I even left the house that day."

"Pity," Lady Grizelda murmured. "Did you notice anything about the paper it was written on? Or the ink?"

James frowned, shaking his head. "No, it was just cheap paper so far as I can recall, probably from the gaming den."

"Perhaps we need another list," Dr. Tizsa said, "of people who attended that party of yours. I know ways to help you remember. But not now. I'm starving, and we brought food."

➤➤➤✦⫷⫷⫷

DURING A QUICK bite of luncheon, it was decided that Lady Grizelda and Dr. Tizsa should take the diamonds to Inspector Harris at Scotland Yard.

"And if we've time," Lady Grizelda said, "we'll drop in on a friend of ours, Sir Nicholas Swan, and see what he knows of Solomon Grey."

"Grey?" Elizabeth said. "The importer of the diamonds? I've almost forgotten he was the victim of the theft."

"Why don't you and I call on him?" Lord James suggested.

"Good idea," Lady Grizelda replied. "Watch his reaction to the news that we've found his diamonds. He could have been the gentleman masquerading as you with Mr. Mason."

"Doubtful," Lord James said wryly. "He is certainly not fair."

Elizabeth had been thinking, too. "Do you know where Constance Silver has her establishment now?"

Lord James choked on his tea, and Dr. Tizsa's lips twitched.

"She had a large manservant," Elizabeth said, "who could easily have killed Joshua. At the very least, she disliked Joshua, and I think she would talk to me."

"You're right," Lady Grizelda said. "In fact, I had thought Dragan and I should go there tomorrow, but she might well talk more to you. I believe the gentlemen are merely shy of admitting they know the address of a high-class brothel."

"Everyone knows it," James said resignedly. He looked directly at Elizabeth. "And I am happy to talk to her. You, on the other hand, will not set foot in a brothel of any class."

"Don't be ridiculous," Elizabeth said. "I hardly think Constance Silver needs to lower herself to stealing unwilling women to work for her."

"I meant," James said stiffly, "it is unsuitable."

It *was* unsuitable, of course. Or it would have been once. Now, she had nothing left to lose. "I don't think we need concern ourselves with that. My reputation was lost the day I left my home with Joshua, and I could never go back if I wanted to. It doesn't matter where I go. Though I suppose your friends might wonder why you trouble to take a woman there with you. Perhaps *I* should go alone."

"No," all three of them said at once.

"Remember she and a minion could easily have murdered Jarman," Lady Grizelda said anxiously.

"Yes, but I don't believe she would murder me."

"Famous last words," James said, rising to his feet. "We go together, or we don't go at all."

Elizabeth acceded to that and went to fetch her cloak and bonnet.

"Just be back before four," Dr. Tizsa said, walking with them to the front door. "I have to be at the clinic, and I won't leave Griz here alone."

James frowned as he opened the front door. "Even so, you've taken a chance, giving this address to Bertie and Barb Sandman. You can't assume one of them will come here alone. One of them probably killed Jarman, and he was considerably bigger than you."

"They'll only come if they recognize the address," Dr. Tizsa said, "and that's what will mark them as the killer. Besides, I always have the advantage of surprise. Do you want to borrow my sword stick?"

"He doesn't need it," Elizabeth said, sailing past them out of the house. "He keeps a wicked-looking dagger in his boot."

# CHAPTER NINE

MR. SOLOMON GREY had unpretentious offices above his largest warehouse near St. Catherine's Dock. The warehouse itself was a hive of activity. Men heaved crates around, loading and unloading wagons. Others, including a few women, scuttled about with clipboards and pencils, or sat busily writing at desks.

One young man, dressed in the dark suit and white collar of a clerk, rose from his desk just inside the doors and bowed politely.

"Sir. Madam. May I help you?" Somehow, his voice penetrated the clatter and cheerful chatter echoing around the building.

"Yes, we'd like to see Mr. Grey, if he's available," Lord James said politely.

The young man glanced down at the open book on his desk. "You don't have an appointment?"

"No," James said pleasantly. "Is that a problem?"

"Probably not, sir." The young man indicated the three comfortable chairs beside his desk. "If you would be so good as to wait here, I'll take your names to Mr. Grey."

James handed him a card. The young man bowed and strode the length of the warehouse, and up a long cast-iron staircase to an invisible floor above.

Taking a seat, Elizabeth watched the activity, following a shout of laughter to its source, wondering vaguely why she found it so fascinating.

"A happy workforce," Lord James said wryly from the seat next to hers. His shoulder didn't quite brush against her, although if he sat back, it might. "A rare enough sight in recent years."

"Does he pay them so well? They certainly don't appear to be lazy."

"I believe the pay is good but within the normal range for the industry. I suspect the secret is that he treats them like human beings. His workers tend to stay."

"You like him?"

"I don't know if like is the right word. He's too...*closed* to like very easily. Mainly, I found him surprising. But I admire what he's done here. He is courteous, or was when I spoke to him a week or so ago, and he struck me as honest."

"Closed and honest?" she queried.

"Like you," he said. "And me, I suspect."

She thought about that. "I expect one is always courteous to a titled gentleman."

"Perhaps."

They didn't have long to wait before the young man hurried back and then led them the length of the warehouse and up the staircase. Beyond the door at the top, a carpet ran through an outer office, in which a middle-aged lady in spectacles sat poring over a pile of ledgers. Another desk was currently unoccupied.

A balding man came out of a door to an inner office and bowed civilly to James and Elizabeth. Their guide knocked and opened the door wide, before bowing and vanishing, presumably to make the long walk back to his desk yet again.

The inner office was as comfortable and unpretentious as the outer. A serviceable carpet, several cabinets and bookcases, and a small mahogany table on which sat a full decanter and several glasses. And dominating the room, a large desk, piled with papers, ledgers, and small boxes. A desk of hard work, not intimidation. Elizabeth's father had possessed the latter variety, she had always thought, at his bank.

From behind this present mahogany edifice, a tall, imposing

man arose. He was younger than Elizabeth had expected, probably not yet thirty years old, although he had the presence of a much more experienced man. His complexion was bronzed, as though by much warmer sun than ever shone on England, and his eyes an all-consuming, deep chocolate brown. Such eyes should, she thought unreasonably, melt with amiability. His did not.

Not that he was unamiable. On the contrary, he came around the desk and bowed to them, and when James offered his hand, he gripped it firmly, if briefly, a practiced smile of welcome on his full lips.

"Lord James, how do you do?"

"Allow me to introduce Miss Barker. Miss Barker, Mr. Grey."

Elizabeth offered her hand, too, somewhat defiantly, and despite her modest appearance, Grey took it and bowed over it with perfect courtesy.

"Please, sit. May I offer you tea? A glass of brandy, perhaps?"

James handed Elizabeth into one of the two upholstered chairs on the near side of the desk. "No, thank you, sir. We shan't keep you, I hope. First, my apologies for disturbing you again, especially on the same subject."

"I heard that he was dead," Grey said, resuming his seat behind the desk. His lips curved faintly although his dark eyes remained steady on James. "Joshua Jarman. I even wondered if you had done it."

"Sadly, someone beat me to it."

Grey's eyebrows flew up. "Sadly?"

"In a manner of speaking. It would have given me some satisfaction, however short-lived. I daresay you feel the same."

Grey shrugged. "Hardly. My loss was minor, since I was insured. The rumors that followed were worse, but we are riding those out, too."

"Then your business thrives, Mr. Grey?" Elizabeth asked.

"My businesses are diverse, ma'am. They are unlikely all to suffer, let alone fail, at once, and so I always have a cushion.

What was it about the diamonds that you wanted to discuss?"

"Mainly that we found them."

Grey's eyes widened. "Did you, by God? In his house?"

"No, in mine," Elizabeth said. James was right—the man was impossible to read. After the first gleam of surprise—and she thought that was genuine, although it might have been astonishment that she was prepared to admit it—his expression betrayed only courteous interest.

"How odd," he said mildly. "Or, at least, it is so to me. May I know what, if any, your connection is to the inestimable Jarman?"

"It's a long story," Elizabeth said, "but I once imagined myself his wife. When I fled from him, I took with me a chess set my father had given me. Unbeknownst to me, that was where Joshua had hidden the diamonds."

"That must have annoyed him. I hope it's a comfort to you."

"It is now he's dead."

"The trouble is, we don't know who killed him," James said. "We are assuming it was for the diamonds, although the killer never got them, but we can't know for sure."

"So, you are wondering if I or one of my stevedores...er—did him in?"

"Something like that," James said.

Grey sat back in his chair, looking neither angry nor amused. "I didn't, but then, of course, I would say that."

"Perhaps you wouldn't mind also saying where you were on Monday afternoon?" James said.

"I wouldn't mind in the least," Mr. Grey replied, dragging a book toward him and flicking through a couple of pages. It appeared to be an appointment diary. "I was here in the office, until about half past three, when I left for a meeting in Mayfair at four. Do we know when Jarman was killed?"

"Not long before four."

Grey nodded thoughtfully. "Have you brought me back my diamonds?"

"Sadly not," James said. "They are with the police, who, I'm sure, will be in touch with you directly."

"I look forward to it. I suppose it is also in my favor that you found them and not I."

"That may yet prove a problem for me," James admitted. "If you're interested, my money is not on you, but you'll understand my need to investigate all possibilities."

"I understand being driven," came the unexpected reply. "I can only advise you to let go. There is more to life."

"Such as?"

The ghost of a smile touched Grey's lips. "When you find out, please let me know."

Elizabeth glanced from one to the other. James was also right that there was something likeable if completely unknowable about Solomon Grey. "One more thing, sir. In your dealings with jewels and jewelers, have you ever come across a gentlemanly character, around forty years old and five feet and eight inches in height? Fair and with a neat mustache?"

Grey blinked, allowing a couple of seconds to pass. "I cannot think of anyone. But then, your description is not distinctive."

James said, "Would you keep your eyes open for such a man and let me know if you come across him?"

Grey inclined his head. "Of course."

James rose. "Then we thank you for your time and bid you good afternoon."

"Allow me to show you out."

On the way, Elizabeth asked him civil questions about his business and employees, remarking on their apparent contentment. He answered with equal courtesy.

Only when James turned to say a word to the clerk at the door did Grey turn toward her and murmur, "If you need work or help of any kind, we usually have openings somewhere."

He wasn't looking at her, but at James.

"You don't trust him," she blurted.

He smiled. "Dear lady, I don't trust anyone." He bowed. "Good afternoon, and good luck."

>>>><<<<

"HE ALL BUT offered me a position," Elizabeth said as they walked to the waiting hackney.

James, who had been scouring the surrounding area, presumably for any signs of threat, cast her a sharp glance. "What did you say?"

"Nothing. My life is much too uncertain right now."

"You could do worse." The words seemed reluctant, almost forced.

"Providing he isn't a murderer," Elizabeth pointed out.

Breath hissed between his teeth. "Providing that, yes."

The hackney waited just outside the warehouse yard. James and Elizabeth both scanned the street, but the only passersby, on foot or in carts, seemed to be purposeful if not in a tearing hurry. Before James opened the carriage door for her, she was sure he checked inside, and he definitely peered carefully at the driver before handing her in.

"I've lived like this for so long," she said abruptly when he sat beside her and the carriage moved forward. "Looking over my shoulder, expecting Joshua to appear at any moment. It became just part of my life. And now, suddenly, I want it to be over. I don't want to live like that."

"I don't want you to live like that either. I'm appalled you ever had to."

She smiled. "It's no comfort that I brought it on myself."

"You didn't. Your father should have dragged you back from Jarman's."

"I wouldn't have gone. Not until the second day, at least, and by then it was too late. He wouldn't have me back." She waved her hand impatiently, as if that could banish all the pointless regrets and wishes. "Do you think Grey killed Joshua?"

"Honestly? I'd be surprised. And if it can be proved he was in Mayfair by four, I don't see how he could have, personally, at least. But he says nothing he doesn't want you to hear. I have never met anyone in such perfect control. What did you make of him?"

"Much the same as you. But I wasn't afraid of him." With Joshua, she had learned to read the signs, and had seen them since in other men who crossed her path, always at a safe distance, as she had ensured. "He might even be *kind*."

"That wouldn't preclude him killing Jarman," James said. He consulted his fob watch and tucked it away. "I told the driver to take us to Mayfair. We should still have time to see Constance Silver and get back before four."

"Have you met her before, too?" Elizabeth asked.

His gaze moved from the window to her face. "Not in any capacity."

She dropped her gaze, shifting on the bench, and felt the blush rise to her face. "Of course not," she muttered.

"No of course about it," he said. "I'm no saint. No prude either, but I always found the blatant trade distasteful."

"You prefer to dress it up with gifts and pretend it is love?" As soon as the words spilled out, she could have bitten her tongue. But she couldn't unsay them, so she stared pointedly out of the window as the hackney rumbled westward. She still felt his gaze on her burning cheek and wondered if she should apologize, or if he should for bringing up such a shocking subject in the first place.

"Jarman does not strike me as the kind of man to bother with pretense," he remarked.

"He wasn't. It was one of the reasons I liked him. I thought he was honest." She thought he would leave it there, but he didn't.

"Who was *not* honest?"

She drew in her breath. "My father. He kept another woman, an actress, I think. I saw him with her once, in a jeweler's shop. She was choosing a bracelet, and he was carrying a huge bouquet of flowers, which I knew were not for my mother. I even heard him say, *A token of my love*. It wasn't, of course. He was buying her favors as surely as anyone ever bought Mrs. Silver's."

She felt movement beside her, as though he would take her hand, and her foolish heart leapt, because she liked his touch. She liked the way it made her feel. But then he stilled, and she realized he was moved by anger.

"I'm sorry. Disillusion hurts. Almost as much as hypocrisy."

She turned back to him, relieved that he understood. She touched his hand, a quick, almost embarrassed caress of gratitude, quickly withdrawn.

CONSTANCE SILVER'S HOUSE of ill repute, which was a new address, not the one she had given Elizabeth nearly four years ago, was a mansion in a quiet cul-de-sac. Her neighbors and local officers of the law presumably knew exactly what went on there. But selective blindness and, no doubt, significant bribery ensured its survival.

There was nothing on the outside of the house, or the tastefully decorated front hallway, to distinguish it. The door was opened at the first knock by a liveried footman. Not by the flicker of an eyelash did he acknowledge the oddity of Elizabeth's presence. Instead, he addressed James.

"I'm sorry, sir. The ladies are not receiving."

"Of course not," James replied, offering his card. "We desire a private word with Mrs. Silver, if she would be good enough to spare us ten minutes of her time."

The footman's gaze swept over the card, and the door widened. "Please step inside and I will see if she is at home."

They were shown into another tasteful salon looking onto the street, although fine net curtains concealed the occupants from any curious outsiders. A Turkish rug graced the center of the parquet floor, on which a sofa and three matching chairs had been artfully arranged. A few gentle watercolors graced the walls. Vases of yellow roses were reflected in the highly polished tables at each of the two windows. Constance Silver, clearly, was doing well. No wonder Joshua had muscled in on her profits.

Although the first footman had left them alone in the room, Elizabeth glimpsed another, stationed in the hallway, perhaps to prevent them stealing the silver, or from roaming the house unsupervised. Light footsteps sounded on the staircase, and Elizabeth could not help wondering what her companion would make of Constance Silver, who was, frankly, the most beautiful woman she had ever seen.

She strolled into the room with perfect grace. Crinolines might have been invented simply to enhance Constance's fine figure. Her tiny waist contrasted with the wide hoop of her skirt and the soft curve of her breasts. Her hair was a rare shade of strawberry blonde, elegantly looped about her head in soft braids, her complexion was creamy and without blemish, and her lips were rosy, full, and curved into a tantalizing smile.

Or at least men found it tantalizing. Joshua had almost drooled, and Bertie had stared at her mouth even more than at her breasts. Elizabeth could never work out whether or not she practiced that smile, or if it was just the natural shape of her lips. She rather thought the latter, although Constance was certainly not above enhancing her advantages.

"Lord James?" she drawled, extending her gloved hand. "I don't believe we have ever met."

James bowed over her fingers. He showed no signs of drooling, and he was far too much the gentleman to stare. "We have not, though I believe you are acquainted with my companion."

Constance glanced at Elizabeth, a faint, questioning smile on her luscious lips. She had even begun to look back to James for enlightenment, when her eyes snapped back to Elizabeth's face, widening.

"Yes, it's me," Elizabeth said.

To her surprise, Constance swept toward her and seized both

her hands. "Oh, my dear! Thank God! I thought he had killed you!"

"I ran away to France."

"Good for you," Constance said, her grin warm and triumphant. Then her gaze moved. "France? But Beth, that hat is hideous."

A snort that might have been laughter broke from Lord James and transformed itself into a vigorous throat clearing.

"Is it a disguise?" Constance asked, pulling her down onto the sofa beside her.

"No, it's lack of funds."

"You can stay here as long as you like, but this work is not for you."

"I'm a seamstress, so I'll probably be glad of any work you can send my way. In just a little."

Constance frowned. "You know he's dead? He cannot hurt you."

"*He* can't, no."

"And Lord James?" Constance asked steadily.

Warmth flooded Elizabeth's face yet again, which appeared to intrigue Constance. "Lord James is a perfect gentleman. He has been helping me."

"We've been helping each other," James said. "I expect you know my name, Mrs. Silver, and how it has been connected to Jarman's."

"I know you went to prison for a crime that was almost certainly Jarman's. And were freed only weeks ago." Her eyes narrowed slightly. "Did you kill him?"

"I did not, and neither did Miss Barker, although he was found in her house."

Constance opened her mouth and closed it again. Then she rose. "I have so many questions that I don't know where to begin. Anthony," she addressed the footman in the hall. "You had better order tea. And lots of wine. We're celebrating, after all."

>>>>>><<<<<

JAMES WAS NOT sure what he had expected of Constance Silver, but she certainly surprised him. She was beautiful, supremely graceful, and charming. Her voice was low and well modulated, with no stridency or the vulgar accent that might have betrayed low origins. Instead, she might have been a lady of birth and breeding receiving welcome guests.

She certainly appeared both astonished and delighted to see Elizabeth. On one level, that pleased him, although it also aroused the suspicion that such excessive delight could be faked. Elizabeth had never suggested that they were such fast friends. In fact, she seemed slightly bemused by the courtesan's welcome, although she told her tale readily enough, right up to discovering Jarman's body in her bedroom.

By this time, they had all been presented with wine, tea, elegant little sandwiches, and cakes.

"Good Lord." Mrs. Silver set her tea back on the table that had been placed for the purpose and reached for her wine glass. "What a narrow escape."

"You think Jarman had come to kill her?" James asked nonchalantly, even while the words chilled his blood.

"She left him. He was a vindictive bastard."

The profanity on her lips was somehow shocking. "I know. Why did you believe her to be dead already?"

"Because she disappeared so suddenly. Jarman was humming with fury for weeks, and yet bit off the head of anyone who dared mention her. I was afraid he'd actually done away with you in such fury. I thought if you had run away, you would have come to me."

"It was the first place he would have looked."

"And yet he didn't," the courtesan said. "Which was telling, as I thought."

"He must have known the direction I took," Elizabeth said

slowly. "I was only ever a few steps ahead of him or his spies...
Oh, he wasn't keeping track of *me*," she added, catching sight of
Mrs. Silver's expression, "but of the stolen diamonds I had
accidentally taken with me."

"The only thing that cheered him up," Mrs. Silver said
thoughtfully, "was you, my lord, being charged and convicted of
the theft."

"What did he have against Lord James?" Elizabeth asked.

"Nothing. It just seemed to be the culmination of a plan he
had set up to prevent the law bothering him. They searched his
house and his legitimate business premises, you know, shortly
after the theft, and found nothing. He wouldn't want to put up
with that for long, since it curtailed further thievery."

Elizabeth sat forward. "Did he mention this plan to you? Do
you have any idea who was involved in it?"

"He tried to implicate the man he actually stole from, too,
but that never stuck."

"No, I mean an ally," Elizabeth said impatiently. "Someone
who could at least impersonate a gentleman. A fair man, around
forty years old, with a neat mustache?"

Mrs. Silver thought. "I don't recall seeing him in such company, but then, I saw him increasingly seldom as I wriggled my way
free of him."

"How did you manage that?"

"I paid him off one last time. And told him I'd given my law-
yers custody of evidence of another of his crimes. That evidence
would be given to the law unless he dissolved our so-called
partnership forever."

"Did you have such evidence?" James inquired.

"Yes," she said.

James raised his glass to her, and her eyes twinkled briefly.
For the first time he *felt*, rather than simply acknowledged, her
attraction.

"Well done," Elizabeth said. "I was afraid you would have to
deal now with Porter, or the insufferable Bertie."

Mrs. Silver regarded her. "What will you do, now that the danger is over?"

"I'm not sure it is, quite," Elizabeth said vaguely. "We need to discover who killed him."

"Why?" Mrs. Silver said. "Be grateful. Celebrate."

But Elizabeth was frowning at James. "Why *did* he pick on you? Somehow, he knew your circumstance enough to make use of them, to see that you bought the diamond and were discovered in possession of it. The more I think of it, the more I believe this apparent gentleman is the key to everything."

James nodded, aware of Mrs. Silver glancing between them, and then of the clock he could see above her head. "We should go, Elizabeth."

She stood without fuss. "Allow me a moment to wash my hands."

Constance rose gracefully at once. "I'll show you the way and order the carriage sent round, if you're in a hurry."

James would have demurred—after all, it could easily be Mrs. Silver's way of discovering where Elizabeth lived. Although all she really needed to do was ask Elizabeth. And in any case, having to discover the address at all implied she did not already know it, and so could not have killed Jarman, or be threatening Elizabeth for the diamonds.

While the thoughts flew around his brain, the two women left the room. From their vanishing backs, the contrast between them was stark, and for some reason that annoyed him. Instead of seating himself once more, he paced restlessly to the window, outraged all over again by all that had befallen Elizabeth through Jarman. He wondered if he should have let her go with Constance Silver. A sense of blind panic took him by surprise, and he spun around to stride purposefully toward the door.

Mrs. Silver glided through it, alone. "You are desperate to be off," she observed. "It's not the usual reaction of the gentlemen who come here."

"But then, I didn't come for the usual reason." He gazed

beyond her at the open door, willing Elizabeth to walk through.

"Perhaps on your next visit," she said graciously, as though inviting him to some musical treat.

"No, though I thank you," he said distractedly.

"My lord, I haven't kidnapped her." The voice was deliciously amused and yet not unkind. It brought his gaze back to her face.

"She has been in considerable danger, ma'am. I worry."

"I'm glad to hear it," Mrs. Silver said. The fascinating smile flickered. "That you worry, I mean. I would not like to think of anyone taking advantage of her. Again. She has been through enough."

"I know," James said.

"Do you?" Mrs. Silver took a step closer. "Are you truly aware what a man like Jarman is capable of? At first, he was careful to strike where the bruises wouldn't show, but I could tell by the way she moved that she was in pain. After the first few months, he didn't care. I have no idea what went on in his bed, but I will tell you this—I would not let him near one of my girls."

Nausea roiled in James's stomach. This was just what he had been afraid of hearing. Disgust and fury at a dead man mingled with fresh pity for his victim and drained the blood from his face. He grasped the back of the nearest chair to steady himself.

"I need to know that you will not hurt her," Constance Silver said, a new hardness in her soft, seductive voice. "Ever."

That she had to ask disgusted him, too, though it also steadied him. "I did not leave everything of worth in Newgate."

Her mesmeric eyes searched his with an intensity that was disconcerting. And then, to his massive relief, Elizabeth walked back into the room. She halted rather abruptly at the sight of James and Mrs. Silver confronting each other, but all she said was, "Your footman says the carriage awaits. Thank you for this, Constance."

"My pleasure. Send me a note next time and we can meet somewhere more neutral. You, my lord, are welcome at any time."

He laughed, because it might have been approval or spite, and followed Elizabeth to the door, where he turned and bowed to Mrs. Silver.

# CHAPTER TEN

O N THEIR RETURN to Hanson Row, Dr. Tizsa all but bolted past them with his hat and bag in his hand.

"Take the carriage," Elizabeth called after him, for she had already spoken to the coachman who claimed to be at her disposal for the next hour.

"That is a very fine equipage," Lady Grizelda remarked, closing and locking the door behind them.

"It belongs," Lord James said, "to Mrs. Constance Silver."

"Is Mrs. Silver in it?" Lady Grizelda inquired.

"Would you mind?" James asked with what appeared to be genuine curiosity.

She smiled. "Don't be silly. Tell me how you got on."

They repaired to the parlor, where the fire was lit, and James brought an extra chair from the kitchen while Elizabeth told her about their interview with Solomon Grey.

"We learned nothing new," she said, "except that neither of us think him guilty. Despite a certain lack of openness, he seems honest and even kind."

Lady Grizelda nodded. "That is what Nicholas said—our friend, Sir Nicholas Swan, who is acquainted with him. Apparently, Mr. Grey is on the boards of several of his charities. Grey seemed embarrassed at first to come across Sir Nicholas there, but they have since allied to make progress quicker."

"But can we rule him out?" James asked. "He claims to have

been at a meeting in Mayfair at four o'clock."

"He was," Lady Grizelda said. "Sir Nicholas was at the same meeting—the board of a housing charity. Grey arrived just after four, bemoaning the traffic."

"Then he *could* have done it," Elizabeth said with odd reluctance. "At a pinch."

"It is a lot to fit into half an hour," James said. "And—forgive me—it takes time to strangle a man, especially one of Jarman's size and strength."

"He could have left the office earlier than he said," Elizabeth pointed out. "I'm sure his staff will happily lie for him." She sighed. "On the other hand, I don't really believe he is the culprit."

"It does provide us with a bit of a moral dilemma," Lady Grizelda said thoughtfully. "By everything I've heard, Jarman's death is a benefit to the world. We cannot condone murder, yet do we really want to see good men hang for the killing of a bad man?"

"It's not about morals, though," James said. "It's about the law."

"The law was hardly fair to you," Elizabeth pointed out.

James met her gaze. "And yet the law is all we have to decide who is a bad man and what is a justified killing. We cannot pick and choose which laws to follow and which to punish."

"Dragan would argue that unjust laws must be changed," Lady Grizelda said. "And by the truly representative will of the people, not by a few interested parties. By your arguments, he rose up against the law of Hungary and the Empire and should go home to face his punishment."

His gaze remained steady. "I would not want that."

"Would you want Constance Silver hanged for Joshua's murder?" Elizabeth asked. "If she did it."

"Another whole moral morass. I did not say my argument was perfect. And besides, whoever killed him, it may well be a matter of self-defense. I suspect she is fierce enough in protection of her girls—she told me she would never let Jarman near them. But she couldn't have done it alone."

"I doubt she did it at all. She was stunned to see me alive, never mind in London, so I doubt she sent her bodyguards to abduct me from Hyde Park. And at four of the clock on Monday she was with her entire staff discussing the future treatment of some troublesome client." Elizabeth smiled lopsidedly. "I asked her."

"Did she mind?" Lady Grizelda asked.

"No."

"I daresay her staff would be happy to lie for her, just as Mr. Grey's would for him. We're not really much further forward, are we?"

"No," James admitted. "But at least we found the diamonds. What did Inspector Harris make of them?"

Lady Grizelda grinned. "He *almost* got excited. And then said sternly that he would have to get experts, and Mr. Grey, to confirm that they were the same stones." As her smile died, she met Elizabeth's gaze somewhat ruefully. "I had to tell him the truth about you. How you carried them unknowing across France in the chess set. It helped that you had already told him it was missing, though we *might* have made it sound as though Dragan and I were with you when you searched the house and found them. He said there was no reason to give such details to the press, but no one can guarantee it won't come out via some nosy reporter. At least we have some time, because he won't release the news of the diamonds until Mr. Grey has identified them."

"Thank you," Elizabeth said. She didn't want to be besieged by the press or spat at in the street. She didn't want to bring shame down on her family who had so assiduously avoided it for four years. She knew those things in her mind, and yet life seemed to be in too great a muddle for her to *care* right now.

Abruptly, James sat up in his chair. "I've just realized. Once the news of the diamonds' return comes out, there will be no need for anyone to pursue Elizabeth for them. She'll be safe."

Elizabeth tried to smile. "Then you can all go home to your own comfortable beds, with my thanks." *And I can go back to my sewing. Which was once all I wanted, and now...*

Now some unspecific dissatisfaction with such a life dragged at her. Bizarrely, she had enjoyed these last few days, being with the Tizsas, and with James, who had once terrified her. With a purpose beyond simple survival. Although there was that, too.

"Not tonight, we can't," her ladyship said severely. "The news won't be out until tomorrow at the earliest."

⫸⫷

SOME OF THE same vexing questions returned in the evening after Dr. Tizsa returned and he had heard all about the interviews with Solomon Grey and Constance Silver.

"We still need to find Jarman's killer," he said, after a simple but tasty dinner of stew, with rather more beef than Elizbeth had been used to in recent years. "In case suspicion falls back on Elizabeth or Andover, if for no other reason."

"I think we have to leave any further interviewing of Jarman's people and Zebadiah Fisher to the police," Lady Grizelda said. "At least for now. We have no way of discovering where they were when Jarman was killed. We may just have to wait for a few days and bend our minds to the problem. Notes help."

Tizsa frowned. "I think we should concentrate on how and by whom Andover was placed so perfectly to take the blame for the robbery. We know Jarman was involved, to avert the worst of the suspicion from him and let his operations continue unobserved by the law. And we know the jeweler's assistant lied, for whatever reason, and that Mr. and Mrs. Mason were almost fooled into buying the stolen diamonds. And then there is this mysterious gentleman. And how he and Jarman knew your movements and your intentions so thoroughly."

Lady Grizelda yawned. "I've written it all down, in the order

110

everything happened, but I'm too tired to think about it now. I'll begin again in the morning."

"You're right," Tizsa said, putting his arm around her waist with quite unselfconscious affection. "We should talk and think of other things. Read, sleep, clear our minds so that we are fresh in the morning. Come, my wife, bed for you. Andover, I'll take the kitchen this time, and leave you the comfortable parlor chair."

"I'd like to take my turn," Elizabeth said. "I'm happy to scream loudly if anyone breaks in."

"You'll scare them off," James said wryly. "And I suspect we only have tonight for this lure to yield anything."

"Neither of you can have slept much last night," Elizabeth protested. "While I am not tired."

"Then keep me company for an hour," James said. "We can play cards, or I can tell you my best jokes."

"Jokes are good," Elizabeth said, trying to hide her ridiculous pleasure at his casual invitation.

"I made some coffee and chocolate in the kitchen," Grizelda said over her shoulder from the doorway. "Help yourselves."

Ten minutes later, Elizabeth brought in a tray with a cup of hot chocolate and a pot of coffee. James had taken the cushion off her work chair and now sat on it cross-legged on the floor before the fire. Open on his legs was some medical treatise of Dr. Tizsa's.

"Take your coat off and be comfortable," she said. "You don't need to stand on ceremony with me."

"I could. But I have it in my head that no one has stood on any ceremony with you for a long time. To say the least."

"I don't imagine there's much of it in Newgate, either," she retorted.

"Not in the way you mean. Aristocrats are certainly not top of the heap in there by virtue of their blood. But if you don't mind, I will take off my coat."

He removed his coat and loosened his tie with the same grace he brought to everything. Even in his shirt sleeves, sprawling back against the armchair, he was the most elegant man she had ever seen. It was like looking at a work of art—a marble statue or a painting by an old master come to life. Long, lean, and muscled, with that pale, sculpted face and eyes that no longer seemed cold to her at all.

She had almost forgotten her old love of art and beauty. Watching him as she poured a cup of coffee and brought it to him, she felt the old tingle of excitement she had once felt in an art gallery. Well, not quite the old tingle. This one was much more *physical*. And it had been with her in varying degrees of intensity all day.

"Will you have the chair?" he said, sitting up to make way for her.

"No, I believe I will join you before the fire. It's how I often finished my day since the weather turned colder. If you could just pass me the other cushion?"

He did so, and she curled up on the cushion with her hot chocolate, feeling rather like a contented cat. Somehow, in this house that had never been home, and had stopped even being secure, she felt comfortable at last. It had something to do with the man beside her, who was both gentlemanly enough and unattainable enough to be safe.

He sipped his coffee. "What would you do," he asked, his low voice rolling through her, "if money and background were no object? Where would you live? What would you do with yourself?"

"You are asking about dreams rather than reality."

"I lost my dreams, for just a little—beyond getting out of prison and wreaking revenge. I suspect you lost yours, too."

"Beyond escaping Joshua and simple survival." She had rarely let herself look back. She dreaded the nightmares that woke her, sweating and sometimes even crying out before she could bury her face in the pillow. That had been enough of the past for her. But slowly, cautiously, she gave herself permission to remember the time before Joshua, when life was unfurling in new interests and possibilities and the world had been not frightening but exciting.

"Where would I go?" she said softly. "Everywhere. I want to go to Paris, and this time see the art. I want to go to Holland, to Florence and Venice and Rome, to Vienna and..." She smiled self-consciously. "Well, I would like to travel and spend days at a time surrounded by art. And then, full of ideas and contentment, I would like to come home to a modest, comfortable cottage in the country, where I would try to paint the lush green views, my neighbors, and even the dogs and cats. But all that would be in my own precious time. I would like to teach children and fill their minds with enthusiasm and learning... Yes, I think I would run a school, where others could teach subjects I cannot—Latin and Greek and mathematics."

"I am surprisingly learned in such," Lord James said. "Perhaps you would consider employing me?"

She smiled involuntarily. "Of course." A little frisson ran up her spine. To have him under the same roof, working with him on such a noble project, to see him every day... *Stop there, Beth!* She cast him a quick glance to find his eyes steady on her face and the faintest of smiles teasing at his lips. And suddenly she had no breath.

"You've changed your mind," he said in mock reproach. "Perhaps no one will send their children to a school that employs old convicts?"

"You are not a convict, and in any case, it is not that kind of school. It's not for the aristocratic and wealthy, but for people who would not otherwise have much of an education at all."

"Ah, a charitable foundation. You will need a *lot* of charity without fee-paying pupils to bolster your income."

"This is *my* dream, and money will be no object, remember? Otherwise, I could not go jaunting about the world in the school holidays, or employ a marquis's son as my classics and mathematics master."

He set down his empty cup and sprawled against the chair

behind him, raising his arms to support the back of his head. "I quite enjoyed teaching the boys in Newgate."

She blinked. "Were they interested in Latin?"

"My aims were not so grand. I taught them to read and write. A mixture of unfortunates and world-weary little pickpockets."

She shuddered to think of children in such a place. "You gave them a chance," she said warmly, "for when they are released. Was this your dream, too?"

"Lord, no, I was bored." He sat up. "I don't think I *ever* had much of an aim. I wanted to do something, but my father refused to countenance a profession. I began to think of politics, but then there was Cordelia, and I, little more than a dazzled boy, imagined happy marriage to be the height of my ambitions. A contented wife, children running tame about the garden."

"Don't you still want those things?"

"I don't know." He grimaced. "I stopped thinking of anything except vengeance and self-justification. Everyone needs a purpose—Newgate taught me that much—but I should have a better one." He sat up. "What about you? Do you not want a husband and children eventually?"

Her smile was twisted. "A dream is one thing, but be sensible—who would marry *me*?"

"I would."

Her heart gave a great thud, and then seemed to stop in a blare of recognition and longing and grief. She tore her gaze free and jumped to her feet with an admittedly shaky laugh.

Snatched up his cup from the floor, she said lightly, "I wonder what your father the marquis would make of that? More coffee, my lord?"

"You called me James, once."

"There is a certain informality here." She barely knew what she was saying. He hadn't said if he wanted more coffee, but she poured him some anyway, and then, for good measure, poured some into her own cup.

"You needn't panic," he said close behind her. "It wasn't a

proposal, just a statement of delight. You are sweet and strong and kind and beautiful, and any decent man would be proud to marry you."

She set down the coffee pot with a bump and closed her eyes in anguish. She didn't believe him, though the words themselves were soothing because he cared enough to say them. More than that, he stood close enough that his breath stirred her hair. She could smell him—a distinctive scent of lavender and spice that she hadn't even realized she associated with him, and that washed over her now with insidious pleasure.

"I doubt you'll want to rush into those offers," said the voice that reached deep inside her, soft and arousing, "but don't rule a husband out forever. All men are not like Jarman. The experience of a wife need not be of violence and fear."

She could not bear it. She swung around, brushing her skirts against his legs, and stared desperately up at him. His eyes were not hard, but warm and kind, and he made no effort to touch her. Until, unable to withstand her curiosity, she raised one curious, unsteady hand to his pale cheek. It felt a little rough with the day's stubble, but he was warm and real and beautiful. And when his fingertips touched her skin in return, butterfly light, she let her gaze stray to those elegant, fascinating lips.

She couldn't help it—she stood on tiptoe, lifting her face to his. One soft, brief caress would be enough, and then she could laugh and walk away, and they would still be friends. His lips parted to meet hers. They were cool and firm, like the man himself, which made her want to smile, but then they pressed hers in return, just a little, and moved delicately.

He cupped her face, lingering, as though tasting her lips, her breath. He didn't ram his tongue into her mouth or mash his body into hers. Perversely, she wanted to lean into him, to feel what merely tantalized so far. Enchanted, she parted her lips for his, and a new sweetness seeped through her veins.

He raised his head before she was ready, and her fingers curled convulsively in his soft hair—when had they got there?—as though to drag him back. Instead, she let her hand fall.

"You see?" he murmured. "Quite harmless."

He stepped back, and she turned away from him with a breathless little laugh. "Quite." But even as she picked up her cup and directed him casually to his, she knew it was not harmless at all, and neither was he. Because what she felt now was physical desire. Her body thrummed with it. And that had beauty, too.

Of course, she desperately needed a distraction. Perhaps that was why she noticed the moving shadow through the gap in the curtain. And that gave her reason to slip away from him and draw back the edge of the drape. The shadow, a deeper, man-shaped blackness in the dark of the street, vanished into the narrow alley between the houses that led to the back gardens.

# CHAPTER ELEVEN

"THERE'S A MAN," Elizabeth exclaimed.

James, his lips still tingling from her sweet, timid kiss, his body still humming with rising lust, took a moment to adjust to the importance of her words.

She let the curtain drop. "He's gone round to the back lane. It's too dark to see who he was."

James was already moving to the door. "Wait here." By the time he reached the kitchen, he knew she was following him, but it was more important to wake Tizsa.

However, Tizsa raised his head from the table before they even entered, and turned, cocking one questioning eyebrow at James.

"Someone's gone around to the back," James murmured.

Instantly, Tizsa rose and doused the lamp. "How many?"

"Elizabeth only saw one, but there could be more." In the darkness, James found Elizabeth's hand and gave it a brief, gentle squeeze. "Stay by the door. Get ready to shout and lock yourself in the bedroom with Griz if you have to."

He felt her nod as her hand slipped free. James edged forward through the darkness to stand beside Tizsa, halfway between the door and the window above the sink. Straining, he was sure he heard the soft squeak of a hinge—the back gate? He heard no footsteps, but then, the garden was mainly soft earth, and it was not wet enough to squelch.

And then came the unmistakable sound of the back door handle being turned. Tizsa stepped silently toward the door, flattening himself to the wall. The lock rattled as something was thrust into it and turned.

A *key?* James drew the dagger from his boot, and since no further sounds came from the window, he moved beside the door, where he would be hidden when the door opened. Which it was doing now. A pale sliver of moonlight fell across the kitchen floor, and a gloved hand snaked around the edge of the door.

Tizsa leapt, grabbing the wrist, which jerked violently. The door slammed against Tizsa, who was left holding an empty glove. Throwing it to the ground, he bolted outside, right beside James. Behind them, the kitchen lamp flared, showing them the figure of a man fleeing through the back gate. The rest of the yard was empty.

"After him," James growled, already heading back for the kitchen. "I'll come from the front."

Without arguing, Tizsa charged through the gate while James strode through the house, yelling, "Lock the doors!" to Elizabeth, though what good that would do when the intruder had a bloody key was beyond him.

In any case, she followed him with the lamp, lighting his way to the front door, which he unlocked and wrenched open. A cloaked man rushed down the street, Tizsa some five or six yards behind. As James leapt into the street, a door slammed and a carriage jumped forward toward Commercial Road.

James swore under his breath. Tizsa, breathing deeply, uttered something in an unknown tongue that James assumed was also profanity.

They glanced at each other, then turned as one back to the house. Elizabeth, still holding the lamp, her eyes wide, backed into the hallway to let them in.

Lady Grizelda stood at the top of the stairs in her nightgown and shawl, clutching the banister. "Dragan? Did we get him?"

"No," Tizsa said, "but we got a glove." He waved it halfheartedly in front of him.

"IT'S A GOOD-QUALITY glove," Lady Grizelda observed over breakfast the following morning, while James was attaching a solid piece of wood to the back door. "Fine leather."

"Bertie *might* wear such a glove," Elizabeth said, "though it's a little restrained for his tastes. He used to prefer more tassels. And it's too small for Porter, who has hands like shovels."

"Grey?" Tizsa suggested. He'd had a better look at the shape of the intruder than James, but it had been impossible to see his features.

"Grey's the one person who knows we don't have the diamonds," James reminded him. "And he knows the police will return them tomorrow."

"Besides, I think he has bigger hands, too," Elizabeth murmured.

"Could it have been a woman?" Grizelda asked.

Tizsa thought about it. "I would doubt it. He was quick and slippery, but the force when he wrenched free of my hold was considerable. I've never met a woman that strong. It could have been Bertie, or Zeb Fisher, perhaps?"

"Or the gentleman who pretended to be me," James added. Whatever the intruder's identity, he was likely to be Jarman's murderer. Jarman must have been using the key, however he had got it, to enter the house at will. Presumably, his killer had taken it from him.

Testing, James pushed the newly attached length of wood, and it fell into the cradle already screwed to the doorframe. A better block to a would-be-intruder with a key than the chair they had shoved under the door last night.

"Oh, well done," Grizelda said warmly. "That should do the trick."

"Thank you," Elizabeth said quietly. He had felt her gaze on him throughout the simple process and suspected he had surprised her. And the Tizsas. At least Newgate had taught him not to be a completely useless aristocrat.

Tizsa nodded and reached for the coffee pot. "Let's think about this mysterious gentleman. As I see it, he is either someone who knows you, or someone who has access to someone who knows you—friends or servants. When you became betrothed, did you have servants who were aware of your movements? A valet or groom or coachman?"

"I had a valet—Matthews," James recalled, though he couldn't picture the man's face clearly. "But even before my trial, he had found a better position with some French baron. I think he went abroad with his new master."

"Getting him conveniently out of the way?" Grizelda said, sitting up. "And he could have come back to the country since. Most valets speak like gentlemen and wear tasteful clothes."

"Yes, but I wasn't in the habit of telling Matthews my movements. I never considered it his business, and he was far too proper to ask."

"But he could have found the note in your pocket about going to Mason's the jeweler," Elizabeth pointed out.

"He could," James agreed. He shook his head. "I just can't imagine him lowering himself to associate with vulgar criminals like Joshua Jarman. Although," he added more thoughtfully, "you did say Jarman could sound like a gentleman when he chose to."

Tizsa reached for his notebook and scribbled down, *Matthews, valet.* "We'll look into him. Give me the name of this baron."

James obliged, after some brain cudgeling.

Tizsa threw down his pencil. "Griz, will you read out the dates and times of the events in '48, from the theft of the diamonds to Andover's arrest?"

Grizelda put down her toast and glanced at her own notebook. "On Wednesday the twenty-third of August, just after two in the afternoon, two of Grey's men set off to take the diamonds to the jeweler who had agreed to buy them. The jewels were inconspicuous, in two small bags, carried in inside pockets. Both men were armed and experienced in transporting valuable items. They were to bring back the banker's draft of the money owed to Mr. Grey for the diamonds. They went in one of the company's carriages. On Houndsditch, another vehicle skewed in front of them, forcing their carriage to stop. Two men, with their faces covered, shot both of Grey's men, snatched both bags of diamonds, and were gone within seconds, vanishing into the panicked crowd.

"On Wednesday evening, the police searched Jarman's business premises—or at least the ones they knew about—and his house in Ellen Square."

"I remember that," Elizabeth said. "It felt like the final indignity. And I didn't even know what they were looking for as they raked through my things. Joshua never told me, and nor did anyone else."

"It was the same evening I celebrated my betrothal," James said.

"And on the following morning, Thursday the twenty-fourth," Grizelda continued, "you took your thick head to Mason's, were shown the diamond, and ordered it to be set into a ring for Cordelia. The assistant told you to collect it on Saturday."

"I preferred Monday," James recalled, "but he was insistent."

"No doubt because Mr. and Mrs. Mason were due to return from their trip to Brighton on Monday and he didn't want his secret deal made public," Tizsa said.

"You duly collected the ring on Saturday the twenty-sixth," Grizelda continued. "On Monday the twenty-eighth, Mr. Mason returned and was immediately offered the diamonds for sale by a plausible gentleman who claimed to be in financial difficulties, which necessitated his selling a set of diamonds he had only just acquired. He claimed to be Lord James Andover, which convinced Mason it would be an excellent and honest deal. Only then he heard about the diamond theft and immediately informed the police. That evening, as you were dressing for dinner with Cordelia's family, the police came to your father's home, found the ring, and arrested you—after Mr. Grey and his jeweler identified the diamond."

Grizelda glanced around the table. "By then, Jarman must already have hidden the diamonds in the chess set and brought it back to the house, for that same day, Elizabeth departed with it for France."

There was silence, then Elizabeth said, "If I were the police, I would arrest me."

"Only Jarman knew," James said, "and he was hardly going to send the law after you. But why pick on me to take the blame? I can't have been the only love-stricken young fool in town."

"That," Tizsa said, "is what's bothering me. The whole thing is so well planned that I cannot believe your involvement was coincidental. Did you have an enemy? Someone you had insulted or won too many wagers against?"

James shook his head. "Not that I can recall. I was a fairly amiable youth, and I never gambled much because I was rarely lucky. Besides, it bored me."

"A rival in love?" Grizelda asked. "As I recall, you were pursued by several young ladies."

"And Cordelia by several men," James said slowly. He met her gaze. "Hampton was sniffing around her even then. And with me out of the way, he eventually won her."

"And," Grizelda added, "he is fair."

"Though not forty. Perhaps he made himself look older..." A resurgence of the old anger swept over James. "I never gave him credit for such brains."

"He never struck me that way either," Grizelda admitted, "but I avoided Society whenever I could and barely spoke to him. Did he know you were going to Mason's that morning?"

James sighed. "I don't know. He was around during the first part of the party at the club. But no one could have known I would go to Mason's, and certainly not in time to learn about Mr.

Mason's trip and the opportunistic tendencies of his assistant."

"No, Mason's part must have been planned even before the robbery," Tizsa agreed. "But whoever gave you Mason's name and got you to write it down must have made an educated guess that you could be influenced in that direction."

James wrinkled his nose. "It was more indolence. My head was pounding. I just did the easiest thing without going to my father's jeweler." He shook his head. "I remember the dinner at the club quite well. I could tell you who was there. We all went on to some gaming hell after that... And it's all a bit of a blur. A sea of faces and cards and bottles."

"We'll note Hampton down," Grizelda said, scribbling in her notebook. "But let's not jump to conclusions. Who else benefitted from your conviction?"

"Honestly?" James said. "No one. My family was disgusted and disgraced. So was Cordelia's and Cordelia herself. My more reckless friends might have liked the notoriety of being associated with a diamond thief who callously shot two men, killing one outright, but it's not as if I died and left them any money."

He felt Elizabeth's grave gaze upon him but refused to look at her as he dragged his fingers through his hair. Her caress of those same locks last night had been sweet and suddenly intense...

"Very well, tell us exactly who was at your club dinner."

"My brother," he began, and his stomach twisted, knotting up as he recited the friends who had been with him that night.

At least, they had called each other friends, but when he had been charged with the diamond theft, not one of them had stood by him or visited him. They hadn't come either when he was released. No one had called or even written, let alone apologized for believing the worst. He had made it easy for them by staying away from his old haunts, and when he did happen to recognize someone, he passed them by as though they were strangers. If it hadn't been for his burning need to prove Jarman's guilt, he would have left London long ago. As it was, he had used the hurt like fuel for his quest.

Grizelda and Tizsa wrote down all the names.

"And they were all at the club with you, too?" Tizsa asked.

James shrugged. "I don't honestly know. I think so. I recall Langley—my brother—being there, but mostly, it's a sea of blurry faces."

"Were you in the habit of getting quite so cast away?" Grizelda asked.

"Never before, that I can recall, even as a student. But I suppose it isn't every day one becomes betrothed."

Grizelda and Tizsa exchanged glances.

"This afternoon," he said, "I think you and I should go to the gaming hell you mentioned, and see if we can't jog your memory. For now, I'd like you to go to your brother and ask him—"

"No," James said flatly.

Tizsa blinked. He obviously knew a resolute negative when he heard one. Elizabeth, however, did not.

"Do you want to get to the bottom of this or not?" she asked irritably. "You are not children to be sulking and refusing to talk to each other. If he can tell you what we all need to know, then you need to ask him. I shall come with you and take notes."

James narrowed his eyes at her. "You will not."

She met his gaze without fear. Even in his annoyance, he was glad of that. He was even ashamed of his feeble attempt at intimidation.

She rose to her feet. "Ten minutes," she said, and walked out of the kitchen.

"And that," James murmured, his ill humor vanishing like mist in the sunshine, "is how she survived Jarman and three years of running. Very well, I'll go to my damned brother. What will you two do this morning?"

"Tidy up the loose end that is the underworld figure of Fisher," Tizsa said.

James regarded them with unease. "I thought you were leaving him to the police? You plan simply to ask him if he killed Jarman?"

"We shouldn't have to," Grizelda replied. "We just need to listen to rumor in the right places."

THE FIRST TIME Griz and Dragan ventured into the rougher areas of St. Giles, they had drawn considerable attention. They began today at the soup kitchen where Griz often volunteered. It was still too early to have opened, but several tattered urchins, desperate mothers, and homeless men were already skulking in the vicinity. Most of them knew Griz by sight. One or two of them had been treated by Dragan, so they were happy enough to talk. Talking about Fisher was a different matter. His name produced a lot of shuffling and head shakes. No one even appeared to know which alehouse he frequented.

Until a dirty boy, wearing a cap several sizes too big for his little head, bounced up and said cunningly, "I'll take ye, lady and gent! But you'll have to give me the price of my dinner, 'cause I'll probably miss it here now."

Griz and Dragan had been caught out by over-helpful urchins before, so they only followed him to the next crossroads, where Dragan stopped him and drew a coin from his pocket.

"We'd hate you to miss your dinner," Griz said kindly, "but you can still have the coin, just for telling us the tavern where we're most likely find Mr. Fisher."

The boy's eyes widened, as if he couldn't quite believe his luck in acquiring such riches for so little effort. "Nag's 'Ead, first on your right down there, next two lefts."

Dragan tossed him the coin, which promptly vanished inside the boy's unspeakable garments. Griz wanted to take him home, bathe him, give him fresh clothes, and send him to her father's estate, where she had sent the last helpful urchin from this neighborhood. She could not save them all, though she'd look out for him next time.

"You want to watch yourself, missus," he said with a cheeky grin. "Fisher likes pretty ladies like you." Then he took off back to his post at the soup kitchen.

"I hope no one robs him," Dragan murmured, as they moved in the suggested direction.

Walking down dark alleys in St. Giles was a hazardous pastime in terms of both filth and crime, and the way described by their informant was increasingly dark and narrow. However, the final turn took them into an alley that certainly was not deserted. A crowd had formed beneath a dingy sign that might once have portrayed the head of a horse. Now, it was largely rust and filth, but it probably was the public house the boy had meant.

"I'd tell you to wait here," Dragan murmured. "But I doubt you'd be any safer."

"They do seem a little angry," Griz noted uneasily, wrinkling her nose as she picked her way through discarded rubbish and rotting food and other malodorous material she didn't care to contemplate.

A loud, indignant voice reached them. "No, we're not giving him to the bloody Peelers! He'd turn in his grave, he would."

"Nothing the Peelers could tell us anyhow," another man growled. "We know who done it."

"Oh dear," Griz murmured. Someone turned and saw their approach, so unless they were prepared to turn tail and run, they had to keep walking forward. Griz drew in her breath and called authoritatively, "Who did what?"

Surprisingly, the crowd parted to show her a body slumped on the tavern steps, his throat slit from ear to ear.

"Mr. Fisher," someone said piously, removing his greasy hat. "Never did nothing to no one, and yet the bloody Jarmans did him in."

"Jarman's dead," Dragan pointed out, inevitably releasing her to go to the body. The men watched him with hostility. Not that there was any doubt about the lifeless state of the body, but he would see what he could learn about the wounds.

"Yes, but his dandy stepson ain't," came another ugly voice. "Yet. Nor Jack Porter, who likes slitting a good man's throat or battering him to death."

"Did anyone see the killing?" Dragan asked, rising back to his feet.

A few heads shook. Someone said, "Found him this morning when I came to open up."

"Don't need to see it to know it," the first man snarled, glaring at Dragan. "Are you a Peeler?"

The moment was nasty. Griz gripped her umbrella, ready to use it on anyone who raised a finger to Dragan. But he had once kept a company of desperate revolutionary soldiers in order, and he didn't look remotely intimidated.

"No. I'm a doctor, as it happens," he said mildly. "Nothing I can do for this fellow. But for you... I can only advise you: don't look for trouble with the Jarmans. I suspect the Peelers are already all over them for something else entirely. My sympathy on your loss."

Slightly bewildered, they didn't prevent him rejoining Griz, and though she felt their eyes on the back of her neck all the way back to the end of the alley, no one gave chase.

"Revenge for killing Jarman?" Griz suggested when she could breathe again.

"Possibly. Or perhaps designed to look that way. Either way, I expect the police have an underworld war on their hands. Let's go back to Hanson Row. I have work to do before I drag Andover off to his den of iniquity."

Griz squeezed his arm. "I miss being home."

"So do I," he murmured. "And I think we can probably go back today if the word is out about the diamonds."

The news seemed to be all over all the newspapers they discovered on their return journey to Elizbeth's little house. They found it empty, so Griz made tea while Dragan scoured the newspapers for any mention of their hostess.

"None of them mention her," he said, "though Andover gets

several mentions as the man who was originally and wrongfully imprisoned for the theft. They all name Jarman and Connor as the robbers and remind their readers that the diamonds resurfaced only days after Jarman's own murder."

Griz poured his tea. "Probably good for James *and* Elizabeth. Dragan, do you—" She broke off as a peremptory knock on the front door shook the house. "Who the devil...?"

"Does not sound like a friendly neighbor," Dragan said with a hint of grimness. He pushed Griz's bag nearer her, for it contained her gold-plated little pistol, and rose, picking up his walking stick before going to the front door.

# CHAPTER TWELVE

EVERYTHING HAD CHANGED with a kiss. As though in some children's fairytale, Elizabeth had been wakened in James's embrace, not just to sweet, arousing sensation but to emotion. To unspecific hope and awareness of life. The man walking at her side this morning remained unattainable, but he was not distant. He was a symbol of what life could be.

They said little as they walked north along the canal side. Elizabeth didn't mind. Although the weather was cloudy, the world seemed brighter. Birds sang above, and the men on the barges passing up and down the canal were cheerful. She didn't pretend James was hers, but she wouldn't have swapped these minutes for anything.

Only as they eventually turned into Grosvenor Place did he say, "Should I apologize for kissing you?"

*Only if you want to break my heart.* "I'm not offended, if that's what you mean." She stole a quick glance at him. "Nor do I make any silly presum—"

"I don't regret it," he interrupted.

"Then why apologize?" she retorted.

His lips quirked. "I didn't. I would apologize for offense, but since you've taken none, I am happy." He took her hand, drawing it into the crook of his elbow, and breathless warmth spread through her. It felt like contentment.

"People will find me an odd, poor creature to be on your

arm," she warned.

"No," he said. "They're more likely to think me an unsuitable creature to be near any lady. But I'm long past caring what *people* say or think on such matters."

"But it bothers you to be going to your brother."

He didn't deny it, but there was a distinct pause before he said, "That's different. I once cared for his opinion and didn't realize it."

"When did you last speak to him?"

"The day I was arrested. Saturday, the twenty-sixth day of August. And don't lecture me. You haven't seen your family in even longer. Are they still in London?"

She nodded. "I once mended bed linen for their neighbors. As I walked along the street, I saw my mother leave the house, and kept my head down. But she would never have noticed someone like me."

"Does it strike you that you can end the lie now? You are in no danger from Jarman or anyone seeking the diamonds. You don't need to live in such…obscurity."

"No, but I can't go home either. They won't have me, and my father's hypocrisy sickens me."

"There are other options. More genteel professions. Griz has influence, you know, through her family and her charity connections. She can help find you teaching posts if that is what you'd prefer."

"She has already done so much." She shook her head.

"We are both lucky to have engaged the Tizsa interest."

"I don't think you are quite so lucky," she said wryly. "I believe the plan is that you pay for it."

"Funnily enough, I am happy to. My father's house is along there in South Audley Street."

*My father's house.* Not *my family home.* They were both exiles, it seemed, but in James's case, he was innocent, and his family had never acknowledged it. They must, she thought angrily, be the worst kind of people. She was almost surprised that he had tolerated her interference in this visit, but she still sensed he wanted support, to face his family with at least one friend who believed in him. Even if that friend was a badly dressed, lowly seamstress.

He seemed calm enough as they walked along South Audley Street, except that he curled his fingers involuntarily before they turned up the front steps of the imposing townhouse. And he snatched an extra breath before he raised the knocker.

The door was opened swiftly by a liveried servant. Lord James held out his card between two fingers. "Lord Langley, if you please."

"If you step inside one moment, I'll inquire…"

Abruptly, the door was wrenched wide and an older, white-haired man in the dark, perfect attire of a butler stared at James, who was ushering Elizabeth into the house before him.

"Lord Jamie!" the butler exclaimed. "Oh, my lord, welcome home."

"Hello, Clifford, you old rascal," James said amiably, holding out one casual hand. Elizabeth felt his relief as if it were her own, as if he had expected the entire household to turn their backs on him still. "How are you?"

"All the better for seeing *you*, my lord." The butler, clearly an old family retainer, gripped the outstretched hand hard with both of his. There were actually tears in his eyes.

"And your family?" James asked.

"Thriving, sir."

"Excellent. I'm very glad to see you looking so well, Clifford." He extricated his hand. "Is my brother about the place?"

"He is," said another voice before the butler could answer.

Lord James did not start, nor even twitch, but something changed suddenly in his demeanor, almost as though his body was clamped by some iron control. He turned slowly to see the man coming swiftly down the stairs.

Physically, he looked like a healthier version of James, though he might have been an inch shorter, his shoulders slightly broader. His hair was a shade lighter, his eyes a more definite blue, his complexion healthy, like an English gentleman who enjoyed the outdoors. His stride was impetuous as he reached the foot of the stairs, and then slowed, and his expression was no longer eager but uncertain, wary.

"The office will do," James said, turning away from his brother and striding toward the back of the house. At the last moment, he remembered to snatch Elizabeth's hand to his coat sleeve and tow her with him.

There was not really an excuse for such abruptness, nor even for deciding where their reunion should take place, since he was not living there. But no doubt for the sake of privacy—heads had appeared over the banisters above, and a growing bunch of people had gathered about the baize door that led to the servants' hall—Lord Langley allowed it.

The office was a working room containing two desks, twice as many chairs, and a bookcase on which resided several ledgers and a few other books on land management. It may have been the preserve of the butler or a steward, or where their lordships met with tradesmen or men of business whom they did not want to introduce into the family part of the house.

James released her and turned briskly as his brother closed the door behind him. "This is Miss Barker, who is kindly giving me her aid in certain matters. Miss Barker, my brother Lord Langley."

The faint frown on Lord Langley's brow may have been constant or may have betokened consternation or bewilderment. At any rate, he was civil enough to bow when Elizabeth curtsied.

"I need to ask you a few questions," James said, without allowing his brother to speak. "Miss Barker will take notes for me. Please, take a seat, ma'am, and be comfortable."

Lord Langley allowed this, also, though he said sardonically, "I have a few questions for you, too. Where have you been?"

"Newgate," James replied, as though surprised.

His brother sighed. "Since then."

"Henrietta Street, mainly. I sent the address to Father."

"Did you expect him to call on you?"

"God, no," James replied. "I thought he might forward any correspondence, though even there I didn't hold out much hope."

"He isn't here. He's in the country."

"That must explain it," James said without any pretense of belief. "Will you be so good as to answer my questions?"

"If you answer mine with equal honesty."

James turned, throwing his hat on the desk Elizabeth had not occupied, but she thought it was an excuse to hide his face.

Lord Langley's frown deepened. "They did not take your hat."

"Ah well, like you, I expect they were overcome by my presence. I shan't be long. Please cast your mind back to the night of my betrothal party, three years ago. We had dinner at White's."

"I recall it," Langley said warily.

"Do you recall who was there?"

Elizabeth had Lady Grizelda's list, so as James's brother began, haltingly, to recite names, she marked them on the list with an *L* for Langley's confirmation.

"Why was Hampton there?" James asked. "He was hardly a particular friend."

"He called, just as we were setting off, and you were in such good humor that you swept him along with us."

James's frown cleared. "So I did. I felt sorry for him because it was I who'd won Cordelia in the end. I didn't really expect him to come, though."

"No, neither did I, but he proved himself a better man. Why are you asking about this?"

"Because it's important to me, and I drank far too much for my memory to be accurate. Where did we go after White's?"

Langley grimaced. "Some hell—I beg your pardon, ma'am—a gaming den off Drury Lane. Coal Yard Lane."

"There was a waitress there that you liked," James remarked.

Lord Langley colored, though his eyes didn't falter. "I remember being touched that you took us there when you were celebrating something altogether more respectable."

"And yet only a few hours before, I'd been shooting strangers and stealing diamonds," James said. "What an actor I was in those days."

"James—"

"Did everyone who had been with us in White's come to Coal Yard Lane?" James interrupted.

Langley sighed. "Yes, and a couple more besides."

"Who?"

"Darchett, Front. Forsythe Niven—No, we came across Niven in the den and he joined the party."

"Niven?" James repeated, while Elizabeth wrote down the added names. He glanced at her. "He's Lady Grizelda's brother, who might also be able to help. Why did Front come? I wouldn't have thought gaming hells at all his thing."

"I expect he was hanging on the coattails of the nobility," Lord Langley said. "Helen wouldn't look at him then, so he was reduced to us. James, what is this about?"

"It's about whom I talked to that night. What did I do at Coal Yard Lane?"

"We all played cards. After one game, I left you to it. When I next saw you, you could barely walk or string a sentence together. But you refused to come away with me. Niven and Graham promised they would see you safely home, which they did barely half an hour after I got to the house." An unexpected smile flitted across Langley's lips. "I left you in bed, snoring like a pig."

James did not respond to the smile or to the insult. He asked, "Was I still gambling when you left the hell?"

"No, you were drinking, and clearly had been in quite a concentrated manner, in a huddle with Niven and Graham."

"Was I with them all evening at Coal Yard?"

Again, a tinge of color seeped into Lord Langley's face. "I don't know. I wasn't in the same room. But you looked pretty…ensconced."

"Did I ask you about jewelers?"

Langley blinked. "You said you wanted to buy Cordelia a betrothal ring at once, and not wait until the next quarter's allowance put you back in funds. And you said, Godfrey's was too expensive and too old-fashioned, and you'd be damned if Papa got to hear how much you'd spent on it. Therefore, you would go elsewhere."

"Did I mention Mason's? Did you?"

"I certainly didn't, for I'd never heard of it until the trial."

"And when you left the gambling club, was everyone else we've mentioned still there?"

Langley thought. "So far as I can recall. No, Darchett had gone off by the time I returned to the main room."

"And Hampton?"

"Still playing cards. Or was it dice by that stage?"

James moved to pick up his hat then paused. "To your knowledge, were any of our party short of funds?"

Langley wrinkled his nose with an aristocrat's distaste for the subject of money. "Graham, perennially, I suppose. And Forsythe Niven because his father was trying to keep him on leading strings with indifferent success."

James nodded and took his hat from the desk.

Elizabeth said, "To your knowledge, my lord, did any of those men bear a grudge against Lord James? A reason of any kind to dislike him?"

"James and Sir Arthur Hampton were rivals in love. Hampton couldn't have *liked* that James won the lady, but I doubt it was personal. Everyone liked James."

James's lips twisted into a bitter smile. "Oh, *everyone*."

"So far as you observed, my lord," Elizabeth pursued, "did anyone *not* seem surprised by the news of Lord James's arrest? Particularly amongst the people you have already named."

"No." Langley looked perplexed. "But I didn't really see most of them when they heard the news. Cordelia and her family were devastated. As were my parents and my sister."

"I shall be sick," James announced. "Shall we go, Miss Barker?"

Reluctantly, Elizabeth put away her notes and rose.

"Wait," Lord Langley said, scowling. "You haven't answered my questions yet."

"You didn't ask any." The direct clarity of his gaze told her James was referring to more than today, and Langley's shifting feet betrayed the same recognition.

"I'm asking now," Langley said evenly. "Why did you not come home?"

"I was not invited."

"For God's sake, James, this is your home! You don't need an invitation. We assumed you would know that much."

"Yes, you assumed a great deal," James said, brushing past him to the door. "Entirely erroneously. Miss Barker?"

She moved toward the door, remembering to curtsey to the marquis's unhappy-looking heir, and walked beside Lord James out of the house.

"You need to go back and talk to him," she said low, all but trotting to keep up with James's spanking pace.

"Why?" he snarled.

"Because you are brothers, and whatever he did or didn't do, he cares for you."

"Oh, *deeply*," James said with heavy sarcasm. "Like everyone else, he tried and convicted me in the space of two seconds and ignored me thereafter."

"Did he?" Elizabeth asked.

Scowling, James glanced at her, and must have finally realized how inconveniently furious his pace was. He slowed. "What do you mean?"

"When you asked him about Mason's, he replied, *I'd never heard of it until the trial.*"

James's shapely lips parted. His eyes widened. "He was there?" Then the scowl descended once more. "I looked. None of them were there. At least he read it a newspaper, I suppose."

"You need to talk to him again," Elizabeth said. "Not today but some other time, perhaps on more neutral territory. He must have been at least partly in the wrong, from our point of view, but you owe it to yourself to listen to his side of the story."

James opened his mouth to retort, no doubt something off-hand and biting. But before the words were uttered, he blinked. A half-smile tugged at his lips. *"Our point of view,"* he quoted. "I like that. I'll kiss you for it when we have a private moment."

Heat flooded into her face. Memory tingled in the pit of her stomach. "No, you won't," she retorted, wishing her voice sounded steadier. "Kisses of gratitude are neither necessary nor appropriate between us."

"What about welcome?"

A rush of emotion, part panic and part longing, propelled her ahead of him, lost for words, even coherent feeling.

He caught up with her an instant later, catching her hand and drawing it into the shelter of his arm. "There, I've stopped. I didn't mean to distress you. Let's talk instead about what we learned from John. From Langley," he corrected himself at once.

"We have a few more names, but I don't know these people. Who among them is fair? Do any of them fit Mrs. Mason's description?"

"Forsythe Niven is fair, but too young. As is Hampton. And Front. And Lord Darchett."

"But only Hampton bears a grudge?"

"I think I punched Darchett's nose when we were at school. And I once sent Front about his business for importuning Helen at some ball. She was clearly uncomfortable and wanted to marry Lord Eaglesome at the time. But they were old grudges and trivial. Only Hampton is likely to have acted in temper."

Elizabeth shook her head. "I don't think whoever engineered your downfall was acting in temper. It was too well planned."

"I may just have been in the right position at the right time," he said, raking his free hand through his hair. "There didn't need to be a grudge."

"Just knowledge," Elizabeth agreed. "And we still don't know who steered you to Mason's. What about this Graham fellow?"

"One of my best friends, an officer in the Royal Navy. He sailed before I was arrested."

"And Lady Grizelda's brother?"

"Too good-natured, I would have thought. But he's clever, as she is. We can ask her. Or Tizsa, since he's more likely to be unbiased. Although," he added with sudden bleakness, "I have heard that no one ever knows one better than a sibling."

"I wouldn't know," she said, "being an only child." She glanced at his closed profile. "Knowing your brother, then, how would you have described him the day before you were arrested?"

"Annoying," James said at once. "Upright and obedient and eager to please." He hesitated, then added, "A little shy. Less sure of himself than he pretended. Fun when he let himself relax and give his sense of humor free rein. And utterly loyal."

"And that is why you are so angry with him? You believed in his loyalty, and he let you down by believing the worst of you."

James nodded once, then opened his mouth and closed it again. At last, he spoke in a quiet, unsteady murmur that she might not have been meant to hear. "Worse. I feared he knew me so well that I *was* capable of the things they said I had done."

They were on a public street, flanked by windows and carriages and pedestrians. There was nothing she could do to give him comfort and belief, except squeeze his arm and briefly press her cheek to it, as if she had bumped into him by accident.

"No," she said flatly. "No."

He drew in a breath. His free hand covered hers as though hanging on to a lifeline. And then he changed the subject. "What was it like growing up as an only child? Were you lonely?"

For the rest of the walk to Hanson Row, they compared childhoods, which drew understanding and occasional laughter. And so, equilibrium had been restored by the time they arrived at the house. She let them in with her key.

Dr. Tizsa emerged from the kitchen door. "You had better come in," he said, and fixed his steady gaze on Elizabeth. "You have visitors."

Her stomach gave a twist of unease. To get it over with, she walked quickly past him into the kitchen to find her visitors seated incongruously at the table with cups of tea.

"Greetings, dearie," said Barb Sandman with a wolfish smile.

# CHAPTER THIRTEEN

T HE SHEER UNEXPECTEDNESS of it made her head reel. And yet it wasn't really surprising at all. They had all been waiting days for Barb or Bertie or even Porter to make an appearance in pursuit of the diamonds. But why come now, when the diamonds' recovery by the police was all over the newspapers?

"Barb. Bertie," she managed. "You've taken me by surprise."

"Thought we might," Barb said, looking her up and down. "Come down a bit in the world, ain't you, since you ran away from Josh?"

"I wouldn't say that. I see my friends have provided hospitality. What is it you want?"

Barb smiled. Her jet earrings swung as she turned her head toward her son. "What is it I want again, Bertie, love? Oh yes, I want to know why you sent your nobby friends to spy on me, pretending to be collecting for charity."

"And if she gave *all* the diamonds to the police," Bertie reminded his mother, smirking.

"And if you or your nobby friends killed my Joshua."

Elizabeth took the wooden chair James held for her. Grizelda poured them both a cup of tea, and James took his to the back door, where he leaned his shoulder against the wall. Dr. Tizsa lounged in the kitchen doorway.

"I didn't send my—er...nobby friends," Elizabeth said. "Although I gave them Joshua's address, they called on behalf of someone else entirely. And yes, I gave *all* the diamonds to the police, or at least all that I discovered in my father's chess set. Finally, no, none of *us* killed Joshua. Did you?"

"Chess set?" Bertie stared at her. So did Barb. "So that's where the old bas—"

"Robert!" Barb snapped.

"—where the old devil hid them," Bertie finished. "Cunning. So you had them all the time?"

"Apparently."

Bertie's lip curled as he surveyed Elizabeth's old gown and the bare, peeling kitchen. "Keeping your wealth hidden so that those who deserve it don't get it?"

"Don't be daft," Barb scoffed. "She didn't know she had them, did she? Goody two-shoes! Not till Josh got himself killed. No wonder he was so hopping mad when you vanished. The hoity-toity whore thought he'd done away with you, too. Not that I'd have blamed him if he had."

Elizabeth ignored the last part of this speech. Instead, watching them both carefully, she said. "Then you really didn't know where the diamonds were? He never told you?"

Barb sniffed. "A private man, was my Joshua."

"He was certainly private with his wealth," Elizabeth agreed. "So how did you know I was here?"

"Guessed," Bertie said breezily. Too breezily? He jerked his head in the direction of each Tizsa. "*No one* comes to Jarman's house for charity. Until he's dead. Papers won't say where he died, but Ma got the name of the street out of some Peeler, and then we remembered your charitable friends here."

"You only learned about Hanson Row today?" Elizabeth said.

They nodded in perfect time with each other.

"They knocked at the front door," Lady Grizelda said.

Meaning they probably didn't have the key to the back?

"Fine gloves," James said, speaking for the first time as he strolled toward the table, where Bertie's discarded gloves lay beside his teacup.

"Thank you," Bertie replied, reaching for them. He was too slow.

James whisked them off the table and held them up to the light, admiring the tassels and elegant embossing on the leather.

"I can put in a word for you with my maker," Bertie offered with a smirk.

"Oh, I shan't put you to the trouble," James said. "I merely wondered if you'd lost one recently. Your pardon, ma'am," he added politely to Elizabeth as he opened the drawer under the table and removed the glove Dr. Tizsa had yanked off their intruder last night.

"A dull glove," Bertie said dismissively, although his eyes had narrowed and Barb's had widened as James held the two gloves together, comparing sizes.

"I would like to return it to its owner," James said, when it was clear the intruder's glove was rather broader. "Perhaps you recognize it?"

"No, but I recognize *you*," Barb said aggressively. "Where have I seen your handsome face before?"

"He probably collects for charity, too," Lady Grizelda murmured, and Barb cast her a quick glance of dislike.

"Nah. Nothing to do with that. Something to do with my Joshua..."

Elizabeth's stomach tightened painfully. Not, she was almost surprised to discover, because she believed for a moment that James really was involved with Joshua Jarman. But because Barb might accuse him and rekindle all the suspicion that had already sent him to prison, reviled by everyone.

But Barb broke into a peal of genuine, delighted laughter. "Got it! I never forget a face! You're the lord Joshua got blamed for the diamonds! Before they got poor Pete Connor."

James leaned forward, clearly about to ask for elaboration, but straight questioning never worked on Barb.

"I don't believe you," Elizabeth scoffed. "Joshua could *never* have arranged such a thing."

"Bloody could," Barb countered. "You never had any idea what he was capable of. Too high and mighty to look. He could do anything, my Josh, if he just knew the right people."

"My point exactly," Elizabeth taunted her. "Joshua did *not* move in the right circles. Far from it."

"Shows what you know," Barb retorted. "He don't need to *move* in the right circles. He just needs to *know* someone."

"Such as?" Elizabeth asked.

Barb leaned forward, an ugly expression forming around her mouth. Elizabeth was afraid to breathe.

And then Barb's face cleared and she gave a laugh of derision. "That's for me to know. You won't never find out."

*Damn.* Elizabeth tried another tactic. "Did you know Joshua had a key to my house?"

Bertie sneered, but his mother had herself better in hand. "Think he wanted to give you one for the old times?" she said crudely. "He needed to get at the diamonds, didn't he?"

"I don't see how he could have got a key, though."

Barb winked. "Easy enough when you know how."

"But you don't, do you?"

"No," Barb said flatly.

Clearly Elizabeth needed another new tactic.

"Who did he give it to?" Dr. Tizsa asked from the back door. He transferred his gaze from the window to the Sandmans.

"The police must have found it on his body," Bertie said. "Either that or *she's* got it."

"His killer got it," Dr. Tizsa said. "Doesn't that bother you? Don't you want a spot of revenge? In this case, we can see that you get it—for just a little cooperation."

Bertie would have spoken again, except his mother elbowed him none too gently.

"I see," Dr. Tizsa said. "You think you've already taken your revenge by murdering Zeb Fisher."

"Fisher is dead?" Barb muttered. Impossible to tell if her surprise was genuine. "Good."

"Where were you in the early hours of the morning?" Dr. Tizsa asked Bertie.

"In my bed, of course," Bertie said with a smirk. "And I don't need to answer your damned questions."

"No, but you'll need to answer those of the police, so you might as well get the practice in. We might even be able to help you."

"*I* didn't kill him," Bertie said, so smugly that Elizabeth found herself believing him.

"Did you know I was back in London?" she asked.

"Didn't even know you'd left," Barb replied, staring at her. "Why *did* you come back? Had enough of the poor life without Joshua?"

"That must have been it," Elizabeth said, removing her tired old bonnet. "Why are you wasting your time here, Barb?"

"Damned if I know." Barb sighed and rose to her feet.

"Who was with Joshua when he stole the diamonds?" Elizabeth asked. "Was it you, Bertie?"

"Nah," Bertie said with some regret. "Got himself a new partner, didn't he? Did it on the quiet bef—Ouch!" He broke off to glare at his mother, who had kicked his ankle and was all but snarling at him. "According to what I heard on the streets," he added.

"What partner?" James asked. "According to what you heard on the streets."

Bertie shrugged.

"A fair man, perhaps, who spoke and dressed like a gentleman?" James suggested.

"Could have been anyone," Bertie said. "We were never introduced. Good seeing you again, Bethie. You take care."

"Why?" James asked. "Have you got some more thugs lined up to abduct her?"

Bertie curled his lips. "What would I want with her?"

Dr. Tizsa and Lord James conducted their visitors to the front door.

"Do you believe a word they said?" Lady Grizelda asked, low-voiced.

"One or two, maybe, but they're the type of people to lie even when they have no reason," Elizabeth replied. "If I was guessing, I'd say they really didn't know the diamonds were with me in the chess set. And they *do* know who Joshua's gentlemanly partner was. I think Bertie recognized the glove, too, though I can't be sure."

"Do you think they lied about killing Fisher?" Lady Grizelda shivered. "We saw his body in St. Giles."

"I doubt they did it personally," Elizabeth replied. "The police will go to them first. But they could easily have been responsible."

"As revenge?" Dr. Tizsa asked. He and James must have watched the Sandmans walk the length the street, judging by the time it had taken them to return.

"To be *seen* as taking revenge." Elizabeth's lips tightened. She couldn't prevent a shiver as the violent and criminal discussions of the past crept back into her memory. "Or to try to take over Fisher's business. God, I thought I'd left all that behind me."

James's hand closed on her shoulder, gentle yet firm, at once comforting and thrilling. Every time he touched her...

He released her and sat in Bertie's vacant chair. "But you don't think they killed Jarman?"

"I suppose they could have followed him here," she said. "They must have known he had access to the diamonds, because of Pete Connor's arrest. On the other hand, if they'd been caught spying on him, they'd have risked his fury."

"Perhaps they caught that fury and that's why they killed him," Grizelda mused.

"There was no sign of a fight in the house," her husband reminded her. "I suppose they could have tidied up, but they'd have had to be extremely quick about it, and I can't help thinking Elizabeth would have noticed. Did you learn anything useful from your brother, Andover?"

"I learned that I apparently spent some time with yours, Griz."

"My brother?" she said. "Which one?"

"Forsythe."

"Oh. Well, that's fine," Grizelda said in apparent relief. "We can pick his brains easily enough."

"Did you find talking to your brother jolted your memory at all?" Dr. Tizsa asked James. "Have you remembered any more about that night?"

James shook his head in clear frustration. "Very little."

"This happened to my sister once," Grizelda said. "Not from overindulgence, you understand, but from a nasty shock. Going back to the places she had been, seeing the same people, seemed to help."

"Which is why you and I need to find out where you were and what you did," Dr. Tizsa said cheerfully. "Especially after you left White's."

"Oh, I know that, for I'd been before the night in question," James replied. "I can find it easily enough—if it's still open."

"Excellent. We can go this afternoon, if you like. I find myself available, and we should consider taking your brother and Grizelda's with us."

"Mine has had enough of me for one day," James said. Then he frowned. "Besides, we should not leave the ladies alone, not since most of the underworld seems to know of this place."

"You're right, of course," Dr. Tizsa responded. "I think we've learned everything we can from Hanson Row and should now repair to Half Moon Street Lane."

⫷⫸

DESPITE ELIZABETH'S OBJECTIONS—"I have a mountain of sewing to complete and I cannot accept your hospitality"—she found herself duly ensconced in the house on Half Moon Street Lane.

She could not deny that Lady Grizelda's spare bedchamber was more comfortable than her best room, but somehow that made things worse.

"I must not get used to this lifestyle," she said in a rush. "I need my own, bare little house and hard work. If I stay here, I will no longer be content to go back."

"Do you think you will be if you don't come here for a couple of days?"

Elizabeth sat down on the soft feather bed and sighed. "I don't know. My life is upside down again."

Grizelda said, "No one should work so much that they damage their hands and their eyes just to survive. I know it happens to many, even to children in much more appalling circumstances, but this is wrong for you. You are a lady of education and intelligence—"

"I am a fallen woman," Elizabeth said. "Rightly disowned by my parents. I would rather work than beg."

"You are a tricked and cheated woman, and I fail to see why we should let Jarman win, even when he's dead."

Elizabeth blinked. "I can't change the past."

"We can change perception of the past. But I'd rather you think of your future, what you would like to do with your life. I know you'll want to finish the sewing you have agreed to, so I suggest you take this time to finish it, without taking on more. I'm not wealthy, but I'm happy to take you on as a companion for bed and board and a few gowns that you'll have to alter yourself. Dragan doesn't like me to be tired. It will be dull work, mostly, but it will give you peace to think without having to worry if there's a roof over your head or if you'll have enough money to eat the next day."

"My business will suffer," Elizabeth said stubbornly, "just as it's beginning to grow."

"Do you care?" Grizelda asked.

Elizabeth closed her gaping mouth. "No. Not really. But I *should* care."

"I have a large family," Grizelda said, "with a long reach. If you wish to sew, we can recommend you to higher-paying customers. If you want to be a permanent companion or governess or teacher, I can help with that, too. If you want to marry and have children—"

"You're a matchmaker as well?" Elizabeth said with a hint of desperation.

Grizelda laughed. "Who'd have thought it? Seriously, though, I need to speak to some people about this case, and I think you should come with me. We need to know about some of our suspects from Society's point of view. Therefore we need to go into Society, and I will need a companion who doesn't say the wrong thing."

Elizabeth narrowed her eyes. "You are trying to manipulate me."

"Come and look at my feeble wardrobe. And then we need to visit my sister Azalea."

Half an hour later, wearing one of Lady Grizelda's plain but excellently made gowns, Elizabeth walked with her hostess to Mount Street and the imposing townhouse inhabited by Lord and Lady Trench.

She felt very self-conscious in her borrowed finery, and yet the soft material, the elegant cut, even when cinched in with a sash to fit Elizabeth's thinner figure, made her feel oddly herself again. Lady Grizelda's maid, who appeared to have many talents, had also pinned her hair into a less severe style. Grizelda had also lent her a hat with ribbons that matched the trim of her gown. Gradually, she felt herself remembering her posture, walking straight-backed with her head up. As though clothes could change what and who she was.

They could certainly change perceptions, though, as Grizelda had pointed out, for neither the Mount Street servants nor Lady Trench herself seemed to see anything odd in Elizabeth's appearance. Her ladyship was discovered playing with her children in a private sitting room, and looked up at them from the floor with an unembarrassed smile.

Lady Azalea Niven, now Lady Trench, was beautiful by any standards. Playing so naturally with her children, she was breathtaking. Elizabeth felt an ache that she eventually identified not as envy but as longing. Not for Lady Trench's beauty, but for her children and the happiness they so clearly brought her.

"Griz," her ladyship said. "Thank God. You have saved me from the wicked pirates."

The pirates released their mother and hurled themselves at Lady Grizelda instead with cries of, "Aunt Griz! Aunt Griz! You must be the enemy pirate!"

"Yo ho!" Grizelda said enthusiastically, waving an imaginary cutlass with one hand while she hugged them with the other.

"Not all visitors are pirates, however," Lady Trench said. "And it's time for lessons before your father comes home."

The children sighed, bowed and curtseyed, cast final grins at Grizelda, and ran off.

Lady Trench rose and smoothed her skirts without apology.

"Zalea, this is Miss Barker," Grizelda said. "Elizabeth, my eldest sister, Lady Trench."

"How do you do, Miss Barker?" Lady Trench said, offering one carelessly friendly hand. "Do sit down and we'll have tea. What can I do for you, Griz? I know that look."

"You sent us a card a couple of weeks ago," Grizelda said, "for a charity soiree or some such thing."

"Yes, we're raising money for a housing charity of Eric's. *You* don't need to pay up to come. In fact, I was hoping you and Lady Swan would play something. There will be a musical part of the evening, supper, and then dancing."

"May I bring Miss Barker?" Grizelda asked.

"Oh, yes," Lady Trench replied, at the same time as Elizabeth exclaimed, "Oh, no!"

Elizabeth blushed. "That is, you are very kind, but I have rather lost the habit of going into Society."

"Then you should find it again in a good cause," Lady Trench said cheerfully.

"Especially as some of the guests will interest you as well as me," Grizelda added. "Did you invite Lord James Andover, Zalea?"

"Actually, I did. I've no idea where he is, but I included him on the card I sent his family. Poor man. It must have been awful for him."

"Did you also invite Sir Arthur and Lady Hampton?" Grizelda asked.

"Why don't I just show you the guestlist," Lady Trench said dryly, "and you can tell me who else I should invite at insultingly short notice?"

Grizelda followed her sister to a desk, where she studied a long list with interest. The tea duly arrived, and she abandoned the list with apparent satisfaction.

"Anything else?" Lady Trench asked sweetly.

Grizelda smiled. "Can we have some of your gowns?"

# CHAPTER FOURTEEN

I N RESPONSE TO Lady Grizelda's scribbled note, sent by urchin
to her father's mansion in Park Lane, Lord Forsythe Niven was
collected from outside White's on James and Tizsa's way to Coal
Yard Lane.

"Andover!" he exclaimed in surprise, although his hand shot
out with no hesitation. "You must have had a grim time of it."

"Not as grim as some." James shook the outstretched hand,
grateful for the normality of the greeting that made no effort to
ignore his past. But then, Lord Forsythe had always been both
good-natured and accepting, with something of Grizelda's
curiosity.

"And as if that's not bad enough," Niven said, "now Griz has
involved you in one of her mad starts?"

"Actually, it seems that Griz—and Tizsa here—have involved
themselves in my madness, for which I am grateful."

"Of course you are." Niven grinned at his brother-in-law,
with whom he seemed to be on friendly terms. "Where are we
going, then?"

"A gambling den in Coal Yard Lane," Tizsa replied, setting off
in that direction.

"If it still exists," James added.

"Oh, it exists," Niven said uneasily. "It was raided by the
Peelers and shut down two years ago, but then it popped back up
again, somewhat changed. Different fellow in charge, different

members, including some very shady characters I wouldn't like to sit next to, let alone play cards with."

"Then it no longer boasts gentlemen members?" Tizsa asked.

"A few of the fellows who like to live dangerously."

James raised his brows. "Have you grown staid, my lord?"

"Apparently, *my lord*," Niven replied with a lopsided smile. "I have enough trouble dodging the matchmaking mamas without having the criminal fraternity on my coattails, too. Why do you want to go there?"

"We want to know how Andover came to take the blame for the diamond theft," Tizsa said. "And we think something might have happened on the night of his betrothal party while he was at this den of vice."

"I was there," Niven said in a pleased tone of voice.

"You were," Tizsa agreed. "And for once, we are relying on your sobriety to tell us what happened."

"Lord, yes, you were three sheets to the wind," Niven recalled, giving James a friendly nudge in the ribs. "In fact, as I recall, I helped take you home."

"For which I remain eternally in your debt. Did I ask you about jewelers?"

"Shouldn't think so. Don't know anything about 'em. My valet makes that kind of purchase for me, since, apparently, I have no taste."

"What jeweler does he use?" James asked, since, after all, Niven had fair hair and was undoubtedly a gentleman, although he couldn't imagine him killing or robbing or lying to send an acquaintance to jail.

"No idea," Niven replied. He was frowning. "You were going on about a ring at one point, though. For your intended, who was that beautiful girl..."

"She's still a beautiful girl," James said, almost surprised by how little the thought of her hurt. "Though she wears someone else's ring."

"Sorry, old fellow."

"Don't be. Do you remember other people giving me advice about jewelers?"

Niven scratched his ear. "Not really. Don't pay much attention to that kind of talk."

"What did you do at the den?" Tizsa asked his brother-in-law.

Niven shrugged. "The usual. Played dice, played cards, flirted with the girls."

"When did you first see Andover there that night?" Tizsa asked.

"When he first arrived, I think... Yes, you came in in the midst of a big, noisy group, just as my card game was finishing up. You were with your brother Langley, and a naval officer whose name I've forgotten—he helped carry you home, though—and several other fellows. Hampton was there, which surprised me, given that you'd just won the lady he was madly in love with. I waved to you and your whole crowd came over. Since my game was breaking up, you all sat down with me instead."

"Who did Andover sit beside?" Tizsa asked.

Niven groaned. "Lord, how am I supposed to remember that? It was three years ago, and I've sat around a lot of gaming tables since then." Nevertheless, he scratched his ear some more, knocking his hat sideways to a very rakish angle as he did so. "Me," he said at last. "And I think Darchett was on your other side."

"Where was Hampton?" James asked.

Niven cast him a disapproving look. "How in Hades do you imagine such details could ever...? Wait, though, he was on the other side of the table, I think, next to your brother, who had that banker fellow on his other side, the one who married your sister."

"Earnest Front," James said.

"That's the chap. Amiable, decent kind of man. Though I barely knew him then."

"Did you converse during the game?" Tizsa asked.

"Must have done," Niven replied, "though I'm pretty sure we

were all concentrating on the cards."

"How many games did you play?"

"Oh, the devil, I can't remember such... Two." Niven sounded faintly surprised. "Langley abandoned us after one, and a shiftier fellow took his place."

"What shifty fellow was this?" James broke in.

"No idea. Never seen him before or since. In any case, I went off to pursue my favorite waitress, and the rest of you moved on to some serious drinking, or playing in some cases, though I didn't see you at the tables again."

Tizsa glanced around Niven to catch James's eye. "Do you remember any of this?"

"Parts of it. Like disjointed photographs." Which wasn't comfortable at all. He must have got ridiculously drunk, appallingly quickly, and he hated to think of himself with so little control.

"When did you next notice him, Forsythe?"

"Must have been an hour or so later," Niven said. He cast a quick grin at James. "You were with Hampton. No idea what you were saying, but the fellow looked pretty disgusted, so I went over to defuse the situation before it got out of hand."

"What *was* I saying?" James asked, though he wasn't sure he wanted to know.

"No idea. Your naval friend had the same idea as me, and when we arrived, Hampton made his excuses and left."

"Left the club?" Tizsa asked. "Or just your company?"

"The latter. I think. Didn't pay any attention, to be honest, because Andover was in such a state he could hardly slur his words together."

"Christ," James muttered.

"Sorry, old chap. Been there too, and it's never fun afterward. Your brother Langley tried to persuade you to go home with him, but you weren't having it. We said we'd take you when you'd finished your drink. Which was odd, because you didn't have a drink just then. Probably thought another few minutes would make you more pliable."

"Was I *fighting* drunk?" James asked, appalled.

"Lord no. You could barely stand, let alone take a swing at someone. You just seemed pretty determined to stay where you were. Probably because you were almost asleep. About a quarter of an hour later, we heaved you up, and you didn't object. We all but carried you into the hackney and then up to your bedroom. Left your brother to put you to bed."

"Thank you," James muttered. "And my apologies."

"None necessary, old fellow, it's what friends are for. Besides, it's not every day a fellow gets happily betrothed." Niven grimaced. "Sorry."

James stopped. They had turned into Coal Yard Lane, and he recognized the gambling den only too well. It was housed in a tall, old, ramshackle building, with steps rather like the area steps of a big house, leading down to a lower-ground floor and an unexpectedly grand front door with a small square window. The porter, he recalled, peered at everyone before he let them in or sent them about their business. The ground floor at least had also been part of the club, housing private rooms for rent, though James had no idea about the rest of the building.

Niven, who apparently was still a member of the club, led the way down the steps.

"Do you remember coming this way that night?" Tizsa murmured to James as they followed.

James nodded.

"Then keep me informed as we go," Tizsa instructed him. "Everything that you recall, whether you've mentioned it before or not."

James remembered the block sliding back and the perusing eye of the porter, although it was not the same porter who let them in now.

"Welcome, gentlemen. Please sign in the book."

Niven signed for himself and his guests, though Tizsa peered over his shoulder, no doubt taking in the other names on the page.

The slightly dingy passage was familiar, as was the main room into which Niven led them. Only, no candles were lit in the daylight of the afternoon, making the room gloomier as well as much emptier than James recalled. No one sat at the large gaming tables, or the roulette wheel. Only two debauched-looking young gentlemen sat at one table, playing piquet with a large wine jug between them. By the state of their posture, hair, and clothes, to say nothing of the stubble on their jaws, they had probably been there since at least the same time yesterday.

Otherwise, a waiter sprawled at a table by the window, yawning over a newspaper, although he sprang to his feet as the newcomers entered.

"Gentlemen, please sit where you will. What would you like? Some wine or ale? A little dinner, perhaps?"

"Bottle of decent claret, if you please," Niven said cheerfully.

"And a pack of cards," Tizsa added.

Niven turned toward one of the smaller tables, but Tizsa caught his arm to stop him. Catching on, James glanced around to recall where he had sat before. The positions of the tables were much the same. He walked to the large table in the center of the room and chose a chair in the middle of the near side. Tizsa and Niven sat down on either side of him.

The wine was brought and poured, and at a nod from Tizsa, Niven dealt the cards. Yes, this had happened before, only the chandelier above their heads had been lit and a lamp had glowed on every table and in the wall sconces around the room.

"Recall things as they were that night," Tizsa said. "Where did your brother sit?"

They went through it all without playing a game, although Tizsa then asked unexpectedly, "Who won that first game?"

"He did," James said, jerking his hand at Niven, who nodded modestly in agreement.

After that, they went through what James recalled of the second game, and, considering three years had passed with many more events to obscure the trivia, he was surprised by how much he could recall. The momentary images that had previously flashed through his mind had become in places a much steadier, continuous memory.

"Who won that second game?" Tizsa asked.

James wrinkled his nose. "Hampton."

"Did that annoy you?"

"No, but his smug expression did. Then Earnest Front said something like, *Lucky at cards, unlucky in love,* and Hampton glared at him. I felt it was tactless of Front, to say the least, and felt more charitable toward Hampton."

Niven sat up. "I'd forgotten that, but you're right. Bad form, kicking a fellow when he's down."

"Was that why you stopped playing?"

James shook his head. "I don't think so. I was just bored. Graham and I took our wine to a quieter table and talked, because he was leaving in the morning for his ship and probably wouldn't be back for the wedding."

"Where did you and Graham sit?" Tizsa asked. James stood and looked around him, before walking toward a small table at the back corner. Niven picked up the cards, and Tizsa brought the bottle. As they resettled, the waiter looked slightly bewildered, then returned to his newspaper.

"Did you have a bottle with you?" Tizsa asked.

James stared at the table, remembered the glass in his hand and Graham's face opposite, laughing as they clinked glasses over an empty table. "No, just the glasses in our hands."

"Did you order a bottle, then?"

"Not that I remember, but I suppose we must have... Wait, though, a waitress refilled my glass with brandy and sauntered off. I called her back to pour one for Graham, too, and she laughed and said it was from an admirer and Graham could get his own. So he did."

"Did you drink from his bottle, then?"

James rubbed his forehead. Images flashed behind his eyes,

the splash of wine and brandy in glasses, laughing friend's faces, a girl tossing her head and swishing her skirt provocatively as she moved away from him. A blur of noise, voices and clinking glasses that sounded too loud, piercing his brain. A blur of faceless people that were increasingly hard to recognize. And yet his mind had hummed with new and interesting thoughts, and though he knew he should go home, he had felt too good.

"I was happy," he said in disbelief. "How the devil could I be happy in that state?"

"Did you go anywhere else?" Tizsa asked. "Or did you just sit here?"

A foggy memory flitted by James. Weaving unsteadily between tables, an arm holding him up.

"Whose arm?" Tizsa asked. "Graham's?"

"No... That is, I don't think so. I sat somewhere else."

"There?" Niven said, pointing to a table nearer to the waiter. "That's where I found you."

Tizsa lifted the bottle once more, and they moved to the table Niven indicated. The waiter began to look decidedly wary.

"We're chasing memories," Tizsa said to him. "My friend hasn't been here for three years and is piecing together one memorable night. Have you worked here long?"

"A bit more than a year. After it changed hands."

"Who owns it now?" James asked.

"There are a few partners," the waiter said. "I only know Mr. Gorman."

The name meant nothing to James. Nor, looking about him, could he remember more than blurs. Once there was his brother's voice, and James had determined to stay with this good feeling and not obey John, who was just plain bossy—but beyond that, only a pressing blackness that suddenly frightened him.

He sprang to his feet. "Going for a walk," he muttered, and all but bolted from the main room in search of fresh air.

In the passage, however, he halted. Here, the smell of stale alcohol and cigar smoke was less. A cool draft drifted through from the back of the house, where the kitchens were located, bringing with it fresh cooking smells. A staircase led to the floor above, where private rooms could be rented for games or supper, or less respectable activities. James was fairly sure his brother had made use of one of them on the night in question. John had always been terribly respectable, which was what made his obsession with that little waitress so rare.

*Did I go up there, too? Was that where I got so drunk and so happy that I couldn't walk?*

Try as he would—he even set his hand on the banister and his foot on the first step—he couldn't recall ever climbing those stairs. He turned away, facing the front door, and realized the porter had gone from his post. Well, it was early and things were quiet. No doubt there would be little break for him later on.

James took the opportunity to go up to the members book, which went back years, and began to scan the pages at random. Voices and the clatter of pans drifted through from the kitchen, then hurried footsteps coming toward him.

Rather than bolt out the door or try to hide in the porter's narrow box, James decided to brazen it out, and continued turning and scanning the pages. The footsteps paused. The hairs on the back of James's neck prickled and the draft brought another scent, of male cologne, familiar and yet unplaceable. Abruptly, and yet furtively, the footsteps began again, this time receding.

James spun around in time to see a dark gray coat and a flash of blond hair vanish to the left of the kitchen. James started after him, since the man was clearly even more reluctant to be seen than James.

The blond man had turned left into a narrow passage that was empty by the time James got there. A door at the end led, probably, to a backyard. Apart from that, James found only a broom cupboard. Hastily, he tried the back door and found it locked. There was no sign of a key.

He returned to the main passage, where he found Tizsa peering out of the gaming hall.

"Are you well?" Tizsa asked.

"Fine," James said impatiently. "But a fair-haired man just bolted from the sight of me."

"Did you recognize him?" Tizsa asked.

"I only caught a glimpse of him from the back. It could have been anyone."

As they talked, the porter ambled toward them from the kitchen. "Can I help you, sirs?"

"No, we just thought we might leave quietly by a back door," James said.

"Sorry, sir, the back door is for staff only. It's kept locked."

"But you must have a key," James replied.

"I'm staff," the porter pointed out, making no offers.

"Of course you are. I suppose the owners use the back door, too?"

"On occasion."

"Satisfy my curiosity. Who is the owner with the fair hair?"

"Oh, I think they all have fair hair." The porter and James regarded each other with dislike.

"You're a close-lipped fellow," Tizsa observed. "Secretive business, I suppose, running a club like this."

"Your hats, gentlemen," the porter said with finality.

❯❯❯❯❮❮❮❮

"THE NIGHT OF your betrothal party," Tizsa said to James, "did you sleep all night?"

It was after a simple, pleasant dinner in Half Moon Street, and the four of them sat in the drawing room. Elizabeth, surrounded by glowing lamps, was sewing with swift efficiency, her eyes intent on her work, although she was clearly listening.

There was something different about her appearance, although it took James until now to realize what it was. Her hair was different. No longer scraped back from her face in a severe knot, her riot of curls was confined more loosely, allowing a soft frame for her face that emphasized the delicate beauty of her features. She also wore a much newer, better-quality gown that was slightly too big for her. Not that it seemed to matter what she wore or how she pinned her hair. He liked to look at her too much. It gave him a warm, tingling feeling about his heart that was as addictive as the earthier desire thrumming somewhat lower. The faint color staining her cheekbones told him she was aware of his scrutiny. She didn't look up, but nor did she seem upset or unhappy.

"Sleep," James repeated, aware that Tizsa had spoken to him. He blinked, absorbing the rest of the question and trying to think back. He frowned. "Yes, I think so, but to be honest, my head was so fuzzy and I had such awful dreams that I'm not sure. Even without the fiendish headache in the morning, the dreams would have been enough to turn me sober for life. Why do you ask?"

"Because I'm pretty sure you were drugged," Tizsa said. "Probably with laudanum, although there are other substances that could have the same effect. Probably after you stood up from the gaming table and before your head started spinning. My guess would be it was in the brandy the waitress gave you when she gave none to your friend Graham."

James blinked. "Isn't it more likely I was simply drunk as a wheelbarrow?"

"Excessive alcohol can lead to blackouts," Tizsa allowed. "But what you describe—the flashing images, the increased sensitivity—are not normal symptoms of simple drunkenness. Do you know who the waitress was?"

James shook his head. "I didn't go there often enough to distinguish, and anyway, my head was too full of Cordelia to notice other women. John—my brother Langley—is more likely to know, but I don't believe he was in the room at the time. But why would anyone trouble to drug me? Just so that I'd make a fool of myself?"

"Or so you wouldn't remember who recommended Mason the jeweler. And if you did remember, no one would believe you because of the state you were in."

Elizabeth lowered her sewing to her lap, gazing at James with distress.

Grizelda said, "And so you would feel so dreadful in the morning that you would take the easiest path to your committed intention of choosing a ring for Cordelia."

"None of that was guaranteed," James protested.

"But it worked," Elizabeth said. "You do have an enemy among your friends."

"Jarman's gentlemanly ally," James said slowly.

They thought about that for a while. Then Grizelda said, "The likeliest candidates will all be at Azalea's soiree on Wednesday. James can look them over, and we can observe their reactions to him. And, of course, Dragan can sketch their portraits. And then we can show them to witnesses like Mrs. Mason."

James and Elizabeth both gazed at her in consternation.

"In a nutshell," Tizsa said.

# CHAPTER FIFTEEN

OVER THE NEXT day, Elizabeth worked her way through her remaining sewing and mending tasks. The day after that, accompanied by Lord James, who had returned to his own rooms but called each day in Half Moon Street Lane, she returned the finished items to their respective owners. To each of her customers, she said she was spending a little while away and would let them know when she was available again. However, she increasingly liked the idea of never being available for such work again. The prospect of returning to Hanson Row made her feel unspeakably lonely, and yet she could not bring herself to live off Grizelda and Tizsa for more than the few days until Lady Trench's party.

"Are you nervous about the party?" James asked her once, as they walked back from Kensington, through the park.

"Inevitably, but I'm excited too. I have a feeling we'll learn a great deal. And besides, I've been altering an evening gown of Lady Azalea's for myself. Griz extracted several gowns *and* hats from her."

"I don't imagine you accepted them for nothing."

"I'm mending some linen for her," Elizabeth admitted.

"And for Griz?"

"Letting out some gowns so that they'll be more comfortable as her baby grows."

He looked at her. "Griz and Dragan might live a little hand-to-mouth by the standards of the wealthy, but the Trenches are, in vulgar parlance, stinking rich."

"That doesn't matter. I don't like to take something for nothing. Pride, I suppose." She cast him a rueful glance. "You don't want to go to the party at all, do you?"

"No. But since a large part of our aim seems to be to let people gawp at me, I shall just have to put up with it."

"I'm sure you'll repel the gawpers with one lift of an eyebrow." She gave his arm a little shake, since she was holding it at the time. She liked the feel of it, solid and protective. "I don't believe your old friends are rejecting you, my lord. But your protective indifference makes it seem that *you* have rejected *them*. In the case of your brother, there is more to the story than we know, because he clearly cares for you. You should take the opportunity to speak to him."

She thought he might be thinking about that, but then he said, "I like it better when you call me James."

"A slip of the tongue," she muttered.

"I'll forgive you if you dance with me at the soiree."

"Don't be silly, my lord. You will dance with ladies of your own rank."

"I'll dance with whom I like, providing the lady agrees."

"We'll see," Elizabeth said primly, taking the coward's way out, because in truth she wanted to dance with him far too much, and the last thing she needed was to fall any deeper into...whatever this feeling was.

"You're right about one thing, though," he said, gazing straight ahead. "My body might be free, but my mind is still in prison. Instead of making the most of my freedom, I've been obsessed with the past, with vengeance that can change nothing for the better."

"Be kind to yourself. You've only been free a matter of weeks."

"My first duty should have been to the people I am responsible for. I own a decent little estate in Kent. I have tenants and dependents that I haven't gone near."

"Go now," she urged, although she would miss him. "Go before the party."

"I thought I might. May I ask a favor of you?"

"Of course."

He looked down at her, his eyes unreadable. "Come with me?"

Emotion hit her in a torrent. Intense pleasure that he would ask. Deep disappointment that she could not accept. "I can't. Whatever I do, I will need my reputation. Wherever Miss Barker has been for three years, she has at least been out of the public eye. She cannot be seen gallivanting with you now."

"I don't mean to stay there this first visit, just post down there, have luncheon at the house—in the presence of my very respectable housekeeper—and return before dark. I would like to see it through your eyes." His lips quirked. "I would like your company. But if you would rather not, I shan't sulk."

She drew in a breath rather than give in to temptation. "I will ask Lady Grizelda what she thinks," she said at last.

A hiss of laughter escaped James's lips. "You do know that Griz never paid attention to convention? If she wasn't a duke's daughter, she would have been ruined several times over. You would do better to consult Lady Azalea."

He told her that, even though it worked against him. And for that reason, she decided to go with him before she had asked anyone's advice.

THEY LEFT AT first light, in a comfortable closed carriage that protected them from the threatening fog in the city, and from any rain encountered in the country. As they left London behind, she sat forward in excitement, gazing eagerly out of all three windows in turn. It was so long since she had been in the countryside that her heart lifted immeasurably. She even pulled down the window and took off her bonnet to feel the wind rushing against her skin and tugging at her hair.

Watching her, James smiled and poured her coffee from a flask. He sat on the back-facing bench, which was quite proper. As much as the country views, she found she liked the glimpses of his lean body swaying easily to the movement of the carriage. Their conversation was desultory yet comfortable, with just that edge of physical awareness she always felt in his company.

Eventually, after they changed horses, the flat, bucolic scenery gave way on one side to the sea.

Elizabeth inhaled the salty tang. "Do you live near the sea?"

"Yes, just another few miles beyond Rochester. Gailsham Court is away from the main roads, so it's quite peaceful."

"Was it your childhood home?" she asked.

"Oh no. We lived mostly at my father's main seat in Staffordshire, or in London, when we weren't at school. We only visited Gailsham occasionally, but I always knew it was mine. I imagined I would live there with Cordelia once we were married, though to be honest, I never thought about the place as much as I did in Newgate."

She glanced at him. "Did you make plans in Newgate? For *after* revenge?"

"Not really. I vaguely—very vaguely—vowed to do something worthwhile, something good and selfless if only I could be free again." He gave a dismissive, self-deprecating wave. "You can't make deals with the Almighty."

The horses slowed and turned into a road that was more of a track. James leaned forward and pointed out the window. "Look, there's the house. You can just see it through the trees."

The first glimpse of golden stone and shimmering water beyond caught at her breath. The second, clearer view from the drive left her speechless. A pretty, stately manor house overlooked a fountain and well-kept gardens, woods to the back and fields to either side, and the sea in the distance. For some reason, the whole place just seemed *warm*.

"Oh, James, it's beautiful," she said at last. And she—or the house—received one of his rare, melting smiles.

When the carriage pulled up at the top of the drive, he alighted unhurriedly and turned to hand Elizabeth down before he glanced up the house and at the housekeeper waiting to welcome them. His manner was tranquil, unemotional, but it seemed Elizabeth had learned to read the signs, for she sensed the pleasure, the excitement rushing beneath his surface calm. It seemed to hum beneath his light touch, showing outwardly only in the slight stiffness of his posture, as though he held himself under rigid control.

Even the housekeeper, whom he introduced as Mrs. Fairley, and who had dashed down the front steps in welcome, seemed compelled by his manner into a more distant welcome than she had intended. On James's request, she swept Elizabeth up to a bedchamber to wash and be comfortable before luncheon.

"I'm sorry, we don't have a full staff here just now," Mrs. Fairley said, "so I can't offer you the services of a maid. However, I am happy to help with anything personal you might need."

"Thank you, but I'll only be a minute or two."

It was as she re-emerged from the room that the housekeeper blurted, "How is he?" as though the words would no longer be contained.

"Well," Elizabeth replied, and then, since she could see the genuine concern in the older woman's eyes, added, "Adjusting."

"Of course."

There was something of the old retainer in her clear affection, and yet James had told her he rarely came here. The house had always been more in his plans than in his life.

"Have you been in this position for long?" Elizabeth asked.

"About five years." Three of which James had spent in Newgate. She must have seen the question in Elizabeth's expression, for she smiled. "I came when my husband died. He was the vicar of Gartside in Staffordshire. I was provided for, of course, but I had nothing to do, and the new vicar's wife resented my involvement in the life of the parish. Lord James offered me the position here, and I jumped at the chance. I hope he will live here at least part of the time, for..." She broke off as James came into view, wandering from one of the rooms to the foot of the stairs. "Luncheon will be served directly, my lord."

"I wish I'd known you before," Elizabeth blurted as he led her into a bright, pleasant dining room with views over the lawn. A fire burned in the grate, providing a welcome warmth and homeliness to a house too little lived in.

He didn't ask before what. Before his world had betrayed him. Before prison had changed him.

"I am not destroyed, Miss Barker," he said mildly. "I was always like this."

"Like what?"

He poured a glass of sherry and handed it to her. "Introverted. Self-contained. If anything, that gave me strength in prison."

She took the glass carefully, and yet their fingers still brushed in passing, like the wings of some fleeing butterfly. "No youthful wild oats for you, then?" she asked lightly.

"I didn't say that." Something changed in his eyes that sent her stomach diving.

He must have been irresistible to women, all curiosity and passion beneath a formidable self-control. She felt it now. Even knowing what she did of men, she felt the dangerous tug of physical attraction and wondered what intimacy would be like with him.

Shocked at herself, she turned away to hide the heat flooding up from her toes, and was relieved to see Mrs. Fairley carrying in a soup tureen while a little maid scurried at her side with a loaf of new bread that smelled delicious. The round table had been set with two places, gleaming silver, and fine china.

James held Elizabeth's chair for her then sat beside her, a more comfortable kind of intimacy. For a week now, she had not eaten alone, and more often than not, this man had been among her companions. And he kept his word. The proprieties were observed, with the maid hovering by the door whenever Mrs. Fairley was out of the room. The conversation frequently included the housekeeper, who answered his questions about local matters and brought one or two tenant disputes to his attention. He listened and promised to speak to the steward.

"Excellent luncheon, Mrs. Fairley," he said when they had finished. "Especially produced at such short notice. Thank you. Would you care for a walk, Miss Barker? It's a pleasant stroll toward the village."

Elizabeth agreed to this with alacrity. Though, of course, strolling was not enough.

"I want to run," she confessed, after a few minutes of decorous perambulation on James's arm.

"So do I," he admitted. "I used to dream of it in Newgate—literally dream. Exercising in a cell is not the same."

"A lady never runs," Elizabeth said.

"Foolish rules." He glanced behind them, and then all around. The harvest was in, so the fields were quiet. "I don't think anyone will see. Shall we?"

His eyes danced beguilingly. There was no way she could resist now. Catching her breath, she released his arm and untied the ribbons of her hat—Lady Azalea's hat. She whisked it off with one hand. He took the other, and as one, they began to run.

"To the trees!" he shouted. It was the first time she had ever heard him raise his voice.

The run was brief, joyful, exhilarating. Even beneath all those skirts, her legs stretched and pounded over the uneven ground while the sharp wind whipped through her hair and over her skin. His hand steadied her when she stumbled, though his pace never let up, and neither did hers, until she realized his longer legs needed more, and she wanted to weep for his long confinement, unbearable to a young and active man.

"Go," she gasped, releasing his fingers. "Go."

But he held on, shaking his head before casting her one indecipherable glance. "With you," he said into the wind, pulling her on. A whole tangle of emotions surged, pushing her onward until she didn't know whether she would laugh or cry.

She did laugh when they made it to the trees, because he did, and for a few moments they held on to the broad trunk of a tree, panting.

"That," Elizabeth gasped, "was happiness!"

"Is," he corrected her, swinging up their still joined hands. He turned his head against the bark of the tree, smiling at her, and her bones seemed to dissolve. He moved, reaching up to her cheek. His handsome face, haloed by the autumn sunshine, swam before hers—and then his mouth covered hers.

A sound like a sob escaped her because she had wanted this so much, and when he would have drawn back, she grasped the back of his neck and clung to him. His body enveloped hers, pushing her against the tree, and she felt no threat, only wild arousal and pleasure. Deliciously aware of every inch of him, she opened her mouth wider, welcoming him in, glorying in his soft, responsive groan. He caressed her throat, and slowly, tenderly, over her shoulders and breasts to her waist and hips, where they lingered, holding her steady while his body began to move in time with his mouth.

"We could show each other such new worlds," he whispered against her lips. "New wonders, new joys... You bring me *life*, Elizabeth Barker."

His words struck some chord deep within her that tightened her arms around him. Her body felt on the verge of disintegration, every nerve alight with delight and desperation. She knew he felt it too, for his breathlessness was different now, and the intense, clouded heat of his eyes betrayed a smoldering desire that excited rather than frightened her.

He kissed her again, trailing one finger from her lips down her throat to the covered hollow between her breasts. "I meant to be good today, gentlemanly and honorable, and now all I can think about is taking you to bed. Or at least to some soft, hidden place in the woods..." Leaving her lips, he rested his forehead against hers. "Don't worry. I won't."

She swallowed. "I'm not worried."

A breath of laughter that was part groan escaped him. "Don't tempt me."

For a moment, all she could hear was the drumming of her heart, while his beat strongly beneath her fingertips. Then she realized the fallen leaves were rustling gently in the breeze and the birds were singing sweet, gentle songs above.

He said, "I am a reticent man, a flawed man. But I refuse to be a fearful one. Could you ever love me, Elizabeth?"

She closed her eyes, letting warmth and gladness and loss overwhelm her passion. "I am a fallen woman and a seamstress. Even before that, I was a mere banker's daughter, unworthy of a marquis's son."

"You are avoiding the question," he observed, stepping back, and in spite of herself, she panicked and seized his hand.

"No. I am trying to make you face reality."

His fingers caressed hers. A smile tugged at the corner of his devastating mouth. "Then there is hope for me?"

*I love you. God help me, I loved you from the first.* "For us," she got out, slipping free of him and picking up her fallen hat. "Now, where is this village of yours?"

⇥⇤

IF JAMES HADN'T already had leanings toward egalitarianism, Newgate would have taught him. No one cared about your birth or whether your spilled blood was blue. Only the strongest and the richest survived. Elizabeth had left her safe, respectable home for a man her parents considered beneath her—rightly, as it happened, but if they hadn't been so quick to judge, perhaps she would have discovered for herself before it was too late. But that she should hold up his superior birth as a barrier to their being together now seemed preposterous.

Of course, that might not be the only reason. He was experienced enough to recognize a willing woman, and Elizabeth was far from indifferent to him. But attraction and physical desire were not necessarily love or commitment. She needed time. After all, they had barely known each other a week, however much of that time had been spent together. This feeling between them had grown from an instant spark to a consuming fire, at least for James. He hadn't consciously given her his heart, but it seemed she held it anyway, this quiet, strong woman who had not only survived but thrived, quite alone in a world that was scarier than any female of her class would normally ever discover.

He showed her the village, made conversation with the locals, and nodded to curious passersby. In between times, they talked of impersonal things that nevertheless revealed her opinions and her compassion and her processes of thought. James drank everything in, but they were almost back at the house before he realized another barrier to their being together, perhaps they only one that mattered.

He had never mentioned commitment or marriage, only love. Given how she regarded herself, this was a catastrophic mistake, and one he instinctively knew he couldn't mend convincingly now by making promises. How many girls had been ruined by false promises of marriage?

Instead, as they approached the front of the house, her arm properly on his, he said casually, "I'm a fallen man too, you know."

She blinked. "I beg your pardon?"

"I fell when I was sixteen," he explained. "I enjoyed it so much I fell many times after that." He met her stunned gaze. "Youthful wild oats," he quoted. "Now I lean more toward mutual fidelity, along with all that wonder and joy. You know, you could divide this house in two quite easily."

"Why would you want to do that?" she asked, bewildered.

"So that our school full of noisy little brats doesn't overrun the civilized drawing room, of course. Look, I'll show you. There's a side entrance here…"

Although slightly bemused, she followed him around the house and in through the side hallway to the back of the building and the other staircase.

"Are these the servants' stairs?" she asked, surprised.

"No." He pointed to the green baize door. "The servants' stairs are through there. This is just another family staircase for convenience. But we could block this part of the house off with a partition and a door. The rooms here could easily be classrooms."

He leapt up the stairs, two at a time, and was relieved that she followed him and even peered into the large salon at the top.

"For play sports on rainy days," he said gravely.

"Nonsense," she protested. "It is clearly the music room where they will learn to dance like little ladies and gentlemen. Oh, very well, and play sports on rainy days, too. It is an excellent room."

"With a teachers' sitting room opposite, and even a dining room."

"Not with a carpet! Think of the ground-in mess after the food fights."

"My dear Miss Barker, there will be no food fights in our school."

"Then we shall have to ensure the food is too good yet not too abundant to lose value."

"Excellent plan."

Their ideas became gradually more ridiculous and so amusing that there was barely time to show her the rest of the house— "Where we shall live in peaceful and civilized opulence," he declared—before it was time to go.

"So, what do you think of my house?" he asked as the horses pulled them down the drive.

"I think it's beautiful but needs to be lived in," she said. "And I think you could be very happy there."

He sat back, prepared to settle for that. For now.

# CHAPTER SIXTEEN

O N THE EVENING of Lady Trench's soiree, her ladyship sent
the carriage to collect them early, so that they were all
comfortably ensconced where they wished to be before the other
guests arrived. Elizabeth was glad of the time to settle her nerves.

When she had emerged from Lady Grizelda's spare bedroom
and come downstairs to join the others, Grizelda had beamed
approval at her. "Why, you look lovely, Elizabeth! Doesn't she,
James?"

"Yes," James had replied. "But then, you always do."

It was mere politeness, of course. But there had been those
kisses she really must not think about tonight, of all nights, when
it was her greatest wish to see him restored to the family and
Society from which he had been deliberately isolating himself.

In the couple of days since their trip into Kent, she had forced
herself to avoid him, to concentrate on altering the evening gown
and morning gowns given to her by Grizelda and Lady Trench.
To avoid the memories intruding—sweet, arousing memories for
which she would always be grateful—she had tried to think of her
future.

She thought she would gladly accept Lady Grizelda's help in
finding alternative, more congenial employment, as a governess
or a school teacher. The trouble was, she could no longer think
about teaching without remembering James's country house, and
their half-joking visions of the school they would create there.

Why had he brought the subject up? Why had he kissed her? Why had he confessed to his youthful indiscretions? Just to show her that he was no purer than she? Men were not expected to be pure, of course, particularly not men of his class, but it was hardly gentlemanly to talk about it. On the other hand, she could not shake the belief that he was being deliberately, calculatingly honest. So that she might believe everything else he said.

*"Could you ever love me, Elizabeth?"*

Lady Trench, who seemed to be very tolerant of her sister's investigative oddities, was discovered in the main salon enjoying a quiet glass of wine with her husband—another fair man. Both came at once to welcome their early guests. Lord Trench greeted Grizelda casually with a kiss on the cheek and shook hands with Tizsa before the introductions were made. He shook hands with Elizabeth, too, and said to James, "Very glad to see you here, whatever Griz has inveigled you into."

"Dragan just needs to draw some people whom James will point out to him," Grizelda said as though this was perfectly natural behavior. "Miss Barker and I shall observe."

"You won't start a fight, will you, Griz?" Lady Trench asked with vague unease. "Because Eric's sisters will never forgive me."

"Of course not," Grizelda said, shocked. "We shall be positive souls of discretion. Show me where you and Eric will greet the guests…"

By arrangement, all four of them began the evening close to the door. James lounged elegantly in conversation with Elizabeth, so that the arriving guests would see him at once. Grizelda lurked to the side of the door, seated by Tizsa, who had his inevitable notebook and pencil at the ready.

"Here they come," James murmured as the sounds of arrivals reached them from the staircase and hallway. Elizabeth felt a stab of panic, shot through with disappointment because her time enjoying James's exclusive attention was over. He touched her hand. "You are a charming, beautiful lady," he murmured. "With as much right as everyone else to be here."

There was no time for more, although she soaked up the compliment like a needy sponge. The first people to arrive were total strangers to both Elizabeth and James. Grizelda shook her head surreptitiously and waved to the couple behind, who appeared to be family. As they swept past Lord and Lady Trench into the room, Elizabeth got a clear view of the two people next in line.

Her parents.

Words deserted her. But she must have made some sound of distress, for James glanced down at her and said something, just as her smiling mother curtseyed to Lord Trench—and looked past him straight to Elizabeth.

Her mother's jaw dropped. She stopped so suddenly that her father had to swerve very neatly to avoid collision. Then, of course, he followed his wife's frozen gaze to their daughter.

They hadn't changed a great deal, except that they had clearly come up in the world to be invited to Lady Trench's event, charitable though it was. They still looked healthy and prosperous, and the sapphires around her mother's neck and in her ears were familiar. They even looked almost as horrified as when she had last seen them, when she had told them she was going to marry Joshua.

They had been right to forbid her. The knowledge kept her as paralyzed as them, until James murmured in her ear, "Elizabeth?"

It broke the spell enough for her to take a stumbling step forward, and then they moved, too, sailing forward with grim determination like warships into battle.

"Mama," she said, her voice uncharacteristically husky. "Papa."

James stepped back again, no doubt to give them privacy, and Elizabeth almost panicked.

"What are you doing here?" her mother whispered furiously. Her gaze swept the room. "Don't tell me *he* is here, too?"

"Joshua is dead," Elizabeth said flatly, "so no."

"Then why on earth—*how* on earth—are you in this house?"

her father demanded, his voice low and furious. "Do you think to embarrass us, blackmail us?"

She had been foolish all over again. Just for an instant, when she had first seen them, she had longed for them like a child, imagined that things might be different.

"No," she said, glad to hear that steadiness had returned to her voice. "Lady Trench invited me as a friend of Lady Grizelda."

Her parents looked stunned. And then, with relief, she felt James at her side once more, the back of his hand brushing against her fingers, lending her strength.

"I think you are not acquainted with my parents, sir?" she managed. "Allow me to present Mr. and Mrs. Barker. This is Lord James Andover."

James did not offer his hand to her now completely flummoxed parents. His demeanor was that of the cold, sardonic man she had first seen emerging from the fog, and he merely inclined his head. "How do you do? My compliments on your charming daughter. Perhaps you will excuse us? I see another friend has arrived, Miss Barker."

He threaded her numb hand through his arm, urging her to walk away toward Grizelda and Tizsa, who stood now with a handsome couple and a darker man she recognized as Solomon Grey.

"I'm sorry," she whispered, "I didn't mean... It was so unexpected, and now we've missed several arrivals. We should return to our previous—"

"In a moment," he said. "I will still be seen. Let us greet Mr. Grey. Did Griz know he would be here?"

"She didn't mention him." Grizelda hadn't mentioned Elizabeth's parents either, though she had studied the guestlist carefully enough that she must have seen their names.

"Hmm... Do you think we're still on trial?"

Startled, Elizabeth met his gaze. "No, they would not be so kind if they thought..." A breath of laughter escaped her. "I think they like to be sure, but I doubt they really believe in your guilt or mine."

Mr. Grey bowed to them. "Miss Barker. My lord. A pleasure to see you again." He seemed perfectly at ease in this aristocratic company, more so than Elizabeth, who was now introduced to Sir Nicholas and Lady Swan, a handsome couple who were clearly friends of Grizelda and Tizsa, although to the sensitive Elizabeth, Sir Nicholas bore an edge of danger that made her wary.

She was glad to see him shake hands in friendly fashion with James. But then another distraction occurred at the door, in the shape of Sir Arthur and Lady Hampton. James turned toward them and was seen immediately.

Lady Hampton's step faltered. The sight of James clearly affected her. Which may have been the root of her husband's angry flush and the hardening of his thin lips. Nevertheless, they exchanged minute bows as Hampton tugged his wife forward and off in the opposite direction.

"You are a remarkably speedy and accurate artist," Mr. Grey said to Tizsa, who smiled faintly without looking up.

"My husband does not care much for the social events I drag him to," Grizelda said brightly. "So he occupies himself thus. My family is inured."

"Is there one of me?" Grey asked.

Tizsa paused in his portrayal of Hampton and flipped back a page to allow everyone a glimpse of Grey's slightly haughty face, cleverly shaded to show his darker complexion.

Grey raised his eyes to Tizsa's face, intent now on Hampton's picture once more. "Do you show them to other people?"

"Sometimes," Tizsa replied.

The Swans wandered away. More guests arrived.

"Do you mind?" Tizsa asked Mr. Grey.

"No. Though for some reason, they remind me of the 'Wanted' bills on lampposts."

"Very astute," Tizsa said. "They have been used as such."

"You are, perhaps, Lord James's ally in his search for truth about the diamonds?"

"As I said, astute," Tizsa murmured.

"Did you get your diamonds back?" James asked.

"I did," Mr. Grey replied. "I hope you have similar luck with your reputation, my lord." With a graceful bow to the ladies, he moved away.

"Do you still suspect him?" Elizabeth asked uneasily.

Tizsa looked beyond her to the door. "Not really. I can't see where he would fit in to either the theft of his own diamonds or the murder of Jarman. But he has an interesting face."

"James, it's your father," Grizelda murmured, which was more warning than she had given Elizabeth about hers.

But James had already seen. His father was a stout man of dignity with receding iron-gray hair and a magnificent scowl. Beside him walked his eldest son, Lord Langley, who lifted a hand in greeting to James. James nodded curtly in return, just as his father caught sight of him and halted, as though waiting for his son to go to him, though his expression never changed.

James bowed to his father, who waited one more instant in vain, before Langley murmured something to him and they turned aside to greet someone else.

"He's waiting for you to forgive him," Elizabeth said.

"My father has never sought forgiveness in his life. Nor has my sister."

Elizabeth recognized the couple greeting their host and hostess—James's sister, Lady Helen, and her husband, Earnest Front. Helen pretended not to see him. Front gave an unsurprised yet slightly embarrassed little half-smile and an inclination of his fair head before being towed off to the other side of the room.

Tizsa sketched some more.

As AN AWKWARD debutante, James recalled, Lady Grizelda had

never shone. Like him, she had never wanted to be there, on show at what had once been known as the Marriage Mart. She had never said the right things or made unexceptionable conversations. In fact, she knew astonishing amounts about unlikely subjects, from classical texts to the plight of the poor. After that first season, he had seen her less and less, except by accident in unlikely locations like the British Museum. or obscure afternoon musical concerts, and once, from a distance, in a soup kitchen.

Lady Grizelda, he suspected, had somehow managed to step back from the social whirl and create a pleasant life for herself, probably without the rest of her busy family even being aware of it. Which must have been how she met the revolutionary refugee almost-doctor, though how she'd made him acceptable to her family or the rest of Society was another matter. Perhaps even her ambitious family had seen how curiously right they were for each other. And, of course, the heroic Hungarians were fashionable, from their exiled leader Mr. Kossuth down.

As Grizelda took up her violin beside the piano, at which was seated Lady Swan, another memory intruded. One of those excruciating evenings when young, marriageable ladies were meant to show off their accomplishments. Most people had cringed, or even laughed behind their hands, as Grizelda had sat down at the piano, and certainly she had galloped through her piece at breakneck speed. But even so, she had displayed skill and even feeling, and no one had laughed as she had stood and marched back to the duchess, her mother.

Now, he heard that skill honed and comfortable. She and Lady Swan had clearly played together often before, and this, an adaptation of Chopin's violin concerto, was breathtaking. Beside him, Elizabeth surreptitiously wiped the corner of her eye with her finger. He loved that the music could move her.

Tizsa, meanwhile, stood apart from the audience, leaning one shoulder against the wall while he scribbled away at his book. It wasn't clear whether he was sketching his wife or catching more details of some of their suspects.

Two rows in front of James was the back of Hampton's head, and the swanlike neck of Cordelia that had once moved him to passion. They hadn't known each other at all, he realized now. He had loved her as one loves a beautiful painting, not as a real, flesh-and-blood woman, and he suspected she had seen him in a similar light. A marquis's son, after all, even the younger son, had been a catch. And she had undoubtedly liked the way he looked.

She turned her head and lifted her hand, as if she were rubbing some vague irritation on her shoulder, though she used the moment to glance fleetingly at James before she faced forward once more.

Something about his return troubled her. The nostalgia of lost love? Shame at not waiting for him? Or did she know that her husband had been involved somehow in James's arrest? In the theft of the diamonds? She was certainly on his list of people to talk to this evening. As were his sister and her husband, although it seemed Helen would only speak to him under duress. Perhaps he should leave her to Lady Grizelda.

Why *was* Helen so standoffish? Just because the scandal of his arrest had scared off the earl who had been courting her, reducing her to the nouveau riche Mr. Front? Judging by the silks and jewels she was awash in, she had found a very comfortable life. And yet she sat on the end of his row beside people he didn't know, her lips thinner than he recalled, and even in repose pinched with discontent.

Releasing the hurt of her determined rejection, he realized that she had never used to look like that. They had been allies in mischief. Once.

The piece came to a delightful conclusion, though not the ending Mr. Chopin had written. It was, after all, merely an excerpt from the concerto. The applause was rapturous, as it should have been.

Beside him, Elizabeth had jumped to her feet, her face shining as she clapped enthusiastically. "I never dreamed she was so talented! *And* Lady Swan…"

"Azalea knew," James said wryly, for Lady Trench looked positively smug as she thanked the duo and introduced the operatic tenor who was to follow. Lady Swan returned to her smiling husband, and Grizelda went to peer at Tizsa's sketches while his arm crept around her waist, a casual, affectionate marital intimacy that made his longing for Elizabeth suddenly fierce.

But it seemed he was no longer the young man he had been, constantly looking forward, desperate for tomorrow. Now he knew to appreciate the present, and so he let her closeness seep into him, inhaled the clean, fresh scent of her, enjoying the occasional glimpse of her lovely profile and the changes in her breathing as the music affected her. There was a delicious, tortured pleasure in being this near and unable to touch her.

"Perhaps you would join me for supper?" he murmured as the final performance was applauded. "I thought we might attach ourselves to my brother."

"By all means," she said. She lowered her voice. "Although he might find my presence odd."

"He is too much the gentleman to notice." He was, too. James took a moment to wonder why his brother was not married, for he was, surely, the most eligible bachelor in the country. And yet James had never seen him pursue any woman except that waitress at Coal Yard Lane.

Supper was laid out buffet-style in the next room, with trestle tables set up along the wall and spilling into the room beyond. At first, Elizabeth seemed uneasy, almost embarrassed that he should serve her from the opulent dishes.

"Did you not have some kind of Season in your youth?" he asked.

A smile flitted across her face. "It seems like another world. In any case, the company was never quite so…distinguished."

"You mean aristocratic. It is not at all the same thing, less so all the time. My brother should not be tied to land or politics just because our father is a duke, any more than the footman there should be tied to a life of service because of *his* birth."

"You are a radical," she observed, with a quick smile of amusement that he imagined also held a hint of pleasure, or even admiration.

He shrugged. "I am a realist. I see the progress of the world and where the impetus is. Which is too serious a subject when what one really needs to decide is between these elegant vol-au-vents or the more substantial pie..."

By then, she was either comforted or had remembered her early training, for she betrayed no unease as they wandered through the throng in search of a place to eat. They found his brother in the end, supping opposite Solomon Grey. There was space at the table, so James pretended not to see the young lady and her mother making a beeline for the same seat and laid his hand on the back of the chair next to Grey's. "Don't tell me. You're on the same charitable board."

John looked up quickly and stood.

"Several, actually," Grey replied, also rising.

"Miss Barker," John said, bowing. "Won't you join us?"

James deposited their plates, then held the chair for Elizabeth before taking the one next to his brother. For a little while, as they ate, they discussed the musical performances and the charity it was all in aid of. Then Elizabeth asked Mr. Grey something about his workers' conditions, and in the ensuing lively discussion, James and his brother fell into silence.

At last James said, "You came to my trial?"

John glowered at him. "Of course I came to your damned trial."

"I didn't see you there."

"I came in quietly after everyone else, with my hat down and my collar up. A concession to Father's order that none of us go near the Old Bailey on the day." His gaze flickered and he mumbled, "I wanted you to have someone there."

"I was always receiving callers," James said sardonically.

"That's not what I heard. I sent you a note, and Father said you wanted nothing to do with…" John laid down his fork and sat back, staring at his brother. "I thought you were ashamed, but none of it made sense, which was why I tried to see you."

"And you never guessed that Father might try to stop you? Even though you believed the worst of me?"

"Damn it, James, I knew how desperate you were to impress Cordelia. And I knew how reckless you could be. I assumed it was some wager, some prank that had gone horribly wrong."

"Anything but the truth," James mocked.

"You wouldn't return the diamonds or say who your accomplice was. I know why now—because you had nothing to do with it. At the time, I was bewildered and angry—"

"Me too," James said mildly.

John's eyes closed. "I can't change it. I can apologize."

"Can my father?"

"Yes, if you give him the chance. He only came this evening because I told him you would be here."

"And how did you know that?"

John's lip quirked. "Lady Azalea told me." He drew in an unsteady breath. "If I could, I would give you back those three years. I'm sorry, James, for what you went through."

James was silent. He realized he was gazing at Elizabeth's fingers trailing around the stem of her wine glass. He raised his eyes to her face and then shifted to his brother's. "It's funny, but I'm increasingly less sorry. Oh, I hated it, loathed it, but the longer I'm away from it, the more I think it might actually have been good for me."

John's eyes widened. "And for Cordelia?"

"Hmm. I'd say yes, except… Is she happy with Hampton?"

John shrugged. "I think so. Though I imagine seeing you again upset her. After all, she didn't wait for you, even if she professed to believe in you."

"Did she?" How much such knowledge would once have meant to him. Now it was a minor mystery.

"Will you speak to the old man?" John asked.

James sighed. "Yes, I will speak to the old man."

If nothing else, their few words, and his father's brief grip of his shoulder, gave the gossips something to chew upon. And brought James, unexpectedly, a modicum of peace.

By the time he moved on, both John and Elizbeth had left his side, and were dancing—John with Lady Azalea and Elizabeth with his brother-in-law Earnest Front. Tizsa was dancing with Lady Swan, Grizelda with Solomon Grey. Cordelia Hampton sat beside a grumpy-looking old dowager who seemed vaguely familiar to James. He decided to rescue his one-time betrothed, but as he moved toward her, among all the other expensive perfumes, both male and female, one made him halt and discreetly sniff the air.

He had smelled it in Coal Yard Lane the other afternoon. For some reason, it meant something to him, but he couldn't remember what.

He wrestled with it as he crossed the room. Cordelia saw him coming. A moment of panic lit her face. She excused herself to the dowager in such a rush it was barely courteous. But then, when he fully expected her to hurry in the opposite direction, she came toward him instead.

"My lord," she said, with that same look of panic.

He bowed. "My lady. We seem to have missed the start of the waltz, but perhaps you would take a stroll with me? We might hunt down some wine."

He offered his arm with a sense of challenge, daring her to take it. But she didn't even think about it. Her gloved hand clung to his sleeve, and they began to stroll around the perimeter of the dance floor, past the trio providing the music.

"How are you, James?" she whispered.

"I am well." This close, there were lines of worry around her mouth, dark shadows beneath her eyes that spoke of too little sleep. "Are you?"

"I hate to think of you in that place."

"I am not in that place. Unless you mean *this* place, which is hardly complimentary to our hostess."

"Don't joke," she begged. "You must hate me. You must hate all of us."

He sighed. "Hate gave me something to do in prison," he said. "But none of it was aimed personally at you." Well, not much of it. "Most of it was for those who put me there. What is upsetting you?"

She veered away from the entrance to the card room, where-in lurked her husband, and tugged James toward the open doorway leading to the hall. A few people milled there, but it was much quieter than the main salons.

"Arthur was always jealous of you," she blurted. Color seeped into her face and the swanlike neck that had once entranced him, even into the part of her chest visible above the deep V of her gown. "Because you were my first choice. It has made our marriage...difficult."

"Then I wish you hadn't chosen such a weasel."

"He isn't a weasel," she said, though without the conviction, let alone the anger, he had expected to provoke. "Indeed, I made my bed, as they say, and I am content to lie in it, but our lives—my life—would become unbearable were he ever to find that I... That you and I..."

For a moment, stupidly, he couldn't even think what she meant. And then he didn't know whether to laugh or flounce away in high dudgeon that she really thought so little of him. But the genuine fear in her eyes overrode both impulses.

He lowered his head to say quietly, "My dear, there is no need for him ever to know. It is our secret and no one else's."

She seemed to sag on his arm. "Thank you," she whispered.

"There is no need of thanks. I should never have taken ad-vantage. I wouldn't if I'd known I would be arrested only days later."

A hint of laughter trembled on her lips. "You didn't exactly take advantage, James."

"I only wish you well, Cordelia," he said gently, and was surprised to discover how true it was.

Returning to the main room as the music came to a close, Cordelia was almost immediately swept away to dance by an eager young man. James strolled on, inclining his head to anyone who caught his eye. Elizabeth had been right. No one cut him. They all bowed in return, as though they had merely been waiting for him to make the first move.

A rueful smile tugged at his lips. He might not have discovered a great deal in his quest to find out who killed Jarman and set him up to take the blame for the theft, but he seemed to be putting things right on a more personal level.

Hampton crossed in front of him and went into the card room. James followed, interested to see whom he talked to, if he could sustain looking James in the eye. For the first time, it struck him what he would be doing to Cordelia by exposing Hampton as a thief and murderer—if that was truly what he was.

Lord Trench was in the room, not playing but rattling the bowl on the first table in mock demand for money, for the gamesters would pay a fee, and a percentage of their winnings to his charity. Earnest Front sat at that table, and beside him, rather to James's surprise, sat Elizabeth's father.

Hampton took the vacant chair beside Barker, and as James strolled around the table to stand opposite them, memory inevitably intruded. At the beginning of that evening in Coal Yard Lane, Front and Hampton had sat in similar positions, with James's brother between them. Then John had left to go in search of his waitress, and the shady character Niven couldn't remember had taken his place.

James had barely noticed him—his mind hadn't really been on the game—but the man had been acknowledged by both Front and Hampton. No one had objected to him joining the table. Had James known him, too? From where? What had made him "shady"?

Both Front and Hampton noticed his observation at the same

time. The former nodded to him. Hampton frowned. Barker looked up, and his eyes widened. James nodded to him, too.

If James had been drugged that night, the early part of the evening had surely been unaffected. Except that what happened later seemed to have given the whole evening a weird, dreamlike quality, interspersed with flashes of loudness and blurry images. The man's face still eluded him.

He walked on around the table, waiting for it to come to him. He exchanged a few words with Trench, meandered around the other tables, and then, having no reason to linger, headed for the door. At the last moment, he glanced back over his shoulder, just as Hampton threw down his cards with annoyance. He did it with a certain flamboyance that James recalled because it always seemed an overly dramatic gesture, and he had done it that night at Coal Yard Lane, just before James stood up and left the game.

James had excused himself to all with a quick sweep of his eyes around the table. And the face between Front's and Hampton's had been…

*Jarman's.*

# CHAPTER SEVENTEEN

F OR AN INSTANT, he forgot to breathe and had to grasp the
door to steady himself. Then he moved, knowing only that
he had to tell someone, particularly Elizabeth. His hungry gaze
found her in an instant, as she laughed at something Forsythe
Niven was saying to her. James strode up to them and, without
ceremony, took Elizabeth's hand, placing it firmly on his arm.

"Sorry, have to talk to Miss Barker," he said curtly.

A hint of annoyance crossed Niven's face, and then he just
laughed. "High-handed, Andover."

"At least he apologized," Elizabeth pointed out over her
shoulder.

"Don't defend me. I'm being unforgivably rude, but I have to
talk to you. I've just remembered who else was at the gaming
table that night, the 'shady character' Niven recalled. It was
Jarman."

By then, they were in the hall, where he had earlier spoken to
Cordelia. It was quieter now, but even so, he swept Elizabeth
away to the darker area beside the stairs leading upward, and
behind a pillar.

"Joshua?" she said breathlessly.

"I didn't know him then, had no reason to remember his face.
And yet I did feel a vague familiarity when I first saw Jarman,
when he was pointed out to me as he swaggered up some alley by
the docks. Not enough to concern me, but when I saw Hampton

throwing down his cards, the whole scene came back to me. The man sitting between Front and Hampton was definitely Joshua Jarman."

"Then you think he was there to meet someone? Or that *he* was the one who drugged you? And urged you to go to Mason's for the ring?"

"He might have. It might *all* have been Jarman. You said yourself he could appear gentlemanly on occasions."

"He could assume the accent and the manners," she agreed. "But he wasn't fair."

"He could have worn a wig."

"He could... Whatever he says, Bertie or Porter could easily have been his accomplice in the robbery, and Mrs. Mason would have no reason to recognize her gentleman as Joshua."

"No." Frowning, James rested his forearm on the pillar above her head. "But then, if it was all Jarman, who the devil killed him? And who left that glove when he tried to break into your house?"

"Do you care?" she asked.

He looked down at her, realizing at last how close they stood, and how predatory his stance might seem to any inconvenient observers. And yet there was no fear in her eyes. Awareness, yes, a swift shallowness to her breathing, but no alarm. Slowly he lowered his head, until he rested his forehead against hers.

"I do care. It would be convenient to simply blame Jarman for the whole and assume he was killed by some underworld enemy. But it wouldn't necessarily be the truth. After all, it was convenient once to blame me. I can't imagine Jarman would have gone to the trouble of picking me out without some pointers. No, we can't rule out an accomplice."

He smiled, because things were clearer, because there was fresh hope. And because he was close to her, too close not to be affected. A quick glance assured him no one was near, no one could see, and then he moved nearer still, crushing her gown until his body fitted to hers. She let out a little gasp of shock, and he kissed her parted lips.

The kiss was too brief, and so much less than he craved, but her response was sweet and heady. He had to stifle his groan as he forced his mouth to release hers. "Say you'll dance with me."

"I'll dance with you."

Smiling, he stepped back, fiercely glad to see the trembling of her hands as she smoothed out her elegant skirts. He offered his arm once more. "Come, we'll stroll a little further before the last waltz, just to calm my wayward body."

Her gaze dipped, and she blushed even more fierily as she grasped his arm.

*Marry me, Elizabeth Barker, please marry me.* But she could not and should not be rushed. And for her, he could be patient.

≫≫≪≪

ELIZABETH'S EVENING FELT like some mad horse ride of emotion, with soaring jumps and a few nasty falls. Seeing her parents and facing their continued rejection. The beauty of the music. Watching James reach the beginning of understanding with his brother and father—and then watching him leave the room with Cordelia Hampton. Jealousy was not an emotion Elizabeth was used to, and she hated it.

He had implied he no longer felt anything for Cordelia. But the concern in his face had proved he did still care. If Cordelia crooked her finger now, even though she was married to another, would he be able to resist? Would he even want to?

Then, of course, he had kissed *her*, and danced with her, and jealousy had vanished into a sea of silly happiness just from being in his arms.

"I never cared much for dancing before," he'd murmured as they waltzed around the floor. "Yet with you, I could dance all night."

"I think Lady Trench might throw us out."

Even as Lady Trench's carriage returned them to Half Moon

Street, she was aware of James on the opposite bench, lounging gracefully in the corner with his face in the shadows, and yet she knew he was watching her. She could almost feel his eyes caress her skin.

"So what did we learn?" Grizelda asked brightly.

"James remembered more about his time at the gambling den," Elizabeth said, glad to have something else to focus on. "Joshua was there, playing in the same game."

"Was he, by God?" Tizsa sat up straight. "Then we should track down the staff who were there that night. They're bound to have known who Jarman was and noticed whom he talked to."

"My brother Langley might be able to help there," James said, sounding oddly reluctant. "I'll go and see him tomorrow. There's something else. I'm pretty sure Cordelia Hampton is afraid of her husband."

Elizabeth's stomach twisted, as though cords of jealousy, pity, and anger knotted together. "Then she should leave him."

"I don't think she wants to leave him. But if we prove he is the man who stole the diamonds and killed Jarman, the matter will be taken out of her hands."

Elizabeth said, "There is also Earnest Front. I danced with him, and he spent much of the time asking me about James."

"Did he?" James asked.

"He's married to your sister," Grizelda pointed out. "It's natural he should be concerned. Did he ask you if James was pursuing the reasons for his arrest?"

"No," Elizabeth replied. "He isn't someone I took to. He...flirts too enthusiastically. But that is hardly proof of theft or murder."

"He has no need of theft," James said. "His family could buy and sell us all."

"I'll make inquiries tomorrow," Tizsa said. "When, sadly, I am forced to go to the office. We should know who owns the gambling club at Coal Yard Lane by then, too. Nightcap, Andover?"

James hesitated, then he said, "No. But I'd like Elizabeth to come with me to Gartside House tomorrow."

"Excellent idea," Grizelda said, and yawned while Elizabeth blushed with pleasure and alarm. "I shall have to be busy on other things tomorrow."

>>>«««

IT WAS EARLY when James called for her the following morning. Even so, the Tizsas had already left the house about their own business, while Elizabeth tried to finish the mending she had undertaken for Lady Trench. In fact, there didn't appear to be much wrong with the linen she had been given to repair.

The Tizsas' maid, with all her mistress's cheerful ignoring of convention, simply showed James into the drawing room, where Elizabeth sat by the window, trying to find something to sew.

She jumped up. "Oh! I wasn't expecting you so early."

"Do you mind? I want all this finished with and behind us."

"No, it makes sense, only... Why do you want me with you to visit your brother?"

"Because you might see things I don't." A smile flickered across his face. "And because I want my family to know you."

A helpless flush of pleasure and pain consumed her. "James..."

"Shall we go?"

As they walked to South Audley Street, she realized the pain was receding into something very like hope, even wonder. James was not foolish or naïve. He understood the world in which he lived. Yet he wanted her to love him. A gentleman did not take a mistress, or even a prospective mistress, to visit one's family. Did he—could he?—want to *marry* her? In the teeth of his family's disapproval? Was this love possible in spite of everything?

*Don't hope,* she told herself fiercely. *Don't dare. Not yet...*

Instead, they talked about "the case" and where their discoveries might lead until, by the time they reached Gartside House, she felt able to concentrate.

This time, the butler, looking delighted, led them upstairs to a breakfast parlor, where Lord Langley and Helen Front sat at the table, leafing through newspapers. It was a quiet, domestic scene, though it brought James to a sudden, surprised halt.

Langley stood at once. "James! Miss Barker. Have you broken your fast?"

"Yes, but a cup of coffee would be welcome," James replied.

"Thank you," Elizabeth murmured, taking the seat Langley courteously held for her while she watched a fascinating array of emotions flash across Lady Helen Front's face.

At first there seemed to be a smile of surprised pleasure in her eyes, swiftly followed by a stare of something very like hunger, and then the fear of a hunted animal before her eyelids swept down and a frozen calm returned. Ignoring James, she nodded distantly to Elizabeth.

There were no servants in the room, presumably by the family's choice, so Lord Langley poured coffee for his guests and returned to his place, before folding up his newspaper.

"You've missed Father, I'm afraid. He's off to foment chaos in the Lords."

"Any sign of life would be an improvement in the Lords," James observed wryly. "But it was you I came to see. I want to ask you about the gaming club in Coal Yard Lane."

Helen was stirring her freshly poured tea as though trying to wear a hole in the cup.

"What about it?" Langley asked warily.

"I was wondering," James said, "if you might know what became of the staff who worked there on the night of my betrothal party."

Langley blushed. He knew exactly which staff member he was being asked about—his inamorata of three years ago. "I believe one opened a hat shop," he said evenly.

Abruptly, Helen stood up, as though she recognized they

were discussing matters unfit for a lady's ears. "I must go, Langley. My love to Papa. Miss Barker, James..." The last name was little more than a whisper, mumbled as she was already turning away and making for the door.

She was a well-dressed woman of ladylike posture and grace, and yet there was something stiff in her movements. Perhaps it was outrage at her brothers. But Elizabeth, abruptly remembering her dance with Earnest Front, who had set up all her hackles, suddenly didn't think so. Alarms rang through her head, depriving her of breath, and yet she could not just sit there.

With a murmured "excuse me," she rose and followed James's sister from the room.

"Mrs. Front," she called, and the woman halted at the top of the stairs. Hurrying toward her, Elizabeth ascertained there were no lurking servants in earshot. Helen waited for her, her expression wary and a little haughty.

"Miss Barker."

"Don't tell him," Elizabeth blurted.

Helen opened her mouth to deliver what would surely be a blistering retort. Yet what came out was, "I cannot tell anyone what I do not hear."

"Leave him," Elizabeth pleaded.

Helen stared at her. "You know the signs, don't you? I could see it in your face last night when you danced with him. I don't know how you escaped your fate, but there is no hope for me. My father would send me back to him as law and custom dictates."

"Your brothers would not."

"And if they kill him?" Helen said. Clearly, she had thought about this. "Langley might be acquitted in the Lords, but James..." She drew in a shuddering breath. "He has suffered enough."

"So have you." Elizabeth met the other woman's stare. "Mrs. Front, do you know where your husband was on the night of Monday the sixth of October?"

→»»»«««←

"You set Rosie up in a hat shop?" James said in amusement when the ladies had gone.

"She needed to get away from that hell. It was being frequented by criminals who were pressuring the girls to prostitution from which they wanted their cut. Most of the girls there were willing enough for the right man, but this was something else entirely."

"These criminals," James said, "wouldn't have been Joshua Jarman's gang, would they?"

"His name was mentioned. I just wanted her out of there."

"Do you still see her?" James asked.

His brother shrugged. "Now and again. I like to be sure all is well with her."

"No more?"

"Not that it's any of your business, but no more. She needs to be respectable, and I need to marry one day, if only to stop you succeeding me."

"I'm all for that. Will you take us to see Rosie?"

"Does Miss Barker need a new hat?"

"God, yes," James said fervently enough to make John grin.

"Who is she, Jamie? What are you up to?"

"She's Barker the banker's daughter. I mean to marry her if she'll have me."

"Why would she?" John asked. "She seems intelligent as well as pretty."

"Thinking of cutting me out, your lordship?"

"Think I couldn't?" John retorted.

"I don't know," James said ruefully. "Which is why I'd rather you didn't try."

After a moment, John finished his coffee. "I used to think you needed taking down a peg or two. And now I find I'm sorry for it. If you want the truth, she can't take her eyes off you. No one could cut you out with her."

James felt color rise into his face, and quickly drained his cup before rising. "Can we go and see Rosie now?"

When they emerged onto the landing, Elizabeth and Helen stood at the top of the stairs, gripping each other's hands. The sight was so surprising that James came to a halt. He didn't think either woman had seen him. Then Helen turned and fled down the stairs. For an instant it struck him that she might have been happy, which was when he realized that each time he'd laid eyes on her since Newgate, she had been extremely *unhappy.*

"Rejoice, Miss Barker," John said. "You are to have a new hat."

⤜⟫⟫⟩⟨⟨⟨⤛

THE MILLINER'S SHOP had customers when they walked in—a matron with her two daughters, all of whom appeared to recognize John, judging by the deep curtseys and blushes.

The smart and respectable young woman helping them smiled with much more ease. "My lords, ma'am, welcome. I'll be with you shortly."

It took James a moment to recognize the laughing, flirty waitress in this prim being, but she was there.

"No rush," John said amiably. "Miss Barker is merely browsing."

Obligingly, Elizabeth lifted an elegant hat from its stand to admire it. James enjoyed making her blush by untying the ribbons of her own borrowed hat, letting his knuckles brush for an instant against the soft skin of her throat. Then he turned her to face the mirror on the counter as she placed the shop hat on her head.

"No, something more open, I think," John said.

"Langley is good with hats," James assured her. "He chose all my sister's for her first Season."

Elizabeth was tolerantly trying on her third hat when the

proprietress finally showed her other customers out and bustled over to join them.

"My lords." She smiled. "A special pleasure to see you again, Lord James."

"And you, Miss Rose. What a fine establishment."

"His lordship helped me find my niche," she said, "as I'm sure you know."

"Miss Barker, allow us to introduce Miss Rose Smith," John said. "Miss Barker needs a new hat."

"Several new hats," James murmured, provokingly, and won a scowl of irritation from his beloved.

"And James, unfortunately," John continued, as though his brother hadn't spoken, "needs to ask you a few questions about the old days in Coal Yard Lane."

The light faded from Rosie's eyes.

"There's no trouble," James assured her quickly. "I'm just convinced that the accusations made against me are connected to the night of my betrothal party. Only I can't remember most of what happened."

"You were drunk as a lord, my lord," she said wryly.

"A doctor friend of mine thinks I was more than drunk. He thinks I was drugged."

A hint of outrage sparked in Rosie's eyes.

"No, I'm not accusing you," James said at once. "Not for an instant. I'm just trying to find out who I sat beside, who served me after I stood up from the card table."

"I didn't see you leave the card table," she said coldly. "When I came back into the room, you were three sheets to the wind, along with two other gentlemen."

"Niven and Graham, I know. I was hoping you could remember which other waitresses were on duty that night."

"It's important, Rosie," John said quietly.

"Lila," she said reluctantly, "and Jenny, I think. They don't work there anymore. Lila left before I did and vanished. Jenny left when it changed hands. I think she went home to Berkshire, but she doesn't write."

"Do you know who bought the club over?" Elizabeth asked.

Rose shook her head. "No. The police shut it down before that. I keep well away from there."

"Did Joshua Jarman ever appear in the club?" Elizabeth asked, and Rosie swung on her, glaring.

"He's why I left. He was making the owner pay a protection fee to him and was trying to get us to whore for him. Some of the girls had no choice, but I did, thanks to his lordship. And if you—" She broke off, frowning. "He was there that night, the one you're talking about."

"Did he speak to Lord James?" Elizabeth asked.

"Not in my hearing. But he spoke to Lila all right."

"What about?" James asked urgently.

"Whoring, I imagine," Rosie snapped. "He certainly scared her, and she had to get out."

"Did you know, by name, any other patrons there that night?" James asked, taking some of Tizsa's sketches from the inner pocket of his coat.

Rosie shook her head. "No, they were mostly new faces to me. I think Jarman's presence scared off the regulars. But then, we might have dropped them a word. With Jarman, there was bound to be cheating and stealing."

"Do you recognize any of these men?" James asked, spreading Tizsa's portraits across the counter.

Rosie glanced at them impatiently. "I'm sure I've seen him before." She pointed at Sir Arthur Hampton. "And him." She tapped Earnest Front. "They were in your party that night, weren't they? Don't know him," she added, touching Solomon Grey, "although I wouldn't mind. *That* fellow came in with Jarman once."

James wasn't surprised. It was Jack Porter, Jarman's lieutenant. "Did you see me speaking privately to any of them?"

Rosie shook her head.

"Did I ever ask you about jewels or jewelers?" James asked,

almost apologetically.

Rosie laughed. "What would I know about such things? Of course you didn't. You didn't even ask me about hats." She reached beneath the counter and placed a rather fetching creation before Elizabeth. It was cream with a graceful feather and dark red silk roses. "Try that one, ma'am."

Blinking, Elizabeth obeyed, and James smiled because she looked so bemused and hopeful and pretty that he wanted her to wear it for their wedding.

"We'll take it," he said.

"We shall not," Elizabeth exclaimed. "I can't afford such a thing!"

"It's a gift," James said. "With an ulterior motive. Where did your friend Lila go?" He was guessing, but Rosie's eyes had dropped each time she mentioned her. Like the less hardened convicts who hadn't learned to lie convincingly when they stole from you.

"I told you, she vanished," Rosie said. "Could be anywhere. She doesn't want to be found."

"Rosie?" John said quietly. "Please?"

"I promised!"

"You know Jarman's dead?" James said. "He can't hurt her or anyone else. Besides, I won't tell a soul. I just need to talk to her. And if we're right, she's among those who will be made all the safer for what she can tell me."

Rosie glared at him, then glanced from Elizabeth to John. She marched across to the other counter, taking the hat with her. "You had better be right," she said grimly, seizing a pencil and scribbling on a piece of paper. "And you can't take *her* there," she added as they followed her.

Elizabeth raised her eyes from the paper to James. "I know that address. It's Constance Silver's house."

# CHAPTER EIGHTEEN

L ORD LANGLEY SEEMED more stunned than appalled that not
only did Elizabeth know Constance Silver, she had been in
her house before.

"Thank God we took the carriage with no crest," he muttered. "Have you no veil to hide your face, Miss Barker?"

"Not this time, but if you have a book I could pretend is a
Bible, or a prayer book, I could try to look like a reformer of
fallen women."

James laughed, a rare, unexpected sound that closed around
Elizabeth's heart and made her smile. "We'll be inside so quickly,
no one will see any of us," he told his brother. "The staff are most
discreet."

Constance greeted them in the same room they had met
before, looking perfectly untroubled to have a marquis's heir
calling upon her. Most of her attention, in fact, was on Elizabeth,
who said bluntly, "We need your help locating someone. A girl
called Lila who fled from a gambling den in Coal Yard Lane."

"My ladies never use their own names," Constance said
pleasantly.

"*Please*, Constance. We're sure she knows something that
could solve several different crimes and clear Lord James's name
completely."

Constance stared at her a moment longer, then said, "And
what of *her* name?"

"It need never be mentioned beyond these walls," James said. "Is she here?"

Constance turned her attention on him. She was, Elizabeth suspected, a formidable judge of character. "Do I have your word as a gentleman on your silence? Do I have your promise not to bring the law down upon our heads?"

"Both," James said.

"And yours, Lord Langley?"

"Of course," Langley said haughtily.

Constance sighed. "I hope I shan't regret this." She rose, went to the door, and spoke quietly to the footman waiting in the hall before returning to them. "She won't be long." She sank back into her chair, all smooth, sensual grace, and met Elizabeth's gaze. "Is this still to do with Jarman?"

Elizabeth nodded. And then quick footsteps sounded in the passage before a young woman burst impetuously into the room. She wore a respectable dark blue gown and clutched a ledger in ink-stained fingers. She looked nothing like Elizabeth's hazy idea of a gaming hell waitress, let alone a woman of ill repute.

"Mrs. Silver?" she said cheerfully. "I was just about to take the books back to..." She trailed off as she realized there were other people present and, with a faint, quizzical smile, glanced at each in turn. Until she came to James.

Her eyes widened with something approaching horror. The book fell from her hands to the floor, and she bolted.

Elizabeth froze with shock. Memory rolled over her in waves. Old fear, old hurts she would never accept again for herself or anyone else. Newer dread when she had first seen James looming out of the mist, the hardness of his eyes and the strength of his rage beneath the pale, haughty exterior.

Why was this girl so afraid of him?

"Lila!" Constance exclaimed before the girl even reached the door. Both the men were on their feet, but not, Elizabeth was relieved to see, in pursuit. "Where are you going? You know *no harm will come to you here.*"

As if those words meant something important, Lila paused, her fingers grasping the door handle. She turned slowly to face the room.

James said, "I mean you no ill, Miss Lila."

There was a kind of desperate strain in his voice that caused Elizabeth to turn her gaze toward him. He held himself stiff and straight like a man awaiting a blow. *He* was afraid.

"I wouldn't blame you if you did," the girl said hoarsely.

Constance took her gently by the hand and drew her down beside her on the sofa. Lord Langley sat back down. James did not, though nor did he loom intimidatingly. He kept his place several feet away.

"Did I ever hurt you?" James asked evenly, though his normal pallor looked even whiter than usual. "In any way?"

"No, sir," Lila whispered.

"I ask because there are things I don't remember, and I need to know the truth. Why are you afraid of me?"

The girl's eyes filled suddenly with tears. "Because of what I did to you."

Elizabeth felt herself sag with relief—and shame. She thought she knew the girl's crime, and was sure James had guessed, too. And yet, instead of asking for details, he said in a carefully neutral voice, "Did I behave ill to you first?"

Elizabeth began to understand the full awfulness of his memory gaps. He didn't know what had been done to him, or what he had done to others, and the latter must have been hardest of all to deal with.

"God love you, sir, of course not." Tears coursed down Lila's cheeks, and she clutched Constance's hand as though for strength. "You were always the perfect gentleman to me, to all of us, and generous, too, which is what makes it all the worse."

James all but fell back into his chair, leaving Elizabeth awash with guilt and an aching urge to put her arms around him. But all she could do was give him time to recover his self-possession.

"Are you talking about the night of Lord James's betrothal

party?" she asked. "When he and Lord Langley and their friends came to Coal Yard Lane?"

"Miss Barker," Constance murmured. "An old friend of mine."

Lila nodded.

"What did you do?" Elizabeth asked.

Lila took a deep breath. "I put something in the brandy I gave him."

"Why?"

"Someone asked me to." Her gaze flickered desperately to James and then to Constance. "He paid me. Said it was just a laugh, to help his lordship enjoy one of his last nights of f-freedom."

"Did you believe him?"

Lila nodded once, eagerly, and then fresh tears flowed down her cheeks. "No. No, how could I? I *knew* Jarman had put him up to it. That's why I was scared into doing it."

"No one blames you for being scared of Jarman," Constance said.

"Whom did Jarman tell to drug Lord James's brandy?" Elizabeth asked.

The whole room seemed to have gone still. The waiting was unbearable.

"I don't know his name," Lila said, wiping the back of her hand across her face. Constance gave her a handkerchief. "I'd never seen him there before, but he came in with their lordships, so I told myself he couldn't mean Lord James any harm, not if he was his friend." She swung around to face James. "I didn't know whether to be relieved you weren't dead when they carried you out, or afraid that you would be by the time you got home."

She wiped her eyes with the handkerchief. "I knew I'd done wrong. More, I knew Jarman knew, and through that could get me to do anything he liked. Whoring, thieving, murdering. Rosie told me about Mrs. Silver. I didn't think she'd look at me, but she took me in, and now I'm learning how to keep the books for respectable businesses. And you went to prison, sir. I tried to tell myself that made what I'd done fine because you were a murderer and a thief, but in my heart I couldn't shake off the feeling that what I'd done to you was the cause of it all. Rosie didn't believe you could have done it, and his lordship told her you hadn't."

"Did he?" James spoke too quickly, glancing at his brother, who flushed slightly but held his gaze. James turned back to Lila, raking his fingers through his hair. "You didn't cause my going to prison. They'd have found some other way to manipulate me into doing what they wanted." He delved into his coat pocket for Dr. Tizsa's drawings and stood. Taking the first, he placed it on the low table in front of Lila and Constance. "Was that the man who paid you to drug my brandy?"

Everyone looked at Sir Arthur Hampton's smooth, haughty face. Tizsa had even caught the faint smile that didn't reach his eyes.

Lila shook her head. "I've seen him before, but it wasn't him."

James frowned, clearly disappointed.

Elizabeth rose and slipped the next portrait from his pile. She laid it on the table beside the first.

Lila's eyes widened. She leaned forward and snatched it up. "That's him. Yes, that's him."

Elizabeth looked up at James.

"Earnest Front," he said slowly. "My brother-in-law."

➤➤➤❮❮❮

"Did you know?" James asked as his brother's carriage began its short journey to Half Moon Street.

Elizabeth shook her head. "No. But at Gartside House I suspected your sister ignored you not because she wanted to but because she was too frightened not to. She had been instructed.

Front wasn't there, so she didn't ignore you completely this time, but she still ran before she disobeyed him. I have developed a...sensitivity to violent bullies, and I'm sure Front is one."

"But why would he set out to disgrace a member of the family he married into?" Lord Langley demanded.

"Because I doubt he stood a chance of marrying into it until James was disgraced and the earl who was dangling after your sister got cold feet."

"Violent bully," James repeated, staring at her. "Do you think he *hurts* Helen?"

"I'm sure he does," Elizabeth said.

The brothers looked at each other. "Brook Street," Lord Langley said grimly. "Front's house."

"No, wait," Elizabeth said urgently. "The best way to protect her is to prove his guilt of theft and murder. Beating him to a pulp will not help. Nor will killing him," she added as she caught the murderous flash in James's eyes. "I told her you would help her, even if your father would not, but without proof of his other crimes, the law will only send her back to her husband. Make up some pretense that her father needs her at Gartside House for the next few days, or find a way to keep Front in London while she goes to stay with friends or family in the country. Meanwhile, we will find the proof we need."

"We found Lila," Lord Langley said. "She is our proof."

"It's not enough," James said, throwing himself against the back of the bench. "Lila can swear Front bribed her to drug my brandy. She can even swear Jarman told him to do it, but that's not a hanging offense. We have to prove he was Jarman's partner in the diamond robbery and the killing of Grey's men, *and* that he murdered Jarman. The trouble is, he's a wily ba...brute and has left no evidence whatsoever."

"There is the glove," Elizabeth said thoughtfully. "A word with his valet and even the glove maker should identify it as his."

"He could just say he lost it and someone else must have been wearing it," James said. "Besides, it would only prove he broke into your house. Which will help, especially with the valet's cooperation on timing. But we need more. A *torrent* of proof. Or..." His eyes glazed over for a moment, then refocused on Elizabeth. In spite of herself, she shivered. "Or a confession."

"A CONFESSION," LADY Grizelda said thoughtfully when they had told her everything that had happened that morning. "We should think how to obtain such a statement from him, because he doesn't strike me as the sort of man who would be intimidated by the police or by our accusations. A confession would seal his appointment with the hangman, whereas he must know we have nothing that would convict him. Yet."

Her face lit up at the sound of the front door opening. "But let's here what Dragan has learned..."

Dr. Tizsa's voice was heard in the hall, along with the maid's, and then he ran upstairs. Grizelda met him at the drawing door, to be embraced and kissed without embarrassment.

"It's Earnest Front," she said, dragging him to the sofa to hear what Elizabeth and James had already told her.

"There's another connection," Tizsa said at last. "Front is part of the company that now owns the club at Coal Yard Lane. Jarman bought it for a song three years ago—probably by threats—not long after Andover was convicted. It was raided and shut down, though somehow Jarman wriggled out of charges and kept ownership of the building. Then he sold it to this company made of himself, Front, and a few minor business owners and some slightly seedy characters.

"It maintains a semi-respectable façade, no doubt with a little added bribery to the local officers of the law, but the dice are loaded, the cards frequently marked, and the roulette wheel fixed. Anyone who complains is threatened. Any gentlemanly clientele of your day, Andover, has melted away. Apart from the more reckless, jaded youths with too much money and not enough to do. And anyone drunk enough in the streets and taverns who might be enticed there by the club's employees—including girls."

Grizelda poured glasses of wine and passed them out, while Tizsa sat at one of the desks and stretched out his long legs.

"There is something else," he went on, "which you might like to talk to your father about, Andover. Around five years ago, rumors began to circulate that old Front's financial empire was not as sound as it had been. His children were expensive, and while the sons, particularly Earnest, were given greater control over the business, they appeared to lack old Front's Midas touch. I suspect it wasn't just your sister's nobility the Fronts wanted, but her dowry."

James frowned. "According to my brother, the Fronts negotiated hard in terms of settlements. My father was inclined to admire the effrontery and gave in. So you're saying Earnest was actually pockets-to-let?"

"Heading there. Which certainly gives him a motive to look for a quick injection of cash. Hence his association with Jarman, culminating, probably, in the diamond theft."

James's lips twisted with a hint of savagery. "He must have been mad as fire when Elizabeth absconded with the diamonds."

"Presumably, other joint ventures went better for them. In any case, he married your sister. Perhaps he began to suspect Jarman had the diamonds back. Certainly he must have known by the time Connor was arrested for possession of one."

"Which was why he followed Jarman to your house," Grizelda said to Elizabeth. "He must have killed him thinking he'd find the diamonds easily enough, and before he could, you came home, forcing him to duck out the back door again."

"It makes sense," Elizabeth agreed. "But we still have no real proof."

"I think it's time I spoke to his valet," Tizsa said.

"And I should talk to my sister," James said bleakly. "At the very least, she needs to be safe. At best, she might know where he was or wasn't when Jarman was being murdered. I should go," he added abruptly, rising to his feet and setting his half-empty glass on the table beside Tizsa. "I'll come back tomorrow."

His gaze lingered on Elizabeth, who managed to nod.

Grizelda said, "Yes, do. We must think how to get Front to confess. Good night, James."

James turned slightly at the door, as though he thought Elizabeth might follow him. She didn't, and he went on his way, leaving her heart sore and heavy.

≫≪

IT WAS ALMOST fully dark by the time he got back to his rooms, where he found a scribbled note from his brother. *I brought Helen back to Gartside House. Come for dinner if you can.*

He paused only to wash and change, and then set off again for South Audley Street. His head was spinning with what he had learned today, with anger and pity over Helen's situation and his own lack of awareness. Even knowing what had happened to Elizabeth, it had never entered his head that his sister could possibly face anything similar. Even when he had realized Cordelia was a little afraid of Hampton, he hadn't thought it a fear of physical abuse.

It may have been all the talk of such violence that made Elizabeth so distant since they had left Constance Silver's establishment. Whatever the cause, it concerned him, adding to his anxieties. These days, he was conscious of a slight ache whenever he wasn't with her—which, he supposed, was quite pathetic for a man who had always been so self-sufficient, a trait he had honed to extremes in prison.

Self-sufficiency, it seemed, was another word for loneliness.

Clifford's eyes lit up at the sight of him. "They're all in the drawing room, my lord," he said, taking his coat and hat. "Shall I announce you?"

"No, no, I remember the way." James cast the butler a quick, distracted smile and ran up the staircase, letting memories bombard him.

As he strode across the landing, familiar voices assailed him—John's, quietly humorous, Helen's softer, his father's half-forgotten bark of laughter mingling suddenly with a much higher-pitched and childish giggle.

James stopped, his eyes widening. The footman at the drawing room door grinned at his astonishment and threw open the door.

Helen sat on the floor, the frozen dignity of their previous meetings nowhere to be seen. He should have recognized the signs of her distress. Had he not been dealing similarly with life since his arrest three years ago? In hiding, with contempt for the whole world. He was not proud of such self-absorption, but at least he could appreciate the picture before him.

An infant of about twelve months staggered from his mother's arms to those of his grandfather, who was perched on the edge of the sofa to receive him. The child chortled with delight, and made next for his uncle, who swung him high into the air before he caught sight of James, hovering just inside the doorway.

All eyes turned on James, their fatuous smiles dying into expressions of mingled dread and hope—apart from the child, who grinned at him and reached out his arms for his mother.

"Good Lord," James said mildly, although his insides seemed to have turned to mush. "I have a nephew. You never told me I had a nephew."

"You never asked," John pointed out, passing the child to Helen.

There was a lot he hadn't asked. For now, as the child hid his face in his mother's neck and smiled sideways at him, he settled for smiling back and asking, "What is your name, small nephew?"

"George," said the child, lifting his head.

James offered his hand. "I'm James."

Solemnly, George shook his hand and then grinned, melting the last of James's heart. George wriggled to get down, and as

Helen put him there, James said, "You are staying here, Helen?"

"Apparently Papa needs a hostess for his important dinner tomorrow night," she murmured. "Or at least, John seems to have convinced him he does."

"Did Front mind?"

"No, I think he's glad to have peace for a few days."

"We should have known," he blurted. "We shouldn't have let you stay there. We should have known."

Helen's voice wasn't quite steady. "We let you go to prison. *We* should have known."

"You couldn't have stopped it," he said. "But we *will* stop this. One way or another."

Her face changed. "Without any of us going to prison," she said anxiously.

"Any of *us*," James said grimly.

# CHAPTER NINETEEN

THE FOLLOWING MORNING, James found himself once again in Newgate Prison.

His blood flowed icy cold in his veins, and yet his skin was damp with sweat. His stomach felt so tight he thought he might disgrace himself and cast up his accounts.

"You don't need to come in," Tizsa had said as the prison loomed ominously out of the fog. "Take the cab back to Half Moon Street. I'd rather someone kept their eye on Griz, to be honest."

Tizsa too had been a prisoner at some point, although not in this country, and there was understanding in his carelessly spoken kindness. Perhaps it was that which made it possible for James to move, to alight from the hackney and force his steps forward. Like forgiving his family and recognizing his own failings, this was something he had to face to be whole.

And at least this time, he was entering via the governor's house. The staff bowed low and showed every respect as he and Tizsa were shown into a bare, gloomy room, while a guard was sent rushing to fetch Jack Porter.

James kept his gaze on the open door and imagined himself pushing the walls back and back.

"Will you manage if they lock the door behind Porter?" Tizsa murmured.

"I will."

Porter all but swaggered into the room, his chains clanking. He looked suspiciously from one man to the other. "You ain't the Peelers, but I know you, don't I?"

"We met in Ellen Square," Tizsa said. "I was collecting for charity."

Porter peered at him and allowed himself to be thrust into the chair behind the damaged wooden table. "Didn't get any, though, did you?" he said with a grin. "Tight-fisted, is old Barb."

"My name's Tizsa. On behalf of this gentleman, I'm looking into the diamond theft three years ago, and the murder of your late associate, Mr. Jarman. If you don't recognize this—"

"Andover!" Porter exclaimed. "Lord James Andover. Never thought they'd stick a nob away for old Josh's sins."

"There were two men who committed that crime," Tizsa said. "You still deny you were with Jarman?"

"I was with him in his house by the fireside," Porter said virtuously. "What you raking all that up for, anyway? Everyone knows it was Pete Connor stole the diamonds. And though I'm just as innocent of *this* crime, I'm in here for the murder of Zeb Fisher."

"You were seen, Mr. Porter. By any number of witnesses."

"Yes, well, set up, weren't I?" He sniffed resentfully. "I was promised the streets would be clear, that only our people would be around."

"Who promised you that?" Tizsa asked.

"Barb, of course. Should never have believed her. Woman lies her ti—"

"Did you tell the police that?" James interrupted.

"What's the point? They wouldn't believe me, just think I was paying off old scores or trying to shift the blame. They've got me for the murder, so why would they rock the boat?"

"Because this conspiracy makes perfect sense for Barb and Bertie Sandman," James said. "Jarman's dead. You got rid of Zeb Fisher, making Fisher's gang weak enough to take over, and then the law gets rid of *you*, leaving Barb and Bertie with no competition in replacing Jarman at the head of his questionable little empire."

Porter looked from one to the other. "You want to take down Barb and Bertie?"

"It would be a pleasure, if there was proof," Tizsa said. "Did they send you out to kill Jarman, too?"

Porter looked genuinely outraged. "I'd never have hurt a hair on Josh's head! Looked after me like a father, he did! Tell you what, whatever I hang for, I hope they hang the bastard who did Josh in, too."

"I heard," James said, "that it was a gentleman who killed Jarman."

Porter's lip curled. "Wouldn't be surprised. Can't trust a nob. Meaning no offense."

"Oh, I think you meant quite a lot of offense," James said, amused, "though I can't say I care. Jarman worked quite a lot with this gentleman, did he not? Helped him steal the diamonds, by what I hear."

"Couldn't have," Porter said with no effort at conviction. He was just determined never to "squeal" on Jarman, even after the man's death.

"By what I heard," James continued, "he also killed Jarman for those same diamonds."

Porter stared. "Nah. Fisher killed Jarman. Everyone knows that."

"We have his glove," James said, taking the captured evidence from his pocket and waving it in front of Porter's face.

"And he might," Tizsa said, spreading his sketched portraits along the length of the table, "have looked like one of these gentlemen..."

"Mrs. Mason," Elizabeth said suddenly, dropping her sewing

into her lap.

Grizelda, who was replacing a string on a guitar, glanced up over her spectacles. "What about her?"

"She can identify Front as the man who tried to sell the diamond to her husband."

"That's what we're hoping for," Grizelda said.

"Yes, but Front probably killed Mason so that he couldn't be identified. Don't you think Mrs. Mason might be in danger, too?"

"If Front thought she could harm him," Grizelda said, "wouldn't he have at least tried to do away with her before now?"

"Possibly," Elizabeth allowed. "But if he starts suspecting what we know, won't he start doing away with *any* evidence that might lead to him?"

Grizelda looked thoughtful. "James is a greater threat to him. James could easily recall who sent him to Mason's that day."

Elizabeth's stomach jolted. "You think he'd try to kill *James*. Oh, dear God, I never thought of that. *Why* did I never think of that?"

"Don't panic," Grizelda said calmly. "Dragan is with him. And Front has no reason to fear James. Too many people saw what state he was in that night, and his evidence would always be suspect. On the other hand..." Her eyes began to sparkle behind her spectacles. "On the other hand, Front could be persuaded that James *is* a danger, with other witnesses to back him up. *That* is the way forward!"

"Not for James, it isn't," Elizabeth said indignantly. But Grizelda appeared to have moved on, for she was frowning again, setting her guitar aside.

"Perhaps you're right about Mrs. Mason, too. Maybe we should warn her, persuade her to stay with friends or family for a little."

Accordingly, they set off through the fog for Ludgate Hill and the rooms above Mason's jeweler's shop.

When the hackney let them down, there seemed to be a lot of people in the street, their voices muffled and subdued in the mist.

The shop had lamps lit inside, presumably to be seen through the murk. Elizabeth and Grizelda made their way between gossiping women to the blue door next to the shop. The voices died away and a shiver of premonition passed down Elizabeth's spine.

Griz reached for the knocker.

"No point in knocking, ma'am," one of the watching women said.

"Is Mrs. Mason not at home?" Grizelda asked civilly, knocking anyway. And to Elizabeth she added, "We could leave a message for her."

"She won't be getting it, ma'am, and you'd be wasting your time," said the same officious woman. "Mrs. Mason's passed away."

This time, Elizabeth's whole body shivered. Her gaze clashed with Lady Grizelda's. "When did this happen?" she managed.

"No idea. Haven't seen her since yesterday, but the police were here, and...and she's gone to a better place." The woman nodded solemnly, as did her murmuring acolytes, who looked now like so many crows in the mist.

"Do you suppose we could go in and poke around?" Grizelda murmured.

"Not unless there's a back way in. Let's see if we can..." Elizabeth turned away from the dispersing women, peering through the fog for signs of an alleyway that might lead to the backs of the buildings. A shop bell tinkled, and a man in a tall hat walked out.

The mist swirled around him and parted to reveal the unmistakable features of Earnest Front.

Only clamping her teeth together prevented her from crying out. But he had seen her, too, for he smiled, coming closer and tipping his hat.

*You killed her. You killed Mr. Grey's men for the diamonds, and Mr. Mason. You probably forced Mason's poor assistant to emigrate if he's even alive. And you basically sent James to prison for your crimes. Plus you killed Joshua.* The knowledge, the outrage, kept her rooted to the spot.

"Miss Barker?" Front said pleasantly, his voice grating across her nerves. "I almost didn't see you in this dreadful fog. How do you do, my lady?"

"Sir," Grizelda said graciously. She was clearly made of sterner stuff than Elizabeth. "Yes, the fog makes one sorry to be out and about, does it not?"

"May I escort you somewhere?" he inquired politely.

*No!*

"How kind," Grizelda said, "but we shan't keep you. I'm searching for the perfect gift for my sister. Good day, sir." Grizelda took Elizabeth's arm, which jolted her at last out of her paralysis.

She managed to stretch her lips and incline her head as they swept past Front and into the shop.

"We were too late," Elizabeth whispered in helpless rage and grief. "He killed Mrs. Mason..."

"Yes, I suspect he did," Grizelda hissed back. "He looks far too pleased with himself. Which is why we'll wait in here until he's well away from us. And then we shall go home and decide how to finish this before anyone else dies."

⟫⟩⟫✳⟨⟨⟨⟨

EARNEST WAS INCLINED to think the stars were aligning in his favor once more. He had had a few shocks, and a few anxieties remained, but on the whole, he felt safe.

At home, with the curtains drawn against the foggy darkness and the fire burning cheerfully in the grate, he settled down with a glass of brandy and breathed a sigh of peace. He enjoyed the distinction of possessing an aristocratic wife, and his son was a marquis's grandson, but God, they were annoying and noisy under his feet. Let the brat disrupt his lordship's self-important dinner while Earnest enjoyed a couple of days of quiet and the space to plan his next moves.

He wondered if he should give his staff a day's holiday. He

could then entice the Barker girl here... Or, more constructively, deal with James Andover. Or would staff absence look too suspicious in that case?

One way or another, though, he rather thought he would have to deal with his brother-in-law. Lord James was his one major worry.

The man had been at Coal Yard Lane, nosing about. It was possible he had remembered something, though even the recollection that Earnest had given him the name and address of Mason's was hardly a hanging offense.

But Earnest had been naïve in those days. He had let Jarman persuade *him* to bribe the girl, which left him a little exposed if this ever came out. The girl herself had vanished years ago, which had suited Earnest and Jarman both. What worried him now was that James seemed to be much in the company of that Hungarian fellow who had, Earnest had learned, a growing reputation for solving puzzles and finding people who were better left lost.

Moreover, Tizsa was related by marriage to Lord Horace Niven, who was powerfully connected to issues of law and order. The last thing Earnest needed was either Tizsa or Niven poking about in his affairs.

The question he faced was how to spike James's guns without casting suspicion on himself. The murder of an aristocrat who had already been wrongfully sent to prison would create far too much attention. James needed to die, preferably quietly, of "natural causes." Or a tragic "accident."

Earnest mulled over some pleasingly gory scenarios. Perhaps he could even somehow involve Elizabeth Barker, who was much in Andover's company, and whom he found a rather tempting armful. Something about her manner, both gentle and unafraid, courteous and yet too direct to be submissive, appealed to him. She would indeed be a pleasure to subjugate...

He heard the knock on the front door without interest. He intended to plan tonight while he enjoyed his peace, not go out or entertain. His servants were well aware of the fact, so he was irritated when Soames appeared in the library.

"Are you at home, sir, to family?"

"I'm not at home to anyone," Earnest snapped. "I believe I made my position plain."

"Yes, sir, of course, sir." Soames bowed and backed out.

"Wait," Earnest commanded, frowning suddenly. "What family? It's not my brother, is it?"

"No, sir," Soames said, returning to the room with a white card on his silver salver. "My lady's brother, Lord James Andover."

*Well!* "In that case, you had better send him up."

Too late, it occurred to Earnest that he hadn't asked if Andover was alone. He certainly didn't want the Hungarian on visiting terms, and there was no point in trying to deal with Andover under the eyes of a sharp-eyed witness.

He rose and went to the decanter to refill his glass.

"Lord James, sir," Soames announced, and departed.

"Ah, my lord," Earnest said affably. "A pleasant surprise. Brandy?"

"No, no thank you." His lordship was frowning, his thin, aristocratic nostrils twitching. But at least he had come alone. "I need your help..." The frown deepened to a scowl. "Damn it, it's you I remember, isn't it? You sat beside me in that dreadful hell the night of my betrothal party three years ago. I even remember talking to you about jewelers. How much do I need to apologize to you?"

Taken by surprise when he was half expecting some kind of accusation, Earnest blinked and paused in the act of waving Andover to a chair. "Not at all," he said. "You were hardly the first drunken youth to bend my ear. Or the last. Besides, I can't imagine I didn't behave in a similar manner at the same age. What help do you need?"

Andover threw himself into the chair next to Earnest's. "I'm trying to piece together what happened that night. Not for any great reason, and certainly not because I think it will redound to my credit in any way. I just hate not knowing. Holes in one's memory are most disconcerting, and I want to *know* before I can properly get on with my life. Does that make any sense?"

"I'm sure it does," Earnest said sympathetically, "when one has been through what you have."

"I want to be married," Andover said. "And I need to know the worst before I can think of proposing."

"My dear fellow, what can be worse than Newgate?"

Andover cast him a distracted yet shrewd glance, as though acknowledging the barb, so Earnest added smoothly, "If the lady understands about that, then surely a night in your cups is...ah—small beer?"

"That's what I need to know," Andover said. "I've spoken to my brother. I even dragged Forsythe Niven to Coal Yard Lane with me." His eyes opened wider. "But then, you know that, don't you? *You* were there. Avoiding me."

"I was," Earnest admitted smoothly, while weighing the pros and cons of disclosure, "though not for the reasons you might be imagining. It's not generally known that I own a part share in that not-entirely-salubrious but pleasantly lucrative establishment. And I don't particularly want it known."

"You came from the staff area," Andover said, his brow clearing. "And went back the same way to get out of my way."

"I did," Earnest admitted.

"Will you come there with me now?"

Earnest's glass bumped against his teeth. He lowered it hastily. "Now?"

"I know it's an imposition on your time, but, well, you're my sister's husband, and we ought to know each other better."

Earnest couldn't deny it felt good to hear him say so. After all, this was the man who had once haughtily forbade him from "importuning" his sister with requests to dance at a ball.

Andover rubbed his forehead. "And being there at the club helps me to remember. I recalled odd snippets when I went with Niven, and there is a distinctive scent to your soap that made me recall our sitting together and talking about jewelers."

"Soap?" Earnest said, genuinely startled. "You smell my soap?"

A quick grin flashed across the pale, serious face. "Or whatever it is that smells so pleasant. I only notice it because it sparks memories I can't quite reach. Will you come?"

Assuredly, it was time to shut James Andover up for good. Earnest rather wished he'd done it three years ago rather than arrange such convoluted revenge. But then, nothing about the diamond project had gone right. He still didn't have his hands on the wretched stones and never would now. Time to humor his brother-in-law.

"By all means. Does your family know what you intend? Don't they mind?"

"I told my father and Langley I was going to drag you there if I could." Andover gave a deprecating twist of the lips. "I think they were glad to have me out of the way of this precious dinner. Thanks for this, Front. I appreciate it."

"I hope you still do so by the end of the evening," Earnest said affably, making for the door, "when your memories of embarrassing, youthful drunkenness come flooding back to appall you."

# CHAPTER TWENTY

FOG, THICK AND filthy and evil-smelling, still swirled around the darkness of Coal Yard Lane. It probably scared off all but the most desperate criminals, yet somehow didn't make Dragan feel any safer.

For the last fifteen minutes, he had been skulking outside the club premises, moving from the street through the narrow arch that led to the back alley, which he suspected was the best place to commit murder. Particularly on such a foggy night when very little could be seen from the rows of windows above.

Dragan almost started when the boy touched his arm.

"He got in the hackney, and your friend's with him."

Dragan pressed a coin into the boy's palm. "Good lad. Go home and keep warm."

The boy's eyes gleamed, even in the fog. "There was another cove there, too," he offered. "Watching the same house."

Dragan paused. "Who?"

The lad shrugged. "Never saw him before. Thief, like as not. He shabbed off when I did but went the other way."

"Did he?" Though the watcher made Dragan uneasy, there wasn't much he could do about it from here. With his collar up and his hat low on his head, he strolled toward the back entrance to the club. The door was no longer locked.

"Gentlemen," he murmured without glancing left or right. A foot shuffled in one direction. A brief mutter came from the other.

He encountered no one in the passage, and the kitchen staff glimpsed at the far end paid him no attention. He ambled on to the main gaming room, which was fuller than one might have expected so early in the evening. The fug of tobacco inside was as choking as the fog outside, and the smell of alcohol was profound. It was not well lit for a gaming establishment, which, Dragan supposed, made it harder to spot the cheating.

He slid into the place beside Inspector Harris, who, this evening, was garbed in a slightly smelly working man's coat and cap with heavy boots. Beside him was the normally immaculate Mr. Solomon Grey, dressed like one of his own dockers. He even slouched. Acting came a little too easily to Grey.

"They're on the way," Dragan murmured. "Took the hackney they were meant to, so our man can help Andover if there's any trouble en route."

"I can't imagine there will be," Harris said, "not until he finds out what exactly Andover knows. And as long as you're correct in all your assumptions in the first place."

Dragan wasn't fooled. Harris wouldn't have come, let alone deployed his men, had he not believed in those "assumptions."

"Someone else was watching Front's house," he said, reaching for his ale. "Ran off in the opposite direction. He wasn't one of yours, was he?"

"No. Contrary to your apparent belief, I don't have a limitless supply of men for my own cases, let alone for yours."

"Are we playing cards, or what?" Grey inquired, already dealing them with practiced ease.

Dragan glanced across the small, empty table next to theirs, to the two gentlemen playing a distracted game of piquet while a scantily clad girl batted her blackened eyelashes at them. Both seemed curiously immune. Catching the eye of his brother-in-law, Lord Forsythe Niven, he nodded, and Forsythe murmured something to Lord Langley.

Only moments later, Lord James Andover strolled into the room, with Earnest Front at his heels.

ELIZABETH STARED AT the unrecognizable figures of herself and Lady Grizelda in the mirror. "How do you even *have* garments like this?"

They both wore thin, gaudy gowns, low cut and revealing. Grizelda's, vibrantly purple with pink ribbons, had a curved slit up the side through which, if she chose, she could flash her ripped stocking. Elizabeth's was scarlet with torn black trimming, and, without petticoats let alone crinoline, it clung indecently close to her figure. Their hair was not so much dressed as shoved under a few pins and left to straggle.

"They've been useful in the past," Grizelda said. "Dragan and I tend to stick our noses in places where a duke's daughter might stand out."

"Dr. Tizsa was fairly explicit about your going nowhere near Coal Yard Lane," Elizabeth reminded her.

"Well, he can't turn tyrannical husband on me just because I'm having his child," Grizelda said flatly. "This is who we are as a couple, and he promised me that it would not change, provided I was careful. Besides, I believe James was equally... er—explicit."

"James has absolutely no right to control my movements," Elizabeth said stiffly. Then, ruining the effect, she sagged. "I can't let him be hurt, Griz. I can't."

"Well," Grizelda said, picking two shabby cloaks off the bed and passing one to Elizabeth, "judging by how he dealt with your would-be abductors, I would say it's quite hard to hurt him, physically speaking. And he does have Dragan looking out for him, along with his own brother and mine, to say nothing of half the metropolitan police force. But I don't see why we should be left at home worrying."

"This man killed *Jarman*," Elizabeth said forcefully, "without even making a mess!"

"That's true," Grizelda allowed, taking a small gold-plated

pistol from her dressing table drawer and placing it in her tatty reticule, "and why we are taking this with us. Also, Beth, we must not be separated under any circumstances."

"Don't worry about that. Dressed like this, I'll be sticking to you like a leech."

They fastened their cloaks and pulled up the hoods before they left the house. Elizabeth clutched the cloak carefully around her.

"If our mothers could see us now," Grizelda murmured in amusement as they hurried toward Half Moon Street and Piccadilly.

"Mine would only see what she's been assuming for three years," Elizabeth said with a hint of bitterness.

Grizelda looked at her. "You should let James speak to them. He'll have them on their knees begging for your forgiveness in five minutes."

"I can't."

"Times are changing, Beth. His own sister married a banker. And what happened to you is no one else's business."

Elizabeth shook her head violently. "It's not that. It's... I didn't *trust* him, Griz. When Lila looked frightened of him, I actually believed she must have cause, that she had to be scared of something *he* had done. I cannot be with a man of whom I have such doubts, not in *any* capacity."

Griz raised her eyebrows. "I'm told that's what engage—"

"Beth?"

They both swung in alarm toward the speaker. She had called from the open door of a carriage that had halted in the road, much to the annoyance of the vehicles behind it.

"Quick, get in," Constance Silver demanded, and on impulse, Elizabeth dragged Grizelda by the arm and into the coach, which immediately moved forward, even while the coachman exchanged insults with the drivers of the hackney and the dray behind.

"Um, this is Mrs. Silver," Elizabeth said uneasily to Grizelda.

After all, they might have been dressed as women of ill repute, but that didn't mean a duke's daughter wanted to be introduced to a notorious brothel keeper. "Constance, Lady Grizelda Tizsa."

Elizabeth needn't have worried. Grizelda thrust out her hand at once. "Mrs. Silver! I've heard so much about you."

Constance's finely arched eyebrows flew up. "I can't imagine that's true," she drawled, though she took the offered hand briefly before turning her frowning gaze on Elizabeth. "What are you about? You look like a pair of nuns."

Grizelda snorted. Elizabeth pushed back her hood and parted her cloak briefly.

Constance closed her eyes. "Covent Garden wear. Don't you feel you'd be better off in my establishment?"

"It's a disguise, Constance," Elizabeth said.

"I noticed," Constance retorted. She didn't look amused. "For God's sake, what are you thinking of?"

"That now we know who killed Joshua and stole the diamonds and cast the blame on James," Elizabeth replied. "James and Lady Grizelda's husband have gone to make him confess, and we can't be in such a place without standing out."

Constance looked bewildered. "What place?"

"Lila's old gaming hell."

Constance sighed. "My dears, they're hardly likely to admit the competition. They have their own whores, who're more likely to tear your hair out than share. You won't get in the front door."

"The back door?" Grizelda said hopefully.

"No," Constance said. "You've no idea the danger you'd be in."

"Griz has a pistol," Elizabeth said. "The thing is, I can't—*we* can't—wait quietly at home while they face who knows what dangers from a man who's killed several times already."

Constance lifted a speaking tube from a hook beside her and spoke into it. "Change of plan, Danny. Coal Yard, if you please." She replaced the tube and regarded them. "The best we can do is lurk in the fog outside."

"We?" Elizabeth repeated. "You're coming with us?"

"Someone clearly needs to look after you children."

>>><<<

JAMES TOOK IN the gaming room at a glance. He pretended not to see Tizsa, who, in any case, had his back to the door, and strode straight to the empty table a few feet from John and Forsythe.

Maintaining what was now mostly a fiction of distance between them, James merely nodded to his brother. "Langley. Niven."

"Evening, Andover," Niven said cheerfully. "Don't disturb me—cleaning out your brother's pockets!"

James pointedly sat with his back to them, which meant Front's back was to the disguised Inspector Harris and Solomon Grey. Tizsa hadn't troubled with disguise. He looked, as he often did, like a gentleman fallen on hard times. Or a refugee who had left everything behind when he fled from tyranny.

A waiter, who clearly recognized his employer, rushed over to take their order. Women no longer served at tables, James noted. Instead, they strolled around the room, blatantly flaunting their wares, or sitting in laps. One couple, hand in hand, left the room, heading for the stairs and the private chambers above.

"Brandy, my lord?" Front suggested. "Since I believe it's what we shared the last time."

James nodded curtly, though he added impatiently, "There's no need to *my lord* me. We're family, for one thing, and for another, there doesn't seem much place for formality in this mess." He took a deep breath, scowling around the room, aware of Front's gaze upon him, curious at first and then gradually more amused.

"Remembering anything?" Front inquired.

"Not yet."

"Have some brandy as an aide memoir." Front picked up the bottle that had been left at their table along with two glasses and a pack of cards.

"Did we play cards?" James asked.

Front shoved one glass of brandy toward him. "No, you'd had enough of games by the time you and I had our conversation."

"Did I just come up to you and sit down?"

After the briefest hesitation, Front said, "No, you were with the naval officer whose name I've forgotten. When I wandered over to you, he was being enticed away by some comely waitress. I took his place, since you seemed to want to talk."

"What did I talk about?"

"The perfection of your betrothed," Front said flippantly. He raised his glass. "To the eternal perfections of Lady Hampton."

And at that gesture, one of those elusive flashes of memory struck. James had sat here and raised his glass with Front to toast Cordelia. The smell of Front was the same, the words only slightly different. James took hold of his glass, feeling again the strange, euphoric unsteadiness of that evening, the blurring of the face beside him, the surging loudness of the surrounding voices.

For a moment, it overwhelmed him, and he tightened his fingers on the brandy glass, swirling the amber liquid that he had no intention of drinking.

"I went on about the ring I wanted to give her as the token of my love," James said slowly. "I was horribly maudlin, for which I apologize."

"There is no need. Your sentiments were perfectly genuine, although it was not like you to share them so openly. You wanted the ring to be as special as her, and paid for with your own money, not your father's. You couldn't afford the prices of your family's favored jeweler. So I told you of one I had honored with my own custom, where you could get fine work at rather less cost."

"Mason's... You gave me a scrap of paper and a pencil, and I wrote it down. You even tucked it in my pocket." And that was when, with his peculiarly heightened senses, James had noticed the smell of Front's soap.

"I did," Front said. "You were effusively grateful and then apologized for being so drunk. Which you were."

"Never been in such a state before or since," James said. He raised his glass to drink, though didn't let the liquid more than dampen his lower lip. His glass had been full then, too. Front had toasted his health and future happiness as a married man. And then, rather cheekily, James's sister Helen. James recalled the feeling he should object to that but being far too happy with the world to bother.

And then, laughing, Front had walked away. He had stopped and spoken to a waitress, then dropped something heavy in her apron pocket. Her face remained blurred in James's memory, but he thought it was Lila, the girl who had brought him that first, drugged brandy. And Front, he knew now, had paid her for her efforts.

At the time, no such thoughts had entered his happy, increasingly sleepy head. Graham had come back before he fell asleep. There had been a waitress who sat in his lap and laughed at him before kissing him and skipping off. And then Niven had joined them, shortly before John reappeared. James had been pleased to see his brother, although he hadn't wanted to go home. He'd known he'd needed to—he just wasn't sure he could stand up.

There was euphoria as well as fury in the return of those memories. They would always be blurred and stuttering, but he knew now what had happened.

He frowned at Front, as though still trying to remember. "What did I do then?"

"You told me in strictest confidence that you needed some air. Which you clearly did."

"I don't remember that bit. Did I go?" He hadn't. He knew he hadn't.

"Yes, and I went with you. Out into the back alley."

"What did I do there? More infernal talking?"

Front looked hesitant. "I'm not sure it will make you happier to know. Leave it there, Andover."

"I *want* to know."

Front shrugged. "It's all coming back to you now, one way or another. I'm not going to tell you, but I'll come with you again, if you really want me to."

"I really want you to," James said, standing up. To prove he was leading the way and doing exactly what he was sure Front wanted, he marched straight out of the room.

Every nerve in his body tingled. He felt the hairs on the back of his neck rise as they had done before attacks in prison. These next few minutes, he knew, were when Front meant to silence him. Not because his returning memories on their own could hang Earnest Front, but because they *could* cast doubt. And a man in banking did not need doubt about his honesty being spread around the city. All Front had risked with his criminal adventures would be lost if his family's respectable bank failed.

They were all gambling on Front's attack coming outside, so that the law would not necessarily intrude on the club. Although, of course, once past the kitchen door, and into the narrower passage, he could knife James in the back and haul his body outside…

Trying to breathe evenly, James all but wrenched at the back door. Unlike the last time he had tried, it was unlocked. Had Front done that? Or Tizsa? And if the latter, would Front notice?

James spilled into the foggy alley, instinctively shoving his back against the wall while Front stepped outside to join him, and pulled the back door closed. Another tricky task loomed. To get Front far enough from the door that he wouldn't notice when it opened again to let out Tizsa and Harris, and yet keep him close enough to the building that he could be heard from the doorway and be in no danger of bumping into policemen too early.

Front swung around to face him. James pushed himself off the wall and walked into the swirling mist before pacing swiftly back the way he had come. He sensed human presence there—Front's thugs? Or Harris's men? Both, possibly.

Other shops backed onto the alley, and most of the buildings were tall and thin. This one was broader, with a narrow tunnel running through to the front of Coal Yard Lane. Various faint glows from several windows showed through the fog, but he doubted anyone looking out from them would be able to see who murdered James.

James walked back and forth across the narrow alley, between the club building and the lower wall of the next, just to make sure there was no one behind to attack him. Then he halted about halfway between the buildings, facing the club, and waited.

"Anything?" Front, only just visible at the back door, took a step or two nearer him.

"No," James said. "I don't believe I was ever here at all."

"Ah, everything's coming back to you now?" Front said, not bothering to argue.

"You paid the girl to drug my brandy. I saw you give her a purse."

"I might have been paying her for anything."

"But you weren't, were you?" James said. "All you wanted was for me to be unsure who had given me Mason's address."

"Had to take the suspicion off Jarman and me," Front said, causing James's muscles to relax in relief. He had never been sure this incitement to confess would work. But the danger was hardly over. He could not afford to relax.

"Then you really did steal the diamonds?" James said, allowing a note of disbelief into his voice.

"Of course we did. It all went exactly as I planned, right down to your being arrested for the crime."

"Seems unnecessarily vindictive," James observed, watching Front's hands hanging loosely at his sides. Behind him, he thought something might have moved. Hopefully Tizsa and the police.

Front shrugged. "I needed your family mired in a little scandal so that I would suddenly become an acceptable suitor for your sister."

"You wanted her that much?" James asked. "And yet you treat her worse than I would a thieving cur."

Front's right hand had begun to move upward, but paused now. "She told you that? Well, women need a bit of discipline."

"Did Jarman teach you that?"

Front laughed. "Yes, actually, he did. It's about all he was useful for in the end, because, as I'm sure you've guessed, he managed to lose the diamonds. His whore ran off with them. That's when my doubts hit." His hand glided into his coat pocket.

"How did you know he'd found them again?"

"One Peter O'Connor, whose arrest heralded your rather annoying release."

"So you started following Jarman and thought you knew where they were hidden?" James allowed himself a jeering laugh. "You killed him for the diamonds and still couldn't find them!"

Front twitched, and his hand emerged from his coat with a large, serrated dagger. "The bitch came home, and I couldn't risk her screaming blue murder over Jarman's body. I decided to go after her later."

"When someone else could do the dirty work for you?" James sneered.

"Exactly."

"But now you're reduced to doing your own?" James said, nodding at the dagger, which Front still held poised in his right hand.

Front laughed. "Would I hurt you, *my lord?*"

"What will you tell my brother?" James asked.

"Nothing. I'm not going back in there at all." With breathtaking speed, Front leapt, and the dagger whipped down at James's throat.

# CHAPTER TWENTY-ONE

J AMES ONLY JUST managed to seize Front's wrist, which at least lessened the force of the blow and upset the deadly aim. Still, he felt the cold burn of it slicing against his skin.

Front's eyes were murderous, glaring with spite. "You and I will be seen weaving off together into the night, and someone else will glimpse you a few hours' hence, long after I am in much more reliable company. I have associates in many walks of life. Now, *die*, my lo—"

And then, everything happened very quickly. As Front wrenched his knife hand free of him, James kicked brutally at his ankles, bringing his brother-in-law down beneath him. Panicked voices and hasty footsteps broke through the mist. Still, Front's dagger hand flailed free and rose again. Even as James made a grab for it, a swirl of skirts flashed before his eyes. The dagger spun away into the fog with Front's astonished cry, and James, glancing upward, gazed into the terrified face of Elizabeth—who abruptly disappeared from view as Front rolled, James under him, and reached desperately for the dagger.

And then, finally, Front was plucked off him by a man on either side. Inspector Harris and John, the latter looking both appalled and furious.

Harris barked something at his men, and two tall-hatted policemen took charge of the prisoner, while John dropped down beside him. "Dear God, James, where are you hurt?"

That was when James realized there must be blood. He felt for his neck, which was wet and sticky and had begun to sting.

"Damn it," he murmured, sitting up and reaching for his handkerchief, which he shoved halfheartedly over the cut. "It isn't serious." He twisted around, searching for the vision of Elizabeth that should *not* have been there.

Only she was, the center of a fog-framed tableau, standing, trembling, between Constance Silver and a ragged version of Lady Grizelda.

"That will need cleaned and dressed," Tizsa said, presumably of his wound, as he and John helped James to his feet. "But it isn't life threatening."

James barely heard him. His eyes were locked with Elizabeth's. Somehow, she was here. She had kicked the dagger from Front's hand and saved him. And in this moment of overwhelming emotion, tears streaking her painted face—*painted?*—her expression was naked.

*She loves me. Dear God, she does love me...*

They both moved at the same time. He touched her soft cheek, as her fingertips brushed the skin of his neck. He began to smile, as though the sun had broken through the impenetrable mist and an answering light in her eyes began to dissolve her fear. And then someone shouted.

"Oi! Grab him! Get back here, you—"

"Oh, for the love of...!" Inspector Harris exclaimed. "After him, you bloody dolts!"

"He's gone under the arch, heading for the front," Tizsa said grimly.

And because no one was safe while Front was free, James let his hand fall from Elizabeth and ran after the policemen who'd managed to lose him. Others were charging through the back door to go through the house.

The narrow archway dipped beneath the building and took up part of the ground floor, giving easy access on to Coal Yard Lane. It was a gloomy, noisome tunnel, and the policemen ahead of him were already at the other end, emerging to peer either way up the lane.

James paused. The policemen had moved fast after their escaped prisoner. They would have at least seen which direction he took. And there was nowhere else for Front to have gone. People did not vanish into thin air.

Frowning, James peered at the dark, dank walls of the tunnel. There was surely no space for a man to hide, flattened against the wall, and yet where else could Front be? Wishing he had a light of some kind, James ran his hands over the rough walls, to the left and right, and finally found, to the right, not a body or even an opening, but the texture of wood.

It was a narrow door in the wall, with no handle. He pushed it open, stepping swiftly aside in case Front was waiting to lunge.

He wasn't.

James moved forward warily and bumped his lower shin. Light filtered down from far above, showing him, now that his eyes had adjusted, a spiral staircase made of iron. *It must lead to the roof.*

He hesitated, for he wanted to give Front no warning that he was coming after him—if indeed Front had gone this way. On the other hand, the fellow was slippery and cornered, and at this point had nothing left to lose. James compromised by leaving the wooden door open. That would at least guide his allies. Meanwhile, he ran up the stairs as silently as he could and emerged somewhat breathless onto the roof.

The fog, he thought, might be dispersing at last, for he could feel a welcome breeze stir his hair. However, it was still thick enough to make finding Front difficult—and stumbling off the edge of the roof dangerously easy.

He paused to get his bearings, and to listen for movement, for the faintest sounds of breathing. What might have been an echo of his own shallow panting caused his head to whip around. His skin prickled. Nerves? Or was Front there?

He scanned all the way around him until he could make out

the lower buildings across the back alley, and even the edge of this roof. And then, as the swirl of fog shifted, he made out the figure leaning against the chimney stack.

"You really do bear a grudge, don't you?" Front said amiably. "Are you really prepared to die just to see me locked up and your own family disgraced?"

"Yes," James said, although God knew he didn't want to die, not now that he had found Elizabeth, not now that he had seen that love in her eyes. *Concentrate, you fool!*

"I thought so," Front said conversationally, as James walked slowly toward him. "Which is why I took the precaution of leaving one of these up here, just in case I was cornered."

Front's hand rose from his side, revealing an old-fashioned pistol pointed steadily at James.

"What is the point?" James said. "You confessed to everything before witnesses, including several officers of the law and a peer of the realm. You were seen to try to murder me, and you cannot possibly escape. Enjoy your notoriety. And after all, you might not hang. I didn't."

"My papa isn't a marquis," Front said with a sudden snarl, and just as James charged him, there was a deafening report. James barely felt the jerk of his arm, so intent was he on the man who might not hang. He kept going, and for the first time, Front looked alarmed. It was instinct to step back, and he did, desperately raising the fired pistol like a club—except that he stumbled and wobbled backward, teetering on the edge of the roof. At the last instant, he reached for James, who sat abruptly on the roof, mostly to stop his momentum carrying him into Front, who fell, yelling, arms flailing, into the night.

James peered over the edge. The mist had thinned, and there were lanterns below now, by which he could see the scattered people. Guilt and alarm smote him at once, for he had assumed everyone had gone inside or at least to the front of the building. But there was Elizabeth staring up at him. And surely that was Constance, clutched in the arms of Grey, as though he'd hauled her out of the way of the falling body.

"Dear God," James whispered, appalled by what he could have done in his sudden spurt of arrogant fury.

*"You might not hang."* The sudden realization had been unbearable.

And now his arm began to hurt like the fires of hell. Behind him, a lantern flared, and he turned, blinking toward the light.

"Meant him to fall, did you?" said Bertie Sandman, sitting down opposite him. "Don't blame you. Suits me too, to be honest. In fact, I arranged to meet him up here to see to it. Better for everyone this way." He took a flask from his pocket and unscrewed the top while he peered at James's arm. "He got you, didn't he? Here, this'll help."

He passed the flask to James, who, beginning to feel lightheaded, took it from him with his sound arm and raised it gratefully to his lips. A whiff of something familiar assailed him, giving him pause. He stared at Bertie, whose eyes gleamed avidly in the light of his lantern, and abruptly everything fell into place.

That was how Front—a pretty inept fighter, after all—had managed to kill the vicious Jarman without even making a mess. Because Jarman had been drugged, just as James had been three years before. And Bertie had been there as Front's ally. No doubt they had meant to share the diamonds.

At the Exhibition the day Elizabeth was attacked, Front had been in the Crystal Palace. He must have sent word to Bertie, and Bertie's thugs had tried to abduct her to discover the location of the diamonds. The diamonds were lost to them both, but Bertie and Barb really were making a play for power. Porter's murder of Zeb Fisher had got rid of both a rival gang leader and Jarman's lieutenant. Front had been a troublesome and, no doubt, expensive ally.

Bertie smiled at James. "Go on, takes the edge off the pain. Can't—" Abruptly, he broke off and sprang to his feet, just as Harris and his men loomed out of the darkness and seized him. "Here, get off! I ain't done nothing!"

Tizsa dropped down beside James. Again.

"Opium," James said, holding out the flask with considerable effort. Tizsa seemed very far away. "Enough to kill me, I suspect. I can smell it from here."

Tizsa took the flask from him, and his stern, handsome face faded into the mist.

⟫⟪

WHEN THE MISTS cleared, James was in a strange but bright and pleasant room, enfolded in the comfort of a feather mattress and clean, fresh bed linen. His arm throbbed and his neck stung, but sun streamed through the window, and when he turned his head in search of familiarity, Elizabeth sat in a chair beside his bed. Inevitably, she was sewing.

*We must be in the Tizsas' house.*

Having found his necessary point of reality, James relaxed and remembered. He smiled.

As though she saw it from the corner of her eye, her head jerked around. Her sewing went flying and she all but threw herself upon the bed.

"Oh, James, thank God!" Her voice was muffled in his neck— the safe side of his neck.

His good arm crept around her without his conscious will, and he moved his head again so that he could bury his lips in her hair and inhale her unique, beloved scent.

"Dragan said you wouldn't die. But you wouldn't wake up either, and I was so afraid..."

"Has Tizsa been poking about it my arm?"

"Apparently the ball passed straight through your flesh without touching bone, so providing there's no infection, you will heal. Only you have lost a lot of blood and need rest. But oh, James, *why* did you go up there alone?"

"Why were you there at all? And with your face painted?"

A sob of laughter shook her, and she raised her face, half

weeping, half smiling. "We disguised ourselves as women of ill repute in order to get into the club. Fortunately, Constance found us and convinced us we'd be torn limb from limb by the real women of ill repute if we even tried to set foot in there, so we lurked in the alley instead. No one saw us for the fog, but I could hear your voice, and when you started fighting, I didn't care who saw me. He was going to *stab*—"

"Hush," James said, smoothing her hair beneath his hand. "You saved my life, or at least preserved me from a nasty injury. I won't scold you for being there, even though my heart almost stopped with fear. I went after him because he had to be stopped, and I knew Tizsa and the police would find me sooner or later."

He stared into her face. Although it might ruin the fragile love she felt for him, there had to be honesty between them.

He swallowed. "I knew he would fall. Even after he shot me, I...*made* him." At best, he'd made no effort to save him.

Her eyes didn't change, and for a moment he thought she hadn't heard or understood. Then she said, "Good."

A shudder of shocked laughter passed through him. It hurt, but he couldn't stop, and after a moment, Elizabeth began to laugh, too. Both her arms were around him, and even through the bedclothes and the mirth and the pain, the shape of her shaking body aroused him.

Over her head, he saw the bedroom door push open. Tizsa's head appeared, and then vanished again. He closed the door silently, and as though privacy had been promised with that one soundless act, desire surged through James, hot and urgent, an affirmation of life and love.

He moved, throwing off the covers and pinning Elizabeth beneath him. Only then did he realize he was stark naked.

She didn't appear to mind. The laughter dying slowly on her lips, she gazed up at him without fear.

"I love you," he said hoarsely. "Every moment since you first looked at me in Hanson Row, I loved you. And now I couldn't bear to let you go. Please marry me..."

She gasped, her breast heaving beneath him. "Oh God," she whispered. "Oh James, I…" She lifted her head and fastened her mouth to his.

Her answer was in her kiss, and rightly so. There was so much to say that only their bodies could show their meaning. Pain vanished in hot, heavy kisses and wild caresses that somehow loosened her gown so that she could throw it off.

"Oh, but your wounds," she whispered.

"Make them better," he said, for they were the least of his concerns, "and let me heal yours."

He hadn't forgotten the horror of her experiences with Jarman. Despite the urgency of their embrace and the clamoring of his body, he kept his caresses slow and tender until she lay trembling and eager in his arms as though utterly bewildered as well as wildly aroused.

His fingers found the heat between her silken thighs, and she gasped, arching into his caress. In moments he thrilled to the feel of her coming apart against his hand, the sweet, desperate sounds of her pleasure. Only then, locking his mouth to hers, did he begin to enter her body and rock them both to heady, shattering joy.

⟫⟫⟪⟪

ELIZABETH LAY NAKED on his pillows, stroking his head, which rested on her breast as their breathing slowly calmed. Still astonished by what he had given her—the first physical pleasure she had ever known, and the certainty of his love—she couldn't stop smiling.

At last he moved, propping himself once more on his sound elbow to look into her face. A smile played around his lips, although there was a hint of anxiety in his eyes. "This isn't quite how I intended the first time between us to be. Rushed and silent… Did I hurt you?"

She cupped his cheek. "Don't you know what you gave me? My only hurt is that I might have caused you pain. You were *shot*, James, and I had no idea what I was doing…"

"Oh, my love, you were *everything*," he said fervently. "You *are* everything. I've never found such delight, such pleasure, as in you." He turned his head to kiss her hand. "Forgive my urgency."

She smiled. "Forgive mine."

"Was it acceptance of my proposal?"

"Of course it was," she whispered, and lost herself once more in the wonder of his kiss.

"In that case," he murmured at last against her lips, "you had better dress before the Tizsas decide we've had long enough alone and unchaperoned."

In the event, they were only just in time. Barely a second after she had dressed and helped James restore order to the bed, a knock sounded at the door.

Hastily, Elizabeth went to open it and admitted both Grizelda and Tizsa, who at least pretended not to know what their guests had just done. Tizsa carried a tea tray, which he set down on the dressing table.

Grizelda sat on the chair before it and began to pour tea, while Tizsa sat on the edge of the bed and examined both James's dressings. James tried to look innocent.

"Very glad to see you awake," Grizelda said, passing the first cup to Elizabeth, who ferried it to James, who was now sitting up against the pillows.

"Thank you," he murmured, making sure his fingers brushed hers. His eyes asked a question, and she could only nod. Aloud, he said, "I hope you'll be the first to congratulate me. Elizabeth has just agreed to become my wife."

"Excellent." Grizelda beamed, approaching the bed with two cups, one of which she gave to her husband before settling in the armchair by the bed. She glanced at Elizabeth. "I see all doubts are at an end."

James had been honest with her, so Elizabeth sat at the foot of the bed and met his gaze. "There was a moment I doubted you," she blurted. "When we first met Lila and she was afraid of you. She thought you'd come to accuse her of poisoning you, but there was a moment when I feared you were just like Jarman and Front and all those other men. It broke my heart, and then to have doubted you devastated me."

"And now?" he asked.

She dropped her eyes. "Two weeks ago, we had never spoken," she said with difficulty. "We are still learning each other, but I know enough to trust you. As I hope you trust me."

He held out his hand, and she moved closer to take it.

"There is still your family, though," she said ruefully. "They will hardly be thrilled."

"Well," said Tizsa, "the Nivens were hardly overjoyed when Griz insisted on marrying me."

"They're not above using you, though," Grizelda pointed out.

"Nor above helping me," he returned.

Grizelda smiled. "It's family," she said to Elizabeth and James. "You will find your way, as we do. Do you want to know about Earnest Front and Bertie?"

"Yes," James said.

"Front is dead."

"Good," James said fiercely, then swallowed. "I have a horrible feeling he almost took Constance Silver with him. It never entered my head anyone was down there still. I never looked..."

"Well, it provided her with a rather startling introduction to Mr. Grey," Griz said, "but no harm was done. And frankly, it's better for your family that he's dead. Easier for Helen."

James nodded. "And Bertie?"

"Under arrest," Tizsa said. "So is his mother, though they might have to let her go. He'll be tried for Jarman's murder and your attempted murder."

"I think he'd come to kill Front," James said. "I was just a bonus opportunity. Only, how did he even know Front was going to be there?"

"He had someone watching Front's house," Tizsa said. "My lad saw him. So Bertie went to Coal Yard Lane, left word with the staff to send Front up to him, and went up to the roof to wait for him. He went from inside the house, so he didn't know anything about the commotion outside. Front was already on the roof, but before Bertie could approach him, you appeared."

James frowned. "I *thought* someone else was there when I first arrived, but I assumed it was just my nerves playing tricks. It has all been about Bertie and Barb seizing power in the underworld, hasn't it? Killing Jarman, trying to get hold of the diamonds, sending Porter to kill Fisher, getting Front out of the way."

Tizsa nodded. "I think so. They'd had enough of Jarman's tyranny and fancied a bit of their own. Only, they overreached, and now Bertie can't babble fast enough in the hope of being granted transportation instead of hanging. Harris looks forward to breaking up a lot of crime, including opium smuggling, prostitution, and a whole ring of theft and stolen goods."

Elizabeth drank her tea, one sad thought breaking into her happiness. "I wish we had been in time to save Mrs. Mason."

To her astonishment and not a little outrage, both James and Tizsa began to grin.

"We were in time," he said. "Andover and I went round there yesterday morning before we went to Newgate, and advised her to go to Brighton for a week or two. Her sister is there, and she's thinking of going for good. We hurried her along and...er—told one discreet neighbor that the poor lady had, sadly, died suddenly. We hoped the news would get back to Front."

Grizelda set her teacup down in its saucer with unnecessary force. "It did. Unfortunately, it didn't get back to Elizabeth or me, and we went to Ludgate Hill to discover her 'death'!"

"Sorry," Tizsa said. "It slipped my mind."

"And mine," James admitted. "But then, you forgot to mention to us that you meant to storm the club as ladies of easy virtue."

A breath of laughter escaped Grizelda. "Well, it was worth it to see the appalled face of a genuine madam. Where will you live when you're married?"

Distracted, Elizabeth met James's gaze. Another moment of communication passed between them.

Elizabeth smiled. "James has a house in Kent. It will divide easily into two and has lots of space for a school." *And for goodness and love. And no fear or loneliness, ever.*

# About Mary Lancaster

Mary Lancaster lives in Scotland with her husband, three mostly grown-up kids and a small, crazy dog.

Her first literary love was historical fiction, a genre which she relishes mixing up with romance and adventure in her own writing. Her most recent books are light, fun Regency romances written for Dragonblade Publishing: *The Imperial Season* series set at the Congress of Vienna; and the popular *Blackhaven Brides* series, which is set in a fashionable English spa town frequented by the great and the bad of Regency society.

Connect with Mary on-line – she loves to hear from readers:

Email Mary:
Mary@MaryLancaster.com

Website:
www.MaryLancaster.com

Newsletter sign-up:
http://eepurl.com/b4Xoif

Facebook:
facebook.com/mary.lancaster.1656

Facebook Author Page:
facebook.com/MaryLancasterNovelist

Twitter:
@MaryLancNovels

Amazon Author Page:
amazon.com/Mary-Lancaster/e/B00DJ5IACI

Bookbub:
bookbub.com/profile/mary-lancaster